SONJA & CARL

SONJA
& CARL

SUZANNE HILLIER

BRINDLE
&GLASS

Edited by Colin Thomas
Design by Pete Kohut
Author photo by Magdalena M.
Cover silhouettes by zhaolifang, Vecteezy.com
Quote from Dylan Thomas, from *The Poems of Dylan Thomas*, copyright @ 1939
by New Directions Publishing Corp. Reprinted by permission of New Directions
Publishing Corp. Permission also granted for use throughout the world excluding
the USA by agents David Higham, representing *The Collected Poems of Dylan
Thomas: The Centenary Edition*, published by Weidenfeld & Nicolson and
acknowledging the authorship of the poet Dylan Thomas.

LIBRARY AND ARCHIVES CANADA CATALOGUING IN PUBLICATION
Hillier, Suzanne L., author
Sonja & Carl : a novel / Suzanne L. Hillier.

Issued in print and electronic formats.
ISBN 978-1-927366-56-1 (softcover)

I. Title. II. Title: Sonja and Carl.

PS8615.I422S66 2017   C813'.6   C2017-900374-7

We acknowledge the financial support of the Government of
Canada through the Canada Book Fund and the Canada Council
for the Arts, and of the province of British Columbia through the
British Columbia Arts Council and the Book Publishing Tax Credit.

The interior pages of this book have been printed on 100% post-consumer
recycled paper, processed chlorine free, and printed with vegetable-based inks.

PRINTED IN CANADA AT FRIESENS

17 18 19 20 21   5 4 3 2 1

For all the fallen ice warriors

Light breaks where no sun shines;
Where no sea runs, the waters of the heart
Push in their tides.
                                —Dylan Thomas

THE TUTOR

"PLEASE JUST SHUT UP." FROM her desk in the second last row, Deborah Hanson's irritated voice cut through the stale air of our Grade 12 classroom.

"What's yer problem, on the rag?"

Carl Helbig was one of a group of boisterous boys who sat in the back of our class and seemed unable to concentrate for more than thirty seconds at a time. I thought of them as "The Choir" and assigned them to an eternity singing in a scalding, vacuous hell.

"You will leave the room," admonished Miss Hannelore

Steinbrink, my favourite teacher, "and I'll deal with you later."

As Carl swaggered out, Miss Steinbrink hissed at him, flushed, "You're a disgrace to the German people."

I thought this was strange as both of them were born in Canada, first-generation Canadians.

Carl Helbig didn't care. He was Davenport High's star hockey centreman and a Junior A superstar. He was said to be "poetry in motion" on the ice, though I'd never seen him—or anyone else—play. I was Sonja Danychuk, eighteen years old, the school's number-one nerd, invisible in a school where slim, pretty girls were the popular ones. I was too tall and a little too heavy, so my white skin, ample breasts, and thick black hair, pulled back in a long ponytail and then folded into a large doughnut, went unnoticed.

"Too many cabbage rolls, perogies, and fried cheap food," I complained to my mother, who merely shrugged. A husband who drank himself to sleep each night and a night job cleaning offices meant she had little energy for or interest in cooking anything but familiar cheap food. So the weight and absence of friends continued. Besides, I was shy, although convinced of my own intellectual superiority while well aware I was at the nasty bottom of Davenport's social barrel when it came to money and class.

"If you got it, flaunt it," my classmate Vivian had instructed, flicking open the first button of my white blouse that I wore every day, surrounded by T-shirts, revealing two inches of swelling breasts spilling from a bra at least two sizes too small. But I did not "flaunt it," so when Carl Helbig, who had been told in early February that his chances of passing this year were remote, in fact non-existent, asked me to a movie, I was baffled. So he could make fun of me later, I was sure, or perhaps he thought intelligence was contagious. Yet our eyes had met after his crass rag remark, as if he cared what I thought.

I had never liked him, with his smart-ass remarks calculated to make his choir buddies hoot with appreciation and his inability to give a straight answer to any question. His raw comments made me flinch so I avoided looking at him, never wishing to be the focus of his attention.

"No, I'm busy," I had said, standing by my locker, looking hard at the floor. Going out with Carl Helbig would be worse than never having a date at all.

It was not that he was ugly. In fact, in a blond, large-framed way, some would think of him as good-looking and at least four inches taller than I was, which was a novelty and a plus. It was that mouth of his and his relentless playing the comedian before his chortling tribe that appalled me. I refused to be the butt of a hundred muttered wisecracks every time I answered a question in class that no one else could answer following some disastrous movie date.

IN THE MIDDLE of February, Principal Percy Wheaton, known to the student body as "Wiley Wheaton," who was scheduled for early retirement that June and whose habitual scowl had been replaced by a benign smile, had summoned me to his office during the lunch break.

"Your name," he said, smiling and showing stained dentures washed by dozens of cups of black coffee a day and an occasional smuggled menthol cigarette, "was brought up by Hannelore Steinbrink during a recent staff meeting where scholarship applications were discussed. It was thought by Miss Steinbrink—and by several other teachers—that you possess the originality of thought and the academic diligence that are the criteria for the Imperial Oil Scholarship. This scholarship pays up to five thousand dollars a year for four years' tuition at a university of your choice—provided that you keep an eighty percent average."

I sat silently, my mind racing. Principal Wheaton, his pink forehead stretching into his receding grey hairline shining under the large fluorescent ceiling light, continued.

"This should be no great challenge to you," he said gently, "considering that in the standardized IQ tests taken in Grade 9 you placed in the top two percent in the province intellectually." Then he added quickly, "Not that our school places undue emphasis on standardized testing."

Noting my shocked silence, he continued, his voice even more gentle and encouraging, "And before getting this news, what had your plans been?"

I finally spoke, deciding to be straightforward. Foolish not to be when everyone in Davenport knew everyone else's business, including dates of marriage, birth of first child, gross annual income, and extramarital affairs, which either took place in the back seat of a car parked near Georgian Bay or under assumed names at the Sinclair Hotel.

"Money's always been a problem," I confessed. "I was planning to take next year off, get a job, perhaps take some night courses and save toward university. This makes a difference. I really appreciate you and the staff thinking of me, it's very kind of you." This last comment was said with a catch in my throat. I was appreciative.

Principal Wheaton smiled his encouragement.

"Your future career plans?"

"I want to teach English," I said.

"Ah, teaching," he replied, rolling his prominent blue eyes, "a noble profession."

Wiley Wheaton spent every available moment at the Davenport Golf Club, even during school hours.

"You can do other things, of course," he murmured, as if imparting a serious and confidential secret. "Someone with your intellectual gifts can go far. There are far more remunerative professions than teaching."

"I'll talk to my parents tonight and think about what you've said." We shook hands warmly, co-conspirators in my academic—and possibly lucrative—future.

The scholarship news, together with my high standing in the standardized testing, gave me a surge of unaccustomed lightness and confidence as I tripped back to the classroom, my head buzzing and my heart beating in my ears. That afternoon, Miss Steinbrink asked to see me after class. She sat behind her desk, slim, blond, and smiling.

"Principal Wheaton spoke to you about the scholarship application?"

"He did," I said, returning her smile.

"And?"

"I'll be speaking to my parents tonight, but I may not apply. It depends on a lot of things." I did not want to share with Miss Steinbrink our family's constant concern with lack of money, not wanting her to feel sorry for me.

"I hope, Sonja, they'll be encouraging. Of course you'll apply. Why not? You're such an outstanding student, and so precocious: sometimes when I speak to you, I feel I'm speaking to a colleague—an advanced one." She laughed her tinkling laugh that I loved so much.

It was all the reading: Anna Karenina, Emma Bovary, Catherine Earnshaw, even Dorothea Brooke—their worlds were more real to me than the world of Davenport High, and certainly the Danychuk apartment on Main Street. But I merely said, "I read a lot."

She laughed again. "It shows in your speech. Do you want me to speak to your parents?"

"No, but thanks anyway. The way you've been . . . it's meant so much to me."

We both got up and she walked toward me. For a moment, I smelled her perfume. It was like a meadow of wildflowers.

"I'll miss you," I said. I adored her. She was, after all, my only real friend at Davenport High—Donalda and Margaret, with whom I ate lunch on occasion, not really counting.

"We'll always stay in touch," she replied, rubbing my upper arm. It seemed in a way she felt sorry for me, but it was just a feeling.

I WALKED BACK home from school that cold February afternoon taking a much greater interest than usual in my surroundings. This was a town I could now look forward to leaving, a prospect that I had relished for at least eight of my eighteen years.

Davenport, population twenty thousand, nestled along the coast of Georgian Bay between Parry Sound and French River, was a three-hour drive by car north of Toronto. As such it was in the Snow Belt, and winters, which stretched from early November to late April, were spent huddling against stinging blizzards or at the very least the bitter cold. It had a main street, called Main Street, with one nine-floor apartment building, a Tim Hortons, spelled without the apostrophe, Henley's Hamburgers, and a Swiss Chalet. There was also a string of small locally owned dress and shoe shops, Michelle's Beauty Salon, and Davenport Hardware. O'Dare's Bar, owned by Joseph Dare Manufacturing, known by locals as Dare's Machinery, Davenport's only manufacturing plant, was the busiest place on the street. All would be closed or moving, it was said, once the mall on the fringe of the town was complete. At the New Davenport Mall there would be a McDonald's, a movie theatre, and perhaps even a Canadian Tire.

Surrounding Main Street were several streets lined with weathered red-brick two- or three-storey houses, many at least one hundred years old, with white lacy eaves and shutters. Some were rooming houses, but a dozen had been renovated for the professional offices of doctors, dentists, and lawyers. On Queen Street stood the Sinclair Hotel, recently acquired by the Holiday Inn chain and advertised as "completely renovated."

Surrounding all of this were the new developments: communities filled with the retired who had been lured to Davenport as "the most affordable living in Ontario," together with first-time home buyers. Then there was Knightsbridge, made up of rows of pastel houses, many of them bungalows, representing "the modern aspect" of Davenport. Behind Knightsbridge was Davenport's proudest accomplishment, the Davenport Sports Stadium, right beside the Davenport General Hospital.

We lived on the fifth floor of the only apartment building on Main Street. Prospective renters were assured it was central to everything, but that was its only attribute. It was a run-down and musty-smelling building erected during the Second World War with temperamental electricity and ancient plumbing. It was not a place where you would invite your friends—even if you had any.

Pops was the superintendent. For his services in cleaning the common area and collecting rent from the sixty units, he was given a rent-free two-bedroom apartment and $1,000 a month. Actually, Ma did the cleaning and Pops usually just collected the rent. Pops, Ma had told me once, had led his class in Ukraine where they had been schoolmates, and in fact was entering university in Kiev when he became convinced his future lay in immigrating to Canada. After their arrival in Toronto in the early eighties, there had been one disappointment after the other, starting with a refusal to allow him to attend university unless he could complete a final year of high school in Canada. His pride would not permit it, and instead he drove a taxi until he lost his licence for drinking. They finally wound up in Davenport. Through it all, Ma had always worked, during her pregnancy, and even when I was an infant.

"They want me to apply for a scholarship," I informed them that night.

They spoke to me in Ukrainian, but I usually answered them in English: no excuse to not speak English after twenty years. They sat looking at me blankly. The smell of that night's dinner of fried pork sausage and home fries hung heavy in the air together with the Camels they chain-smoked. Pops had already placed raw garlic in his twenty-six of Smirnoff, "to clean his blood," and sat it next to him on the table. By ten that night it would be empty, and he would lie across the table, comatose, until Ma, who left after dinner and returned home at midnight from her office-cleaning job, woke him up for bed.

"If I do receive the scholarship, and I may not, it would cover most of the tuition, but I'll still need money for residence and books. I'll work every summer and get something part-time in Toronto during the year, but I might need some help." I had switched to Ukrainian, pointless to stick to principle and not be understood.

"We can't help you," said Ma, shaking her head and deeply inhaling her Camel from a hand that had seen too many pails of steaming water and strong detergent. "We'd hoped you'd be going to work to help us."

I felt myself flush with anger. The money that went to

Camels and vodka alone would probably cover the cost of residence and I only needed a modest contribution. I sat with my arms folded, silent and accusatory, my eyes fixed on them. Guilt, I thought to myself cynically, their answer to everything: the dutiful immigrant daughter, seeing to her parents' well-being, paying her mother back for all the cabbage rolls and perogies that had contributed to the buttery roll under her chin and those extra inches on her thighs and upper arms. The least she could do was to see that the Camels and vodka didn't run out.

Ma pushed the remaining inch of her Camel into the greasy aftermath of her dinner plate and got up reluctantly. Six hours of cleaning the five floors of 98 Maple Street were waiting. She was a small, thin woman with faded eyes and sparse grey hair showing patches of pink scalp and her tiny face seemed buried in mottled, puffy skin. On occasion she'd say to me, "Imagine a little scrap like me having a big girl like you." It was the closest she ever came to affection.

I watched her trudge from the apartment carrying her mop and pail full of bottles of cleaning fluids to supplement those already waiting in the basement of the Maple Building. The owners had told her she was a good cleaner, a compliment she had repeated with pride to Pops and me. And she was honest. When she found lost items, she'd place them in plain sight on desktops in the offices. I pictured her, a cigarette steaming from her pursed lips, driving across Davenport in our 1988 Honda Civic, along the frozen streets lined with grey-tinged snow under a sky too cold to show a moon, and I felt a nudge of compassion for this feisty little workhorse. The feeling did not last long.

Pops had finished his first three ounces of vodka. I sat at the table with him although the dishes were waiting to be removed and spring midterms were to take place in five weeks. If I were to receive the scholarship, I could not waste time. But I waited for him to say something.

"You must apply for the scholarship. Your mother does not understand: education is everything. I made a big mistake not continuing my education. I should have stayed in Kiev or done something here. You have my head."

He spoke English well although with an accent. He would never speak English in front of my mother in consideration of her feelings. "You have my head," was an indirect rebuff to Ma, who, by implication, was not scholarship material.

"You must not end up like us."

I got up from the table, piling the plates and picking up Ma's cigarette butt, holding it between forefinger and thumb, and dropping it into the garbage under the sink: a cleaner using her dinner plate as an ashtray, a defiant act against her hours of cleaning. I pressed Pops' heavy shoulder with my hand. His swollen abdomen rose and fell and I could smell the sour of sweat. Later I wished I'd said something, although I knew he did not expect it.

Two weeks later he was dead. Ma found him sprawled across the table, a huge whale with arms like fins sprouting hairs of black wire strangely assertive on pale dead flesh. An empty vodka bottle sat beside him. She woke me immediately. I pressed his cheek, chilled dough, and removed a final cigarette butt from his swollen yellow fingers. When they came to pick him up, I marvelled at his helplessness, his head bobbing from the gurney, and stifled a desire to tell them to be careful. "A massive coronary," we were told later.

Arrangements were made through The Reasonable Alternative, the region's cheapest crematorium. There was no service or funeral, no prayers or tears. He belonged to no clubs and never attended church. Any relatives were still in Ukraine, most of them dead, and he had no friends. I stood with Ma in the small chapel with its stained-glass windows listening to the piped-in organ playing "Bridge Over Troubled Water." Ma murmured that fifty was too young to die, and when I got up at two in the morning, unable to sleep, I saw her sitting where he always sat with his vodka bottle, chain-smoking her Camels and looking into the distance.

There was no money except a death benefit from Canada Pension to cover cremation costs, plus a very small monthly amount. Ma wanted to stay on in our building as superintendent, claiming, quite truthfully, that she had always done all the cleaning. But when I relayed this request to the owner, he refused, stating it was a position only suitable for a couple. We were allowed to stay in the apartment for a month provided Ma continued with the cleaning.

We decided to rent a one-bedroom in the same building. I would have the bedroom and Ma the pullout sofa.

"I will clean at night but also during the day. Some

pay forty dollars for six hours, on some days I can do two houses. We can manage, but you must forget your plans for university. It would be impossible—you can see that." All this was delivered in low and pressing Ukrainian.

I did not answer, torn between the humiliation of having Ma support me by working fifteen hours a day and giving up any future of escape and stimulation. I would, I decided, try to get a part-time job at Tim Hortons, Swiss Chalet, or even O'Dare's Bar. I had heard Timmy's and Swiss Chalet paid between $8 and $10 an hour, and at O'Dare's the drunks might provide decent tips. It would interfere with my studies and any future scholarship. As well, it would provide amusement for some of my class-mates, who suspected that I, the poorest student in the class, looked down on them. But I had to do something. Even Pops had encouraged it. And I missed him, more than I'd ever thought I would.

"Sorry 'bout your father," Carl Helbig said, just as I was about to go into Miss Steinbrink's classroom for a discussion of the Fool's role in *Lear*.

"Thank you." I avoided his eyes. How did he know? We had not even placed a death notice in the *Davenport Guardian* and I had only missed one day of school. Typical of gossiping Davenport. Then that night, a call came from Carl's mother, Mrs. Gerda Helbig.

"You help my Carl pass grade? I give you twenty dollars each hour. Only you and Carl must know. This very import-ant. Carl tell me you very smart. Without help, he not pass."

"Please give me a few hours to think about it," I said.

I had no one to discuss it with. Ma might encourage it, but only if I contributed the money to household expenses. This, after assuring her that I was no longer considering attending university. I had, in fact, applied for the scholarship the day after Pops' cremation, although I knew at the time lack of money might make following up impossible. Ma was limited, even Pops had implied it. I decided, however, I would not discard my university plans, but keep them as a tribute to Pops.

Twenty dollars an hour was enticing, double what I'd get at Timmy's or anywhere else, even counting tips. And I couldn't be sure these jobs were available. And working with Carl meant I'd be reviewing my own work. I marvelled at the amount and then remembered that Mr. Helbig, Carl's father, was general manager of Joseph Dare Manufacturing. I had read it in the *Davenport Guardian* at the time of his appointment, and that Mrs. Gerda Helbig worked for the company as an accountant/bookkeeper. In fact, there was a picture of the plump, smiling Helbigs with a caption underneath reading, "A Family Affair." No doubt, I thought, in a nasty frame of mind, Carl would be headed in the same direction—but as a disruptive assembly line worker.

The nature of Mrs. Helbig's call explained Carl's movie invitation some weeks earlier: he was enlisting me for academic help. It was a better premise than to have him use me as the butt of his comedy routine following some so-called date. I would not admit a sense of deflation in having thought for even a moment that I'd appeal to hockey hero Helbig. But apparently I had my uses.

I did the calculations: three hours a night, five days a week, twelve hundred a month, for four months. It would cover residence—and more. I did not wish to tutor Carl, but then the whole matter of tutoring was to be surrounded by secrecy. He could be relied on to keep his mouth shut, perhaps ashamed that his smirking friends might know he needed help. As if they didn't already suspect it.

I did not want him to come here, view our shabby apartment, meet Ma, and see that she spoke no English. His mother had an accent, but at least she communicated. She did not merely stand there, smiling her lack of understanding. It embarrassed me that I had to phone all Ma's cleaning customers to inform them that she spoke no English, and that I would have to explain the specifics of her duties to her. And then there was the shame I felt at my own embarrassment.

Since Pops' death, Ma didn't cook. There were no more smells of pork sausage sizzling in lard or sharp tomato sauce burping around rolls of cabbage wrapped around ground beef and rice. Instead, Ma told me to help myself to the mottled pink luncheon meat and pumpernickel in the refrigerator. I didn't blame her. I had never appreciated her cooking and her schedule made me ache with guilt. I did not even allow the acrid fumes of her Camels that lingered heavy in the air saturating everything to bother me. I was, after all, losing weight. I decided, however, I'd buy some apples and eggs when I started my new job.

I called Gerda Helbig that evening and said I'd accept the job and would tell no one. There were conditions, however. The tutoring must take place at the Helbig home. She told me they lived in the new Knightsbridge Community Development, several miles to the north of Davenport High, and that Carl was on the hockey team that practised twice a week for the Saturday games. This, I informed her, might cause scheduling complications.

"For real help Carl needs a minimum of three hours a day," I said, marvelling at my own nerve, and thinking that I needed a minimum of $60 a day, a much more pressing concern.

My scheduling meant nothing to Frau Helbig, who assured me transportation would be provided by either herself or Carl, and that on his hockey practice nights I could come directly to the Helbig residence after school. She was relentless, I thought, and I acquiesced. Stopping her would be the same as trying to stop a tank by standing in front of it. I thought of Ma and Pops' tales of the Second World War as told to them by my grandparents, and that only the cold of a Russian winter and vodka had defeated them. I felt some shame at the analogy. After all, I wanted Frau Helbig's money and the job, in that order, and Gerda Helbig was not even born at the time of the Second World War. And neither was Ma.

ON A NUMBING evening in late February, Gerda Helbig picked me up in her shiny new Volkswagen in front of the apartment building. I was relieved. I had worried that Carl would arrive for me.

"Yes, I've eaten," I lied, unless of course you considered

a half-slice of pumpernickel and a Bubbie's Pickle an evening meal. I was thrilled to notice I was losing weight, and I imagined arriving at university slim and attractive, with a shrinking of those unwanted soft curves that had plagued me for years.

Gerda Helbig, cheeks round and apple-rosy, short hair with its golden highlights swept back and anchored with spice-smelling hairspray, gripped the wheel with small, plump hands with square pink fingernails and spoke of Carl. He had never been a student and had squeaked through each year, except for one, but now that he was in Grade 12 he had reached an impasse.

"It is teacher fault," she spat. "There is nothing wrong with Carl. He not schtupid. But he must have high school diploma." Apparently even Joseph Dare Manufacturing, where Carl might eventually be employed, took note of this.

I felt uneasy. Her indignation and blaming of teachers worried me. Could I measure up to this animated talkative woman's expectations? I had decided on my teaching strategies the night before. I would start with *King Lear*, explaining to my student its various themes. There was considerable cruelty throughout, and I felt that he'd respond to that. Putting out Gloucester's eyes with the leg of a stool and the suffering of Lear at the hands of his daughters might appeal to him. I would convey it all as a family tragedy, although a royal one, and get him to understand the plot. I'd then focus in on its more subtle aspects, the irony of Lear finding spiritual insight through madness, the pathos of Cordelia's death, and

Lear's resulting agony. Who knew what this large blond jeering fellow might be capable of when severed from his chortling army camped in the last row of every classroom? Then on to *The Great Gatsby*, with an emphasis on Gatsby's criminal past. That would interest Carl, even the unrequited love that saw Gatsby dead in a swimming pool, all for an ingrate who would not attend his funeral. The decay of the American Dream, the symbolism of East and West Egg, and the flickering green light, even Carl could grasp that. And then the *Prufrock* poem—Prufrock, done in by self-consciousness and society's restrictions. Could I make Carl Helbig hear the mermaids singing? I would, I was hopeful, open up another world—a world remote from the video games and violent movies I felt sure he was addicted to—and transform this hulking hockey player into perhaps a creature of thought.

History and political science would follow, kings and queens and changing governments, together with the concepts of capitalism and socialism. I could get through to him on that, especially after the union problems at Joseph Dare last summer. I did not wish to let Gerda Helbig down.

The Helbig home was a jewellery box of a bungalow, as shiny and antiseptic as our apartment was jaded and sour. There were porcelain ornaments scattered over every polished surface, many Royal Doulton figurines. Ma had broken a Royal Doulton during one of her private cleaning jobs and had offered to replace it, almost collapsing when she found out it would be more than $500. Pictures of Carl's two sisters showing strong white teeth and fair hair beamed from silver frames. One was in a graduation gown and the other, also gowned, had just received a diploma, which she held in her hands.

Both Carl Sr. and Carl Jr. got up when I entered the dining room, and Carl thanked me for coming.

"Come, you taste my dinner," Gerda said. "Carl and Father soon finish."

I knew I should refuse. It was demeaning to go there and gobble down food on my first night as if I were starving, which in fact I was, but the vision and smell of the roast beef with rich dark gravy and a platter of roasted vegetables, together with the leftovers from a Romaine salad saturated with oil, vinegar, and garlic, were overwhelming.

"Perhaps just a little," I replied, attempting to keep the eagerness from my voice. I did, however, decline the apple strudel. There were limits, after all, to what a paid employee should receive. I wondered what Carl would have said but for the secrecy pledge.

Gerda, referred to by Carl as "Mutti" and by Carl Sr. as "Trudy," had arranged the study with leather chairs and a thick polished mahogany table. I reminded myself that Carl would never set foot inside our grungy fifth-floor apartment.

"We have less than four months to get through the three hard courses," I said brightly. "I understand there are no problems with math or science, not that I can help you with math."

Carl nodded solemnly. I looked at him carefully for the first time. At school I averted my eyes whenever I saw him, afraid of calling attention to myself. He was, I decided, attractive, if you liked the obvious Teutonic type. Everything about him was square: his chin, his head underneath the closely cropped fair hair, his jaw line and shoulders. Even his teeth, when he permitted a brief smile in return for my intense scrutiny, were white and square. His nails, pink, clipped, and square like his mother's, were part of large hands that moved constantly in a restless tangle. It seemed he found it impossible to stop moving.

"If you want to, you can get up and move around."

He smiled his relief, got up, and paced the room. No doubt, I thought, for him to be sitting motionless in a classroom would be torture, and I started to understand his classroom restlessness, if not his rudeness.

I would, I decided, give him an overview of *King Lear* and then narrow in on certain themes and paradoxes. "*King Lear*," I explained in a voice that I feared just escaped shrillness, "wanted lavish professions of love from his three daughters, but Cordelia, his favourite, refuses, and says she only loves him as a dutiful daughter. Because of this, Lear gives his kingdom to the other two, Goneril and Regan, and disinherits Cordelia. She had two suitors, but afterwards only the King of France.

"Lear, rejected by Goneril and Regan, is cast out in a storm and goes mad. But in his madness, he gains insight. The Duke of Gloucester, betrayed by his bastard son

Edmond, gains insight upon becoming blind. Both of these happenings are ironic and paradoxical. Cordelia is hanged in the final act on the instructions of Goneril and Edmond, and Lear dies of grief.

"Lear says, 'Why should a dog, a horse, a rat have life, and thou no breath at all? Thou'll come no more, never, never, never, never, never.'"

It was one of my favourite Shakespearean passages, and I was aware I was giving it considerable drama and in the process revealing much too much of myself.

Carl looked at me, alarmed.

"Isn't that sad?" I asked him, my voice almost breaking, "He's so full of grief and remorse."

I saw him watching me in Gerda's gold-rimmed wall mirror, my black hair swept up in its thick coil, my black almond-shaped eyes shining from my white oval-shaped face with, as I always lamented, its puffy cheeks, and wished he could share in one iota of my passion for literature, which, I feared, he inwardly characterized as "crap."

"It doesn't do anything for me," he said carefully, watching my face pucker in disappointment, "but I can see it moves you. To me, it's really a waste of time."

I had obviously failed in my purpose so I would start again at the beginning, clarifying and paraphrasing, then trying the Socratic method that Miss Steinbrink used, drawing out knowledge by asking questions.

"What do you think of Goneril's and Regan's answers to their father? And of Cordelia's answer and implied criticism of her sisters?"

"Not much," he replied.

"How about Lear's reaction?"

"Stupid."

"And of the Duke of Burgundy's withdrawal as Cordelia's suitor?"

"She's lucky to be rid of him; he was only in it for the bucks."

I felt gratified. At last I had elicited an enlightened response—of sorts.

"The King of France still hung around," I reminded him.

"Good for him," said Carl, smiling at me and showing his square white teeth. "He knew a good thing."

I sat frowning at the text. He was detaching himself and making fun of me, as if, because I had a passion for literature, I was in some way naive and childish.

"And there is Edmund, the bastard son of the Earl of Gloucester, who is jealous of his legitimate brother Edgar and who will falsely convince the Earl that Edgar is plotting his death."

"Edmund's a real bastard," said Carl, smiling again.

"Look," I said, attempting to take the edge out of my voice, "we have a test on this in three weeks that counts for thirty percent of the final mark. If you don't care, then I don't, but I'm not going to have your mother waste her money if you don't want me to help you."

It was the first time money had been mentioned and it had a sobering effect. Carl stopped smiling and started talking. "I guess that's why you're doing this, for the money. You didn't believe I'd be such a challenge. That's what Steinbrink said I was, after telling me I was a disgrace to the German people, 'a challenge.'"

I wanted to answer, Of course I'm doing it for the money. My mother cleans floors for a living and my dad's dead. I haven't got enough for university unless I get it for teaching you. But I did not want his pity.

"I do need the money because I want to go to university next year. I've applied for a scholarship, but it doesn't cover everything even if I do get it, and there are others applying. But I do like teaching and that's what I want to do, so it's not all about the money. Understand?"

He nodded, looking serious. He always understood the concrete; it was the abstract he had problems with. It was his way of making me feel like my love of literature was in some way made-up and pretentious.

"I want you to paraphrase for me, in writing, like you would in an exam, all of Act I. I want you to pay special attention to the Fool. It is another paradox that the Fool, who is the court comedian, serves as a touchstone of common sense to Lear, who lacks judgment. Can you do this for me?"

"It's sixty pages."

"It's important," I insisted.

I WAS QUIET as I sat with Gerda Helbig in her scented Volkswagen, returning to the two-bedroom apartment that was soon to be a one-bedroom and that smelled of stale smoke and the liniment of broken lives.

"Study is good?" Gerda demanded.

"Well, I hope," I answered. I was not about to launch into a list of concerns as to Carl's academic shortcomings to his biggest fan.

"I tell them it nothing. He lazy boy," she replied, wheeling expertly and smoothly along the darkened streets with the smooth sheen of winter wet reflected in the headlights and the occasional streetlight.

"Carl must hockey practice at eight o'clock. You come to my house, three-thirty. You have dinner, then work hours with Carl. You and Carl ride in Volkswagen. Again tomorrow?"

I nodded my agreement and thanked her once more for the dinner. That was one thing about Gerda Helbig: she prevented you from making personal decisions. I had only two hours to spend on my other courses and math was always a concern. One thing was certain, however: I would know my Lear.

THE NEXT DAY I followed Carl in winter sunshine to his gleaming blue Volkswagen parked near the teachers' parking, past a cluster of whistling boys.

"Way to go, man," one shouted. Carl merely turned around and grinned at me. I scowled back at him and walked more quickly toward the shiny little Bug, not relishing the thought of being cooped up with this large blond teenager who felt that literature was one huge joke and that my love of it some amusing form of early dementia. I saw Candace Stewart standing on the school steps watching us, unsmiling. She was said to have sex with Carl on occasion and never missed a hockey game. Carl threw her a wave and grin, which she did not return.

"They think we're getting it on," he explained.

I did not answer but looked straight ahead. I had no friends except for my two luncheon companions, Donalda and Margaret, both heading for professional courses, and Miss Steinbrink. *They* would know I would never get it on with someone like Carl.

2

THE STUDENT

"**Y**OUR ASSIGNMENT?" I ASKED. WE had not spoken on the way back to the bungalow, heavy with smells of oven-roasted chicken and furniture polish, except to have him mention the hockey practice at eight o'clock. "Assignment" sounded pompous, I knew that, but I wanted to give the tutorials an air of formality.

"Didn't do it." His voice was cheerful with just an edge of defiance.

"Why not?"

"Couldn't."

"Why not?"

"Can't read it."

Shakespeare was of course difficult, and I was aware that there had been complaints that the twelfth graders would benefit more from modern dramas such as Miller's *The Crucible* or even Williams' *A Streetcar Named Desire*, which would at least have a mad Blanche whose dependency on the kindness of strangers might make more sense to the average teenager than a mad Lear with his dependency on family. And there would be some identification by the male students with Stanley Kowalski, a fact that I had mentioned to a laughing Miss Steinbrink, who had paid me the compliment of consulting me on curriculum choices. I had been fortunate enough to acquire a job at the local library the previous summer and had spent all my spare time reading modern drama. It had been my best summer.

"Shakespeare is difficult," I told him carefully, "but I did explain some of it to you yesterday, and the annotated text should help." I started to question him, and to my surprise he remembered the plot, the paradox of a mad Lear becoming enlightened and a blind Gloucester gaining insight. He even remembered the Fool as a sensible touchstone for Lear.

"You remember it all really well." He smiled and flushed at the praise. "But you've got to reduce it to writing. Exams, remember?"

He stopped smiling.

I decided to have him try a little *Gatsby*. Shakespeare was too heavy for starters.

Rather than lecture as I had the previous day, I started questioning him, even attempting to personalize the West Egg and East Egg, laughing when I compared my apartment with his home in a new development. He did not laugh, perhaps, I thought, out of concern for my feelings. His sensitivity surprised me, as did his moral position on Tom's adultery and the relationship between Daisy and Gatsby.

"But he did love her," I argued. "Everything he accomplished he did for her, even if it was criminal activity. He was even willing to take the blame for the accidental death of her husband's mistress."

He would not be convinced, and I thought of the irony of the virgin, Sonja Danychuk, taking the moral low road with this outspoken student who questioned Deborah Hanson's menstrual periods, and who, as everyone knew, was having sex with the unsmiling Candace Stewart.

We talked about the valley of ashes, the green light on Daisy's dock, Gatsby's parties, and the American Dream, lost among the pursuit of wealth.

"Do you know any symbols?" I asked.

"My dad's Mercedes," he answered without hesitation.

I was pleased, as well as with the roast chicken with mashed potatoes and string beans, followed by cheesecake with sour cream and bottled blueberries. He would, he promised, give me a plot summary of Chapter One of *Gatsby* in writing the next day, touching on the revelation of character and developing themes.

Carl Helbig Sr. drove me home in his Mercedes, sleek,

silver, and purring, which sounded like the shushing of winds through summer branches on the icy streets of Davenport. He was a soft-spoken man with only a slight accent, the opposite of the animated Gerda in every way.

"We are," he told me, "very grateful for your efforts. Carl's not a student, but his graduation from high school is very important to his mother. He is," he continued, "a good boy and a great hockey player. We cannot all be good students."

"We're doing well," I said.

I entered our apartment warm with satisfaction, even looking forward to the next day. I was, I told myself, a great teacher, inspiring and encouraging, opening up new avenues to even the leader of the badass choir. And I had chosen the right vocation, earning a living by teaching what I loved. I settled myself on the faded stale sofa in the still apartment where I could no longer smell cooking, and where sometimes late at night I could still see Pops sitting at the table with his Smirnoff bottle, a glass symbol of unfulfilled aspirations, a much sadder symbol than Mr. Helbig's silver Mercedes.

Mutti picked me up at five-thirty the next day in front of the apartment and informed me they were waiting dinner for me. She had taken for granted that I hadn't eaten, and merely smiled and nodded when I said, "You didn't have to do that," replying only, "Your Mutti work night, yah?" Everyone always knew everything in Davenport. "Guess she glad her daughter so schmart."

I nodded, thinking Ma would have been better pleased

had I been planning to work at the local pharmacy or the Toronto-Dominion Bank rather than planning a university education, even if I did receive an Imperial Oil Scholarship.

Dinner was wiener schnitzel with buttered noodles, carrots, and broccoli, followed by crystal goblets filled with imported strawberries and blueberries with large curls of yellow custard on top. No wonder Carl was so big, stuffed with nutritious food since birth. Mutti, I thought with admiration, could do everything. Wearing my white socks, while carefully placing my boots on the mat inside the front door, I returned the smiles of the two Carls, who stood as I entered the dining room.

I actually loved it all: the food, the shiny surfaces, the scent of money hovering behind it. The day before we'd arrived early, and the cleaning woman, an elderly German immigrant who Carl introduced as Ursula, was rushing to finish polishing our mahogany work table. Polite of him to introduce her, I thought, doubting whether any of Ma's employers had ever seen fit to make an introduction.

I watched her as she bent over the polished surface, rubbing our already-gleaming table, lips pursed and underarms jiggling with effort. I smiled and said, "It's okay," after she muttered, "Sorry" for keeping us waiting. I heard her gathering up the familiar charlady's utensils, heard her close the back door quietly, and glimpsed her through the window, pail by her side, a bowed figure, fumbling for the keys of her decrepit Volkswagen in the pocket of her down duffle with its hood pulled up against the late afternoon chill.

I felt a moment of guilt. It could be poor Ma trudging off with pail and cleaners, after having her evening meal of pickles and luncheon meat, all followed by three Camels, one after the other.

"Husband and I have Rhine wine," said Mutti as she poured two glasses. "You keep clear mind for study. Time to celebrate after Carl pass grade."

Carl led the way into the study and stood looking down at me, his blue pullover showing the fresh checked collar of his shirt underneath. His scoured jeans were tight on his long legs, and even his running shoes were unmarked by the slightest trace of dirt. Now that I'd permitted myself to look at him directly, I decided he was the cleanest person I'd ever known. Even his ears had been soaped to a shine and under the light glowed like the pink inside of seashells. Blonds, certainly natural ones, I thought, always looked cleaner than those of us with dark hair. He always made me feel unclean, although I did my best, fighting with the temperamental apartment shower that had to be cajoled to give more than a lukewarm dribble at morning and night.

"Present," he sang, depositing three white sheets with carefully inked paragraphs on the polished table in front of me.

I leaned over and started to read. "This is wonderful," I breathed and then realized under no circumstances did this sophisticated analysis of the first chapter of *The Great Gatsby* originate with Carl Helbig.

I looked at him steadily when I had finished.

"It's very good," I said. "I wonder who wrote it."

"What do you think I am?" he answered, his voice full of contrived indignation. "A dummy?"

"No," I said quickly, "I don't think that, but you didn't write this."

He had, after all, gone to the trouble of plagiarizing three sheets of criticism, presenting them to me as a gift, and even if the gift was not authentic, it remained a presentation. It was pointless to pull moral indignation—the food and money were too good.

"Why?" I asked, lowering my voice, knowing in some intuitive way the answer.

"I wanted to make you happy, the way you were last night when I answered your questions on *Gatsby*."

"You went to this much trouble . . . to make me happy?" I asked softly.

He looked at the mahogany surface of the table, then back at me, and then looked away again. "It's more than that . . . I can't read. It's like pain. The letters are fucked up and I can't spell, not a damn word. It would have taken me years to do what you wanted, and even then I couldn't do it. I have a hard time sitting still even for two minutes. I can use the computer; I play games on it. I got this off the Internet. I typed 'Gatsby' into Google and there it was under 'Chapter One.' I copied it. It took me three hours."

I'd heard of this problem before. I wished I could afford a computer. I could not be angry with him. Neither could

I give him sympathy, knowing it would anger and embarrass him. He had wanted to make me happy.

"There's a word for this, I believe."

"There are two," he replied. "One is stupid and the other is dumb."

"No, no," I corrected him quickly, "you're anything but. The fact that you've reached Grade 12 without being able to read or spell may mean you're a genius. You gave me great spoken answers. They should let you do your exams that way, but they may not. Not Davenport High. I could go and ask Wiley Wheaton just in case they'd consider it."

"No friggin' way. This was just between us, remember?" His voice had a determined edge I hadn't heard before.

We sat without speaking. And then he said more softly, "I understand when you read or talk. It's just reading it and understanding it on my own."

"Have you ever been tested?"

He smiled and the edge in his voice was back. "In elementary school when I was about ten. The teacher insisted on it, as I was already repeating my year. Mutti got very upset, said they were covering up their bad teaching and my laziness. So nothing was done. They kept promoting me, the class moron. But I had a lot of friends, nothing like being the class comedian, and I could always do math. I was one helluva hockey player from age seven, so they kept pushing me through, probably afraid of Mutti and of losing their top peewee scorer. But now they won't push me through anymore: I'm too much of 'a challenge.' You can't have a high school graduate who can't read or spell—bad for the school's reputation."

"Nice that you can do math, my worst subject. Trigonometric ratios and evaluating logarithms drive me crazy. Perhaps you can tutor me."

I was glad I'd said it. He started smiling and allowed me to continue.

"I'll read the first act of *Lear* to you, all of it. I'll spell out the words and explain every sentence. The test is on *Lear*, so we'll leave the *Gatsby* and *Prufrock* for the moment.

"Not what you expected, eh? Really boring for you. Not even 'a challenge.'"

"No, it's not what I expected, but I'm here to help, not to enjoy myself." Having said this, I was sorry. I made it sound as if I were serving a prison sentence.

"Really earning your twenty bucks an hour."

His resentment was wounding. He had opened up to me. Now he wanted to punish me for it.

I pride myself on my self-control. I am not a crier. I did not even cry when Pops died, enduring his passing like some festering abdominal wound that stirred when I least expected it. Literature, more than life, was moving to me, so I avoided intimacy, although I knew I desperately needed it. I felt sad for him, but I stifled it. Empathy would be seen as condescension. I would be basic and frank, no subterfuge or sympathy. I would even attempt humour provided he did not think he was its object. After all, didn't he use humour every day of his life? Carl Helbig and his chortling choir, background music in the back of the class, guaranteed to drive his teachers into a rock-and-roll frenzy.

"When you need the money like I do, it doesn't really matter how you earn it. This beats Tim Hortons and O'Dare's, and your mom's cooking beats everything. If I were home I'd have a pickle and a piece of processed meat for dinner. I haven't eaten so well, ever. If you didn't have learning problems, think of all the great meals I'd miss and all the money I'd lose."

It was the right approach. "Glad to be of service," he said, and he sat down, smiling.

The reading began. Act I, the Shakespearean rendition and then the Danychuk interpretation, spelling names and having him copy, over and over, then a page and a half, succinctly printed, outlining the plot, the development of characters, and the Fool, who I told him was no fool at all. I had him copy the page, cringed inwardly at his clumsy efforts and the reversal of letters, and then had him read it haltingly back, time and again. Tomorrow he would reproduce and correct what he'd done, and if sufficient we'd progress to Act II; if not, we'd begin again to do the Act I synopsis.

There was still history and political science, which we hoped would be multiple choice since he found that easier, provided, of course, he could read the choices.

At nine we were both exhausted. And now I'd have two hours of studying to ensure my scholarship, should my application be successful.

"Studies go good?" asked Mutti as we cruised through the icy streets in the silent silver Mercedes that Carl Sr., who was watching a hockey game in the living room, had heated up for us. It seemed impossible to me that Carl's Mutti hadn't taken in the fact that she had a son who had, indeed perhaps always had, serious learning problems that had been ignored year after year. Her denial of the situation was cruel.

"Carl," I said, breathing deeply, "has really serious problems with his reading and spelling."

"And that is why we have you, to solve problem." Her voice was harsh, scratching my already stretched vulnerability. Did she want me to saw open the head of her handsome scrubbed son and attack the problem with a screwdriver, tightening some loose screws so all would function, like the Mercedes and the well-oiled machines functioned at Dare's Machinery?

It was useless to argue further. I decided I disliked Gerda Helbig, who could not have an imperfect son any more than she could have an imperfect house. Carl was lazy and his teachers incompetent.

"I'll do my best, Mrs. Helbig," I promised, stifling a desire to say more. Shutting up for $20 an hour and great dinners. But what was the point of arguing with a tank?

We would meet tomorrow.

THE NIGHT WAS heavy with February chill, and the white sliver of a moon in the black socket of a starless sky gave no light. I let myself in and waited in the foyer until a man with long black hair and wearing a black leather jacket and frayed jeans went into the elevator.

Pops had always warned me to never get in the elevator alone with a man at night. Suddenly I missed Pops, with his vodka, swollen belly, and sad dark eyes. Unlike my mother, who was probably too tired to care, he always smiled and nodded his head in approval when I handed him my report cards and essays. He was not a mean drunk, just a consistent one.

The apartment was cold and I pushed up the thermostat. The building was old and needed renovating. Not that the owner would renovate, and if he did it would mean an increase in rent. You made a choice: discomfort or loss of money. I left on my coat and boots and started on my history assignment. I liked British history, with its succession of kings and queens who ushered in new eras reflecting individual politics and religion. I especially liked the Tudors: Henry VIII and his abolishment of the Catholic Church to accommodate his marital choices, and the indomitable Elizabeth I, using her professed virginity to manipulate foreign powers and remain on the throne.

I couldn't focus. The confrontation with Carl, if you could call it that, had upset me, as had Gerda Helbig, with her unrealistic demands. I wanted to use the Internet to further investigate Carl's problem but it would have to wait until tomorrow when I could check it out on one of the five computers in the school library. It was unfortunate that Carl could only use his father's computer to play video games and plagiarize English assignments.

I tossed and turned in the tangled sheets, tired but unable to turn off my thoughts. I smelled Ma's cigarette when she came home at midnight and heard the closing of her bedroom door. Things would be worse when we moved to the one-bedroom next month and she had only the sofa. I woke up soggy and still tired at seven and struggled with the tepid water from the rusty shower, finally giving up and heading to the kitchen sink to shampoo my hair. There, hair wrapped in a towel, I joined Ma, who was already up, cigarette attached, sitting at the kitchen table.

I felt cranky, both at the cigarette smoke and at a refrigerator that contained only Bubbie's Pickles, mouldy cheese, and pumpernickel so stale that it curled from its opened package, the mottled pink luncheon meat long gone.

My crankiness was enervating, almost enjoyable, and I aimed it at Ma, who I secretly blamed for hastening Pops' death by her relentless menu of fried sausages and lard-packed fried potatoes. I spoke to her in Ukrainian, my desire to integrate her into English-speaking Canada gone.

"There's no food in the fridge and you're killing me with your damn cigarettes. I smoke a pack a week in second-hand smoke and this place stinks like O'Dare's Bar. If I didn't eat at the Helbigs, I'd starve."

"You are," retorted Ma in rapid-fire Ukrainian, "getting really high on yourself, all because of your chance of a scholarship and eating with the rich Germans. Losing weight won't hurt you, that's what you always say you want, and when your father was alive all you ever did was complain about my cooking so don't make like you miss it. Cigarettes are my only pleasure and I won't give them up for a spoiled daughter who appreciates nothing. I clean floors all day to keep a roof over your head and all you do is bitch, getting your head turned and eating with the Nazis. If your father was alive, no way you'd dare speak to me like this."

Ma's tirade unsettled me. I got up, still drying my hair, and stamped back to the bathroom. I'd been too harsh, directing my anger at Gerda Helbig and the whole Carl situation at Ma, who, despite her chain-smoking and poor food choices, hardly deserved my condemnation. When I returned, dressed for my library visit, hair blown dry and pinned back in its usual fat doughnut, Ma was gone, but there was a crumpled twenty left on the table. I would have preferred to leave it as a final rebuff for when she returned at five o'clock, but I stuffed it into my jeans pocket. I would pick up a coffee and a doughnut at Tim Hortons on my way to school.

"I want," I told Carl, who had been huddling with his crew before classes started and now separated from them on seeing me approach, "you to pick me up a block from the school this afternoon. I don't need your gang's noise again."

He shrugged his agreement and grinned, his square white teeth shining.

During the lunch hour I used one of the school's computers for research. I needed to find out what I was dealing with, to identify what Carl's problem might be.

After school we went to Carl's empty house, as Gerda and Carl Sr. were attending the Dare's annual dinner. Carl seemed less guarded without his parents and because, I suspected, what he considered to be his ugly secret, coiled in his scoured body, had now become mine. I did not speak of my findings until we had eaten. We sat for once side by side at the kitchen table, helping ourselves from a casserole of beef stew that Carl had removed hot from the oven, and then returned to our study room.

"I went to the library and researched your problem."

He stopped his usual pacing and sat down at the table in our study.

"You're dyslexic. It's neurological."

He did not reply but stared at me, perhaps not knowing what I was talking about.

"The wiring in one part of your brain is a bit . . . tangled. It means you have a hard time processing words and it gives you problems with reading and spelling. There's no cure, but you could have been helped a lot if they had diagnosed you earlier, even as young as five or six. Forty percent of those who have it also have an attention deficit disorder. That's why you're so restless, always moving. Sometimes they give you a medicine for this, to help you focus, to inhibit the inhibitors, if that makes any sense. It may or may not have worked."

"But is there a cure?"

There it was again, the screwdriver mentality. Did he want me to go in and straighten out the tangles?

"No, but it could have been helped. The good part is that it has nothing to do with intelligence. Brilliant people have this: Einstein, Walt Disney, Thomas Edison, and talented actors like Dustin Hoffman and Jack Nicholson.

I read Tom Cruise can't read a word, learns all his scripts by having someone read them to him or by hearing tapes. And Generals Eisenhower and George Patton. Patton had to have his wife read to him. But so many have exceptional talents. You can inherit this."

He shook his head: I had given little comfort. "I guess it's Hollywood or the army. Good I have hockey . . . I love it, you know, the excitement, the cheers, the way we are together as a team, the rush I get after a goal. It sets me free, hockey does."

He looked away, as if in confiding this, he had revealed something of himself that he had not intended me to know. And I already knew so much. I felt a closeness to him, a closeness I had not expected. We sat in silence, and then I said softly, "There's still *Lear*."

So we started again, over and over. I could, I had discovered, give him strategies to help. Finally, at seven o'clock, he produced a printed, memorized version of Act I with only the occasional reversal of letters; then on to Act II with my reading the original and then interpreting it, spelling all the words, and then Carl printing—or attempting to. At seven-thirty, we had to stop; hockey practice was at eight o'clock.

"Fed up?" he asked.

"Of course not," I lied. It was incredibly boring, and the final results, leaking out clumsy and painful, hardly seemed to justify the effort.

"They have talking books on CDs and videos of plays you could see and listen to. They may have a movie of *King*

Lear. I know there are movies on *Hamlet* and *Macbeth*. They have a movie of *The Great Gatsby*, in fact several, but you'd be better with the talking book. Ask Mutti to order it."

"Okay," he agreed, "but it's better with you. You keep my mind from wandering."

Sonja, the attention deficit antidote, the synapse connecter, Sonja with her little hammer and screwdriver.

But I wanted to help.

As we drove back that evening, I thought about his problem while looking out at the long violet shadows from the bare maples lingering over the snow-covered lawns of Davenport's suburbia. I started to formulate a strategy, but I would wait until tomorrow to share it with him. We had done enough today.

"I HAVE AN idea," I told him the next day, after we had settled ourselves in the study. "I'll read the play to you, explaining as I go, then I'll select five questions. I'll write out the answers and you'll memorize them. It means you'll have to copy them over and over, but it's the only way you're ever going to pass. If you listened in class, you could tell what's going to be on the test paper and the exams."

"Isn't it a bit underhanded? Like I'm using your work?"

"Not really. I'll discuss the answers with you. It's just that you'll be able to communicate in writing because you've practised and if she questions you, you're fine with the spoken word."

"I don't want to get you in trouble."

"Don't worry about it, I'll be fine. We have to be practical. We haven't touched the history and political science yet, and we've been a whole week well, four days anyway, because we did some *Gatsby* and one act of *Lear*. That's crazy. We'll never get through anything that way. There's one thing, though: you've got to stop cutting up in class. Just sit there and shut up, or better still move away from your gang and try to answer some questions. Silly to get everyone's back up, especially Steinbrink's, when you're trying to pass high school."

"Yes, boss."

I was aware that I was aiding him and indulging in some convoluted form of plagiarism, and I knew I must try to reduce the answers to as basic and simple a format as possible. Suspicions might surface, but detection must be avoided for both our sakes. I did not know why I was risking myself in this way. Was it because I had become Carl's confidante and cared about him, which was something new for me? I was aware it was for more than the twenty dollars an hour and great dinners.

IT WAS A Friday night and Mutti and Carl Sr. were staying overnight in Toronto, as Carl Sr. had been attending a business meeting for the company that afternoon. It was the second time Carl and I had been alone. Mutti had phoned at five giving oven instructions for the macaroni and cheese she'd prepared for our dinner.

It was strange, just Carl and me sitting at the kitchen table in the silent house. Mutti was such a presence that she made the house come alive with her ceaseless chatter and the cleaning and cluttering of endless pots and pans. Carl removed the macaroni dish from the oven and placed it on the table, but instead of having me serve myself, he spooned it onto my plate.

"Say when."

"When. You'll have me fat as a seal."

"I never think of you as fat, just nice and round where you should be nice and round."

He smiled when he said it.

"Thank you." I was not used to compliments, except of the academic variety, and did not know how to reply—or if, in fact, a compliment was intended.

"My mother used to cook a lot of fried stuff: sausages, fries, and hamburger meat. I sort of blamed her for my dad's heart attack, probably unfair of me. The bottle of vodka he drank every night didn't help."

I didn't know why I confided this to Carl. Perhaps it was because he'd told me so much and I wanted to reciprocate, or I just wanted to talk about Pops. I never had, even to Ma.

"You miss him?"

"Yes, sometimes more than others. He was always proud of me when I did well: Ma was too tired to care." I felt a heaviness in my chest and a suspicious burning under my eyelids. I stopped eating.

Carl got up and stood behind me, his large, warm hands on my shoulders. I felt the warmth spread down my arms and across my chest. Then he gave them a slight squeeze before he sat down again.

"I know he was proud of you. If I'd been your dad, that's how I would have been. That's what you've got to remember, the times when you made him happy and proud."

I was shocked. I had not expected such words of comfort from hockey hero Helbig. I had underestimated him.

"Let's get a little air before we start the *King Lear* waterboarding."

The kitchen door led directly to the backyard, so we stepped outside without our jackets. I wore only my socks, having deposited my boots as usual at the door when I entered Mutti's immaculate house. It was the middle of March and there was a harsh chill in the air, and the bone-like branches of the maples were still bare. The soaked grass on the lawn was flat and brown, and had a stale tobacco smell, while a blurred moon gave little light. We just stood there on the back steps, not speaking, breathing in the silence. I gave an involuntary shudder, and he took my hand.

"You're freezing. I'm such a dickhead. Let's go back in and I'll let you start earning your twenty an hour."

He took my cold hand in his warm one and led me back to the kitchen, where he vigorously rubbed my arms and hands, even rubbing my feet. I was not used to physical contact and it mesmerized me. I stood like a robot and then when I sat down obediently lifted each foot as ordered.

"I'll make you some hot coffee; Mutti's got some Blue Mountain from Jamaica. It's great, it'll warm you right up and even keep you awake while you drill idiot-boy here."

The coffee was hot and rich and we sat sipping it at the kitchen table, delaying going to the study.

"If," he said, looking at me with a smile, "you'd come to the movie with me when I asked you, I could've kept your hands warm all the way through."

I could have told him why I refused, but I didn't. It would sound silly. I merely said, "Sorry, I didn't really know you then."

"Just a stuck-up snotty little teacher's pet," he teased, and he had me smiling as we headed for the study.

After that night I never felt quite the same way about him.

THE NEXT FRIDAY'S session crawled on in its usual way: reading, explaining, writing, spelling, and then the clumsy pain of regurgitation. By nine o'clock the answer to Lear's redemption on the heath in the storm and the Fool's contribution had been condensed to a page and a half of printed discomfort, with no brilliant insights, but readable and hopefully passable.

We drove back to the apartment, fellow conspirators, easy together, the secrets of dyslexia and plagiarism giving us a relaxed intimacy, as had our moment on the back steps a week before under a cold early spring moon. I felt a surge of warmth that I attempted to ignore. We were in it together, working as a team. Two spies in foreign territory moving with stealth through the darkened academic world of Davenport High, with its chipped lockers filled with sour running shoes and discarded lunches. Restless classrooms, filled with slouched, blue-jeaned students with glazed eyes and slack mouths.

"What do you do on weekends?"

"Study. I need the scholarship."

I refused to fabricate a social life. I had never been part of the giggling groups of girls discussing dates and parties, ponytails bouncing with shampooed aggression, ears studded with multicoloured fake jewels, and bright eyes outlined in dark pencil: girls with tight designer jeans, snug T-shirts, and spearmint breath, girls who spoke of "hunks" like Carl Helbig. I was Sonja, number-one Davenport High School nerd, the girl who teachers sought out for the right answer. Sonja, with her black bun, pale face, hidden body, and high clear voice.

"Ever been to a hockey game?"

"No."

I would not say I thought hockey, in fact any sport, silly, but that I was aware he was a very big deal when it came to hockey. His name constantly drifted out from the pockets of gigglers in the school cafeteria as I sat eating lunch with Donalda and Margaret.

"It's not as if I'm not interested," I lied, "it's just that I'm really busy, especially now, because I haven't been putting in my hours for my own studies."

That should stop him from pressuring me, and even deliver a small smack of guilt to that unblemished square jaw of his. He was fully aware why I was not putting my hours in: I was too busy drilling him to pla-giarize my test summaries so he could become a high school graduate.

He ignored the smack as a love pat. He had, I thought,

something of the rigid Mutti, not yet a tank but the parts were in place.

"I want you to come to the game. It's against Mississauga Secondary and they're coming all the way here by bus. It's a top team and these are the playoffs. I want you to come, just this once. The game starts at 2:00. Then I'll never ask you again. It's only fair that you see something I'm good at."

I found the urgency in his voice compelling. Besides, in the pocket of my black duffle coat with its attached hood were $360 in hundreds and twenties, neatly folded. This would be the second in a series of bank deposits, which would build up week by week, paving the way for my exodus from Davenport and a successful future life. No doubt Carl skated well and wanted to showcase his efforts. And I did not want him hurt. Never by me.

"Okay," I said, stifling a sigh and attempting to remove the resignation from my voice. "I'll go."

Just this once.

3

THE GOLDEN EAGLE
OF DAVENPORT HIGH

DAVENPORT WAS PROUD OF ITS arena. Built with
public donations through a series of drives, dinners,
and even lotteries, it was the equal of arenas built in much
larger cities such as Brampton, Mississauga, Markham,
Newmarket, and Barrie. It seated sixteen hundred around
a large rink and had two food and drink concessions at
each end that gave off smells of hot dogs, hamburgers,
fries, and coffee, which wafted toward the long lineups
at intermissions. Its sound system was state of the art and

usually echoed the rich tones of Jim McNeil, who was well known as a sports commentator for professional leagues before retiring to Davenport, where he had been born.

MA HAD LEFT at nine for a prearranged house-cleaning job for a woman I'd spoken to who informed me she wished to be present when "the char woman" was there, "just in case." I watched Ma leave with a mixture of guilt and relief. I wanted to avoid her Camels, coughs, and sharp glances, as this tiny injustice collector never forgot a fight and could recite the hurtful words of any opponent for years to come. On the other hand, she looked like a beaten figure, with her pail of harsh detergents and swollen red hands. Years later, long after she was gone, I always pictured her that way, small and shrunken, her flannel coat falling tent-like from her narrow shoulders, shuffling in her flat boots, a cigarette hanging from lips as grey as oysters.

"I'll get some groceries," I said in Ukrainian by means of apology. Ma merely nodded, obviously still upset by my morning outburst two weeks before. To lessen my guilt, I bought some groceries at the corner store before leaving—some bananas, low-fat cheese, a pumpernickel loaf, a dozen eggs and orange juice. I saw no need to spend more of my hard-earned money when I could be assured of five mouth-watering dinners each week, courtesy of Gerda Helbig.

The bus was full, so I walked three miles to the arena into the bright of an icy March Saturday afternoon, crossing the street so I could catch the remnants of the sun on the other wet sidewalk. My toes and hands were numb and the redemption of spring seemed far away. The cold pricked my cheeks and I held my nose, giving it a temporary break from the chill. Why had I promised Carl that I'd attend? When I reached the arena, it was one forty-five and a FULL sign had already been posted outside.

"Standing room only and very little of that," said the large man at the door. He had a grinning overbite and a wool cap was pulled over his ears. "Mos' everyone's been here since one."

I was relieved. I could now get a return bus, go back to the empty apartment, wrestle with the thermostat, and try to complete the week's assignments. And I could honestly tell Carl that I couldn't get a seat.

"Sonja," said a loud voice, "we got a seat for you right up front. Carl was afraid you wouldn't get a seat." It was a smiling, shuffling Jerry Henley, dumb as they come, his cap with the school colours on backwards. He'd obviously been told by his idol Carl to see to it that I had the best seat in the house.

I followed him awkwardly, pulling the hood of my black duffle toward my face as a form of disguise. There was nothing shameful about appearing to see Davenport High's hockey team compete in the finals, but it was something I'd never done. It might interest Candace Stewart and the group who saluted Carl and me when we left the school for our study sessions. As well, it did not reflect the image of number-one nerd, Sonja Danychuk, whose interests, I thought, should be on a loftier plane.

"Didja hear about Carl being scouted?"

"No." I wasn't even sure what he meant.

Jerry continued with his information, the fact that I wouldn't know about scouting not even entering his mind. Even a geek like Sonja Danychuk would know about scouting.

"There's reps up here from the Pittsburg Penguins and the Ottawa Senators, anyway that's what the *Davenport Guardian* said, and there's only one guy they'd be looking at. Ain't that amazing, really awesome."

I nodded my head, still not certain what I was agreeing with.

The arena was erupting in a kaleidoscope of noise and colour. Shrill whistles tortured the air and assorted chants went up from pockets of supporters of both teams. I was seated in the best seat in the middle of Carl's Davenport following, who appeared to be the loudest group in the arena. The Choir and the girls accompanying them wore large T-shirts over heavy woollen sweaters stating, WE'LL GIVE YOU HEL, or YOU'LL GET HEL ON EARTH. It was a winter circus, with the smell of fries, beer, and packed humanity, chilled and expectant, all waiting for the arrival of HEL.

In his rich, sonorous voice, Jim McNeil announced each player in the lineup, starting with the Mississauga team, who were hailed as each skated forward, accompanied by the applause of the Mississauga supporters who sat directly across the ice from the Davenport crowd. He then started to introduce the Davenport team, waiting for the applause to dissolve before going on to the next player. Then, at the very end, with theatrical bombast, he thundered, "Centreman Carl Helbig!"

The Davenport rows went mad with welcome, and then the chanting started: "Hel, Hel, Hel . . . Big Hel . . . Big Hel . . . Big . . . ."

No wonder he had wanted me to attend: I would be a witness to this veneration.

The national anthem was played, the puck dropped, and soon ten players were moving around the ice at high speeds. The Davenport contingent was focused, however, on number 14. He was a superhero, moving with effortless speed. The eyes and heads of the Davenport groups followed him as he rushed toward the Mississauga goal with the tank-like relentlessness of Mutti transformed into muscle and heft. He could not be stopped. I glimpsed his face, stiff, pink, with eyes focused slits.

The Mississauga goalie sprawled against the onslaught, but the shot was so fast that, like the goalie, I missed the entry. The goal light flashed, the crowd erupted, hooting and hollering their approval, and the chants began again, "Hel . . . Big Hel . . . Big Hel . . . Big . . . ."

"Davenport goal scored by number 14, Carl Helbig, unassisted," shouted Jim McNeil, his voice raw with pride, the contrived Broadway showmanship gone.

His teammates encircled him, closing in on him with a helmeted cocoon, sharing in the triumph.

"You know what I think," pronounced Jerry Henley to Carl's followers, "I think he'll be scouted by more than the Penguins and Senators. I can see the Bruins or Blackhawks." Everyone nodded in solemn agreement.

The goals kept coming and the chanting continued.

The final score was eight to two for Davenport, six goals and two assists by Carl Helbig. He had come over to acknowledge us after it was all over, face maroon, teeth flashing, without his helmet, his short blond hair plastered against his square wet skull.

"Glad you could make it," he said, smiling at me. And then to Jerry, "Some guys are here from away, they want my number."

"I told you," crowed Jerry. "Diddin' I tell you? The paper even said it."

He was, I thought, basking in the sun of the indomitable Helbig, who couldn't have read it in the paper in any event. With Jerry, it was as if some psychic welding had taken place, and there was a dual future for both, full of chants, shared agility—and money.

"I didn't think you'd be into this kind of thing."

It was Candace Stewart in her huge T-shirt with its GIVE 'EM HEL in bright red letters and a snug angora cap with a hole in the back for her long, butter-coloured ponytail. Her eyes were as cold as the icy rink currently in the process of being Zambonied down.

"I was invited," I said, knowing at once it was the wrong answer and that this was a girl who had shared a closeness other than tutoring with Carl Helbig.

"Oh really," purred Candace, not missing a beat, "guess someone was trying to involve you in school activities, to make you a bit well rounded—not as if you do normal."

The obvious reply was that she was quite right and that I did not wish to socialize with the group that made up the Helbig-Henley congregation. They were, I thought, ordinary—childish even—and then I realized with a little shudder of self-awareness that I had become, as Ma had proclaimed a few weeks ago, "high on yourself," high as a result of my hoped-for scholarship, Mutti's dinners, improving finances, and academic kudos—a heady combination. And I was even thinner. No, I didn't want to do normal. Yet I was lonely, not that I'd admit it—not even to myself.

I ignored her. Let Candace Stewart think the Hockey God, Carl Helbig, was attracted by my dark, intense self and not my academic help—although surely Candy must be suspicious of the attraction.

I shuffled with the crowd from the cold arena listening to the excited voices, hearing words like *scouted*, *drafted*, *Bruins*, *Hawks*, and *Senators*. Being scouted or drafted I concluded was similar to being anointed, and from what I could tell the anointment was encrusted with jewels, lined with such inducements as a signing bonus and a contract that could last for years and bring in millions, millions far beyond my realm of thought. Across from the sea of packed bodies I spotted Mutti vigorously chatting with several members of the crowd. I waved at her but she was too preoccupied to respond.

THE PLAYOFFS LASTED for ten days. There was only one more game left, Davenport against Etobicoke, and it was to be played at the Davenport Arena. At school, everyone spoke of Carl Helbig, but he was not there. There had been no tutoring for ten days. Every night he was in a different arena and every day he was celebrated by the school.

I was not, I told myself, one of his puck bunnies. I was, I hoped, someone he looked up to, although sometimes I felt it was more than that. Even more importantly, I needed the money. Nothing had come in for ten days. Six hundred dollars lost and all because of damn stupid hockey.

"Tonight's the last game, you coming?"

He had dropped in after class, probably, I thought, to receive the kudos of his adoring fans. He was their hero, and *Lear* and *Gatsby* could both go to hell. I was standing by my locker, books in hand, surprised but pleased he had sought me out.

"I saw you play at that first game against Mississauga and you were very . . . impressive."

"But not impressive enough to see again?"

I felt his hurt. It appeared vital to him that I see him in a different light than the frustrated and limited student I met with five days a week.

"You'll impress the whole school, even all of Davenport. You don't need me there. I won't be missed. I realize your athletic abilities far outweigh your academic ones. You'll do fine without me." And even saying this I wondered if it were true; perhaps he wouldn't do well without me— except in hockey.

"Great. Thanks a lot."

He turned and stamped away, and I thought I heard a muttered "Bitch." He strode through the door that opened out into the school parking lot where Mutti's Volkswagen stood waiting. I wondered if he was angry enough to stop our tutoring lessons. I hoped not; it would be the height of stupidity to forfeit his chance of graduating from high school because his teacher, and that was how I liked to see myself, refused to attend a final hockey game—important as it may be to him and to Davenport.

I worked on my courses that night in the chilled apartment, occasionally feeling a nudge of guilt, thinking that perhaps I should have attended. It seemed so important to him and I could make up for the sacrifice of three hours. I would hopefully do well, although there was no news on the scholarship.

Davenport won ten to six, and Carl Helbig was awarded the league's most valuable player award. There was a huge celebration and the *Davenport Guardian* carried the victory in headlines on the front page with a large picture of Carl smiling broadly in his hockey gear and a play-by-play description of the game. Too bad, I thought sourly, that it would take him so long to read his own praises. At the same time I was glad for him; it would make up for everything else. I wanted him to be happy.

He was not in class the next day; hungover, I surmised, but he appeared the day after.

"You've become quite the celebrity, Carl," said Miss Steinbrink. No longer a disgrace to the German people, even our teacher was impressed.

But at the end of the day he was there, waiting for me, smiling.

"Still interested?" I asked.

"Of course I'm still interested. What is it with you, anyway? Without you I can't make it. I probably won't make it even with you, but at least with you I've got a fighting chance."

We walked together into the cold. As usual I was wrapped in my black duffle, my head down, and beside me strode the most valuable player of the Ontario Junior Hockey League, earmuffs covering his shiny pink ears, eyes narrowed against the late afternoon chill. He opened the door of Mutti's Volkswagen and I jumped in without even thanking him.

"I've got something to show you when we get back—something exciting."

"You've done some English on your own?"

"I said exciting," he answered with irritation.

We drove in silence, the Volkswagen finally beginning to heat up, our breath clouding the frozen windows.

"Too bad you missed the game," he said.

"Yes, I should have gone. But as your friend Candace Stewart says, 'I don't do normal.'"

"What a bitch." He laughed, not without affection.

We entered the bright little pink box of a house heavy with the rich smells of fried steak and onions, mingling with bubbling cabbage, turnip, and potatoes. I had missed the food.

Mutti was standing there, eyes steady on Carl. "It is time to feed our champion," she stated.

It was not until we were sitting at the study table, stuffed with steak and tapioca pudding, book opened at Act Three of *King Lear*, that he presented me with the envelope.

Inside was a letter printed on the letterhead of the Boston Bruins and signed by the administrative vice president. They were offering him a contract, a projected $1 million a year for three years, with an option for them to extend for an additional three, terms to be negotiated at that time. Prior to this he would attend training camp for three months starting the end of June. A cheque for $300,000 as an advance on the signing bonus of $500,000 was attached to the letter.

"I saw a lawyer about it yesterday, a guy familiar with these things, but he wants me to see a specialist in sports contracts in Toronto. He says the final contract could be worth millions. I heard from the Oilers too, but I'm sticking with the Bruins."

He kept watching me for a reaction.

"It's so much money. I don't even think about that kind of money."

He nodded eagerly, obviously pleased he had impressed me.

"You're sure you want to continue this tutoring? It looks to me like you're going to be just fine without a high school diploma."

"Too boring for you, like watching a hockey game?"

"No, no," I said quickly. "I'll be glad to continue."

I should have attended that final game. It was unsettling that he was so dependent on my approval. This was not a relationship I had sought or expected.

"Oh sorry, I forgot. You need the money."

Of course I needed the money. Was he implying that I should be pursuing this repetitive boredom out of the goodness of my heart? I looked at him closely, standing with his V-necked pullover, as blue as his narrowed eyes, with the usual crisply laundered shirt inside it, blond hair no longer drenched with hockey sweat, standing there looking at me, his mouth tight with annoyance. Or was it hurt? I asked myself whether I deserved his hostility.

"Yes, I need the money, but I'm happy to teach you. I'm really impressed with your offer and you're a great hockey player. I should have gone to the game and I'm sorry, I really am. I don't fit in with your group and I feel awkward."

It was a concession I felt forced to make, but it was only half true. I did not fit in with his group, but not because I felt awkward. I felt, if the truth be known, superior. But my answer had the desired effect. He sat down at the table smiling for the first time and lightly touched my arm.

"No need to feel awkward. You're smarter than the whole crowd of them put together."

I dismissed the comment with a smile and a shrug.

"No one's offering me a million-dollar contract. Now let's start on *King Lear*, Act III."

Of one thing I was certain: at this rate no one would ever know *King Lear* better than I did.

He had forgotten the paragraphs I had drafted that were to be part of the forthcoming exam, the academic plagiarism that made us conspirators against the system, but after a few hours, much to my relief, he started to remember.

"What if the questions aren't on the exam?"

"Don't worry, they will be."

"And if they're not?"

"Then write them down anyway, it shows you know something."

"I may have trouble reading the questions."

"Then I'll ask the monitor to read them out loud."

"And if she won't?"

"You are," I said, suddenly weary of it all, "just making problems. What you're memorizing is what I believe will be part of the exam, if not all at least some, at least fifty per cent."

So it went on—and on. April and May, five hours instead of three, five days a week, and then six days a week, then there was over $5,000 in the bank, more than enough for residence, and the hoped-for scholarship would cover the university fees. I could even buy myself black stretch pants, a black pullover, and a new black duffle jacket for the winter, together with boots, and a cropped black leather jacket for the fall term. I would get my hair styled, shoulder-length, getting rid of the bun. I mentally ticked off all my requirements. It was such a pleasant time-waster and occurred every night before I slept and every morning after I woke up. I would start university as a new person.

The exams were during the first week of June. Following my instructions, Carl moderated his behaviour, no longer leading his congregation of worshippers at the back of the class.

"We won't," I told him, "sit together at the exams. It might cause suspicion, especially if your work shows improvement." But after the English exam was handed out, I turned around and we exchanged smiles. Four out of five questions as predicted.

He was called in and questioned: such a drastic change had to be accounted for. But he answered the questions and got his high school diploma.

Mutti hosted the celebratory dinner, a five-course banquet. "I like your Mutti to come to my dinner?"

"She works at night." I felt shame at my betrayal. Ma could miss work and have a decent meal, but then they would see that she spoke no English, looked like a bag lady, and would wish to smoke, contaminating Mutti's pristine home. Carl Helbig Sr. always smoked his cigars outside, even in the coldest nights of winter.

"I'll ask her," I lied.

After four glasses of wine, the chicken soup, the lobster salad, the fish course, and the filet mignon with Mutti's red wine sauce, the Helbigs gave me diamond earrings for my efforts. I felt myself flush with pleasure: this gift was a first. I pictured myself wearing them, my hair back, the earrings uncovered and sparkling.

"Sonja, the family salutes you," said Mutti, raising a glass of Riesling and beaming at me, her firm, round apple cheeks flushed with wine and pleasure, "You prove vat I always say, there is nothing wrong with Carl. Gut teaching change everything."

I exchanged a smile and glance with Carl. Our plagiaristic

conspiracy had succeeded and welded a bond. This was not the time to disillusion Mutti.

"I'd like to toast Carl, the best hockey player in Ontario." I would not have done it had I not had so much Riesling, and then Moselle, and had I not just placed the twinkling earrings in my shabby purse, pending an ear piercing appointment at Clarke's Jewellery the next morning for $20.

"To Carl."

We all stood and raised glasses. Carl smiled and looked at me. With a sinking feeling, moderated by the intake of Riesling and Moselle, I knew he cared for me and that I cared for him, but perhaps not in the way he wanted. He was leaving the next week for the Bruins' training camp.

We left the house together under a star-packed sky. It was late spring and the air was sharp with new grass, ripe earth, and the distant fragrance of lilacs, sweet, sad, and already dying.

Carl drove more slowly than usual back to the rust-coloured block of an apartment building where he'd never been invited in. Once there he leaned to kiss me, but I circumvented it by deftly turning my head and kissing him lightly on a cheek that smelled of Irish Spring soap and Aqua Velva.

"Perhaps when I come home we can go to a movie at the New Davenport Mall," he ventured.

"That would be nice," I said quickly. "Sure, give me a call."

We both sat without speaking.

"I'll miss your mother's cooking." I was sorry as soon as I said it.

"More than you'll miss me, I'm sure," he said, not smiling.

I didn't answer.

He walked with me to the apartment door and did not attempt another kiss.

Later, as I lay in bed, my thoughts reeling, I regretted not letting him kiss me. I had wanted to kiss him, as I found him sexy and yearned for intimacy, but I knew it would add a new dimension to our relationship. I knew it would be a beginning: it would be more than the "making out" or "getting some" so prevalent at Davenport High. But it was as if getting physical with Carl would be a betrayal. I would be settling for a semi-literate jock who could never share in the things most important to me: my love of literature and my beloved novels, plays, and poetry. I did not want to spend my life watching sports and violent movies. Yet I felt a sense of sadness. I asked myself if I was using my love of literature and my superior intellect as a defence against intimacy or as an excuse for not seeing someone as he really was. I didn't want to think so.

THE NEXT AFTERNOON an official envelope addressed to me appeared in our mailbox. I had been granted an Imperial Oil Scholarship for four years at a university of my choice, a scholarship that would cover all costs of tuition. The week before I'd been accepted at the University of Toronto for the four-year program in Honours English. I felt a surge of happiness I wished to share, but Miss Steinbrink had left town. I wanted to tell Carl, but felt I couldn't, not after what had happened the night before.

The next morning I broke the news to Ma, who sat wizened at the kitchen table, inhaling her second Camel.

"I've been accepted at the University of Toronto and they've given me the scholarship. I don't want to leave you, but it will be better in the long run. I'll help you later on, and you'll be happy I went, just wait and see. It's not that far away."

Ma looked at me blankly. "You didn't tell me. You have money? I hope you change your mind." The word *money* was said in English, which was strange.

I looked at her grained hand holding the steaming cigarette, and it had developed a slight tremor.

"Yes, I have money. What do you think I've been doing every afternoon and night?"

I was ashamed of the sharp impatience in my voice, but I continued. "Pops wanted it for me. He told me. He felt his life was a failure."

I was being cruel. Ma had been the workhorse, never complaining to or of a partner who drank himself into oblivion every night. I was implying that she had brought about Pops' failure, pushing him into a premature death as a result of her limitations.

There was a silence and then Ma shrugged her acquiescence, but when she spoke her voice was bitter. "Do what you like, you will anyway. You're just like your father. You better watch your drinking."

I sighed and reached out my hand to touch hers, but she pulled it away, crushing out her cigarette in her coffee cup.

I got up. My appointment for ear piercing at Clarke's was at ten. "Not to worry, Ma," I said, not unkindly, waving away a cloud of the last drag of her exhaled smoke. "I've seen enough of addictions."

4

THE UNIVERSITY STUDENT

TORONTO IN SEPTEMBER WAS GLORIOUS with bright sunshine, a cool breeze, and a cloudless blue sky. Once I had settled into my room at the residence that I shared with Sandra, a physiotherapy student from Sudbury who told me after a brief introduction that she'd be spending most of her time at her boyfriend's apartment, I walked around Bloor Street and then Yorkville, where I had a glass of Riesling in honour of Mutti. From my table I watched the women trot by in their tight jeans with high heels or boots and freshly coloured hair. I loved it all.

I entered Holt Renfrew, Bloor Street's most exclusive store, and the smells of dozens of costly cosmetics and perfumes wrapped around me. Like a perfumed heaven, I thought. Going up on the escalator to the second floor I looked down at the dozens of immaculate and expensively dressed women who sauntered from counter to counter. The second floor was filled with designer clothes, elegant and unattainable. I looked at the price tags and caught my breath—glamour, but at a price.

I paid for my first half-year of the residence and was relieved to see that I should have enough to cover the entire year. Now I was able to buy some clothes, and I would get my hair styled at one of the expensive and exclusive salons in Yorkville. The bun was so out of date, in spite of the fact that it showcased the diamond earrings that I never removed.

I sauntered through the campus, admiring the old stone buildings and the surrounding lawns and trees. I had picked my classes with my mind on the Honours English degree but took a psychology and French course as well. My scholarship depended on my keeping an eighty per-cent average. Not difficult for me surely.

It was an all-girls residence and I felt my usual sense of personal isolation. There were groups, laughing knots of girls, some who I assumed had gone to high school together and who gave off an easy sense of familiarity and confidence. None of them, I was certain, came from as poor a background as mine. Sometimes I would hear them discussing social events and certain sought-after on-campus males. I would sit detached, munching my lunch and dinner in the cafeteria, casually reading a newspaper. The cafeteria selections were fair, some fresh fruit and vegetables, better than stale pumpernickel and a pickle, but far inferior to Mutti's dinners. For several weeks I sat alone, my newspaper replaced by required reading from my English courses; then, slowly, I was joined by two other misfits.

"May I sit here?" She was drab but neatly dressed in tailored pants, a striped shirt, and a cardigan. Her chin-length hair, straight and shiny ash blond, fell forward, partially concealing a taut, pale face.

"Reading for English 120? Too bad we have to take medieval studies for an honours degree. It's that or Old English, and I'll take Chaucer before *Beowulf* any day." Her voice was high and precise, like a little girl at a school concert.

"Yes, certainly," I answered, delighted that I finally had company; it was no longer necessary to disguise my isolation by flipping through my study books.

Her name was Janet Murdock, and she came from London, Ontario, where her father was vice-president of London Life Insurance Company. She intended to enter law should her LSAT be high enough once she had completed her degree.

"I'm going to teach high school," I muttered. So ordinary, I thought.

"Oh lovely," carolled Janet. "All those summers off to go to Europe."

"Yes, I've thought of that," I lied. It might have been true if I'd had a father who was a corporate executive rather than a rent collector who drank his life away in Davenport.

Finally we were joined by another student, a Johanna Borden from Calgary, overweight, with short hair and a uniform of blue jeans and a tan-coloured blazer that I suspected might be cashmere after hearing that her father was a chief engineer with Suncor, an oil and gas company. She was in first year of mining engineering and preferred to be called Jo. She was, I suspected, a lesbian, and she made us both laugh with her vicious remarks aimed at the twittering knots surrounding us in the cafeteria.

"Heavy intellectuals," she would snarl, "all here so they can tell their future bridge partners and philanthropist husbands that they graduated from U of T."

"There are serious students here," protested Janet. "Most of them are focused on their future careers. You're back in my grandmother's era, Jo. Isn't she, Sonja?"

"Sure is," I replied. I liked Janet, and we usually sided together against Jo when there were three of us at the table.

"Are you attached?" Jo asked me one night when Janet was off-campus having dinner with a visiting aunt.

It was an open question, but I realized there might be more behind it than a casual inquiry. I was yet to have a date, a ridiculous admission for a girl of eighteen, but I was not a lesbian. Somewhere in the recesses of my mind there lurked a handsome, dark, brilliant poet or author with whom I could share titillating cerebral conversations and travel all over the world, where we would entertain in our various salons the foremost intellectuals of the day. But I knew I would never meet him in Davenport, home of hockey and hokum—although my mental images at times had a disconcerting way of metamorphosing into Carl Helbig, complete with blue sweater and scrubbed jeans. My answer could hardly be "No, I'm waiting for someone good enough. Haven't met anyone smart enough yet" or "The only one ever interested was a dyslexic hockey hero from Davenport."

So I replied, "My high school boyfriend's been drafted by the Boston Bruins; he turned down the Oilers. He's quite the hero back home. These hockey contracts pay millions. No wonder kids these days are only interested in sports and never read a book."

"Wow," said Johanna, showing her first enthusiasm since we'd met. "What's his name? I love hockey. I'll watch out for him."

"Carl Helbig," I replied. "They think he'll be another Gretzky."

It was good, I thought, that I'd attended at least one game.

AS USUAL, I was alone and lonely. I attended classes, turned in my papers promptly, and received top grades, with the expected comments on my originality of thought. This stemmed, I believed, from both my ability to conceptualize and then to analogize various works with other, very disparate, works. It was less genius but more a creative talent. It was just the way my mind worked, and academics loved it. And I worked like a dog, having no other distractions. There would be no problem keeping my scholarship for next year, although there would be a problem with living expenses unless I acquired a well-paying summer job—a remote possibility. I listened to my two affluent friends speak of travelling to Europe the following summer, and I envied them.

"Could your father get me a job with London Life next summer?" The question formed in my mind and then remained unexpressed, a not only embarrassing but futile inquiry. I would have to find room and board in London, Ontario, and that would erode any savings. There was no London Life, or indeed any other life, in Davenport.

5

THE ACADEMIC ENTREPRENEUR

"WOULD YOU HAVE DINNER WITH me?" Jean Pierre was tall, thin, almost cadaver-like, with thick, dark, oily hair combed straight back into a knotted little ducktail. He wore a long wool scarf looped around his neck and spoke with a French accent. He smelled strongly of cigarettes and I thought of Ma. He was in my Shakespearean study group and his answers to the teaching assistant indicated that all was lost in translation. It was in November, too late for him to change courses. I did not want to have dinner with him but could think of no immediate excuse to refuse the invitation.

We walked from the weathered stone campus building north to Bloor. It was dark early now and fat snowflakes drifted down slowly, disappearing in his scarf and forming blurred hives around the street lights. Our destination, Jacques' Omelettes, was on Cumberland, one street north of Bloor, and we climbed up the stairs to the second floor of the three-storey house. It was only five and the dining room was empty, so we had a choice table looking down on the street. Jean Pierre ordered a carafe of Cabernet Sauvignon in French and lit a cigarette, letting the smoke ooze out of the big, black nostrils of his thin, arched nose. Again, I thought of Ma.

"*C'est impossible*, hopeless," he pronounced. "I will become, what you say, a Christmas graduate."

He had come from Bordeaux to better his English and to acquire a degree as a preliminary step to graduate work at the Sorbonne.

"You should have gone to McGill in Quebec," I chided sympathetically. "It's essentially a francophone province, less of a cultural shock for you."

I felt relieved at the conversation. I found him so unattractive with his greasy hair, cavernous nostrils, and small stained teeth with their enveloping stench of smoke that any thought of intimacy with him, or having his emaciated acrid body next to mine, gave me a psychic shudder. On an academic level, however, I could be forthcoming. I looked down at the street, watching huddled figures walk with their heads lowered through the drapes of clotted snow. It could be a romantic setting, but I was with the wrong companion.

After we had finished our steak and frites, he stretched forth a large cool hand and rubbed my upper arm. "My apartment's near here. Why not come in for a drink?"

"Not tonight, I'm way too busy."

He sighed, removed his wallet from his leather jacket, and handed the waiter his credit card.

Shakespeare 100 was based fifty percent on essay work and fifty percent on the final exam. There was an important essay due the following week. I did not want to hurt his feelings—after all, he had bought me dinner—so I said, "I'll draft your paper on *Macbeth* and you can be assured of a passing grade."

He kissed my hand with the fervour of a man pulled from quicksand.

Better than sex, I thought. Academic payment for the beefsteak, frites, and the glasses of Cabernet Sauvignon. I felt nostalgic for Mutti's dinners and Carl Helbig smelling of Irish Spring soap and Aqua Velva.

The incident inspired me. The next day I tacked a small white card on the bulletin board in the building where our English classes were held. It read: HELP WITH TERM PAPERS. PHONE SONJA. $150 DOWN.

The response amazed me. There were apparently an unlimited number of students lacking either the inclination or expertise to produce an acceptable term paper and who were not above passing off my work as their own. Within two weeks I branched into British history, specializing in the seventeenth and eighteenth centuries. I presented all papers with a flourish—as if for publication—to my grateful "customers." Within thirty days there was $3,600 in a newly opened account at the Toronto-Dominion Bank on Bloor, the same bank that held the monies from the Helbig tutorial funds.

"YOU'VE HEARD ABOUT Carl, I'm sure," said Jo at dinner one night before the Christmas break. "He got his bell rung, just lay there for a while, but was playing again by the end of the game. Bet he had a concussion."

I felt shock. Then shock at my own shock. After dinner I phoned Mutti.

"Not worry," she said, "Carl good. Just a few little head bumps, not serious. Carl let no one down, he top-scoring rookie. And would you like to attend Christmas party, in Carl's honour?"

I assured her I would if I returned home.

I decided that night to go back to Davenport for the Christmas break. My first inclination had been to stay in residence and concentrate on the January exams, but the residence was shut down with only a skeletal staff for the holidays. I had neglected my own work, churning out papers for others, but I could study just as well at home. Then there was Ma, who I could never think of without guilt. Both Pops and I had deserted her, but I had done it more directly. She never phoned the residence because of her English problems, and I had only contacted her once as she was never home. Cellphones, I had read, were on the way.

I would buy Ma a gift. It would be a first. We were not a family who exchanged gifts, small bills perhaps, but not gifts. My diamond earrings, presented at the Helbig house to celebrate Carl's passing grades and never removed, had been a first. Now it was Ma's turn. I would buy Ma a coat to replace that ugly, ill-fitting grey flannel tent she always wore and some good scented moisturizer for her hands. That would please her, I felt sure. And help dilute some of my guilt for leaving.

Even at pre-Christmas sale prices, the coats at Holt Renfrew were expensive, and too tailored and chic for Ma. I saw a black cocktail dress on the second floor, twice reduced and now half-price but still expensive. I tried it on. I had lost more weight but not on my breasts, which rose pale, swollen, and exposed from the low-cut square neckline. I would need a black bra, spike heels, and sheer, barely black hose—and a chinchilla wrap, I thought, making fun of myself, the latter out of the question.

"Mademoiselle is gorgeous, simply gorgeous," cooed the saleslady with an accent like Jean Pierre's but with much cleaner hair. "*Quel décolletage.*"

"I'll take it," I said. Of course, there was the matter of having no place to wear it, but then one never knew in life, although my past had never shown any social activity except for the Helbig dinners. But Mutti was partial to parties and she had invited me to a Christmas party for Carl, whose health I wondered about. Carl and The

Choir would be there, and I would shock them all with my newfound glamour and fleshy exposure. Carl would really be impressed, not used to seeing me as anything but a dowdy academic. And I wanted to see him again. This time we'd kiss, if he wanted to drive me home, and perhaps see a movie together later on. Just a casual date, something I'd never experienced. I picked up the bra and the black patent pumps with the stiletto heels and sharp pointed toes—again, totally impractical. But impressive.

I felt guilty, so I left with my own purchases on my arm to find a less expensive and more appropriate store for Ma. In Yorkville, I passed a display window with a small-sized steel blue coat with a fluffy, grey-white fox collar. I stopped and took notice: a consignment store. It would have been thoroughly dry-cleaned and Ma would never know. I went in. There were racks of clothes, all previously worn, but in excellent condition. Forest Hill rejects, I thought, knowing I would never wear anything previously worn, regardless of the price and source. There was nothing like the arrogance of the impoverished.

"It was purchased new for over fifteen hundred. The collar alone would be worth seven-fifty, and now it's a steal at two-fifty, a real steal. It would have been gone long ago, but it's a *petite*, for a very little person, a four or even a two perhaps. Not for someone like you, of course."

"I'm aware of the meaning of *petite*," I said. "Is this the final price?"

"My dear," purred the saleslady, rolling her eyes.

The store operated on behalf of a charity, and the saleslady was no doubt volunteering her services, which explained the attitude.

"I'll take it," I said.

I would switch the tag of my $850 cocktail dress to this little coat and wrap it in my Holt Renfrew dress bag. I felt no guilt at my subterfuge. The price would impress Ma, even perhaps serve as some solace for what I thought of as my desertion. She would be delighted, having worn her grey tent as long as I could remember, and unlike the cocktail dress the coat could go anywhere. A cleaning woman with an expensive coat in Davenport—not that Ma would wear it to any of her house-cleaning assignments.

I waited at the Dundas Bus Terminal, textbooks in a large briefcase and my clothes in a small suitcase. The coat, wrapped in the Holt's bag, was carried on its hanger over my shoulder. My fellow passengers might wonder how anyone affluent enough to shop at Holt Renfrew would be travelling in a rickety Greyhound Bus to a place like Davenport, but then no one on the bus would ever have shopped at Holt's.

It was a four-hour journey by bus. As the bus left Toronto, I looked at the wet streets lined with store windows shining with Christmas lights and at assorted crowded small restaurants. Inside the cafés and restaurants staff members from the surrounding offices were being feted for the holidays and there would be laughter. I felt depressed. Leaving Davenport had changed nothing. I always felt alone.

As the bus left the city, the lights lessened and I became aware of my fellow passengers. The man across the aisle was already asleep, mouth open, a thin silver thread of mucus stitched between his lips. He drank, I surmised, and would be heading off to ruin someone's Christmas with some drunken violence on Christmas Eve. In the seat in front of him a woman of perhaps thirty-five chewed her gum methodically, puncturing the soft grey wad with greyer teeth. A waitress, a single mother, going up north to see her kids, who were being brought up by her mother. I noticed a bag from Toys "R" Us under her feet. Perhaps she was not a waitress but worked in one of the body-rub parlours near Yonge and Dundas, rubbing baby oil into swollen bodies, not missing any part. Occasionally a police officer was rubbed by mistake and a bawdy house charge laid, with Kleenex stiff with semen from a nearby wastebasket used as evidence. I had heard of this from a police officer who attended my Wednesday-night psychology class and who was working toward his BA. He was trying to impress me and he did, but not in the way he intended—nauseating stuff.

I needed a car. I could have driven to Davenport in three hours, listening to "easy jazz" on the car radio and stopping off for coffee at a McDonald's or Tim Hortons in the various small towns on the way. Then I would not be inundated with what I mentally called "the great unwashed," or the "toiling masses," or was that from Karl Marx and his silly manifesto? I did not accept the Dickensian concept of mankind marching together in united humanity toward the grave. A motley army, I thought at the time. I could not think of myself as being part of this great fabric of humanity. I had once read of the rich inner life of the only child. What they meant was that you were forced to be introspective so that your mind, spirit, or whatever it was that made up your intrinsic essence curled inward like an ingrown toenail and festered its own way into eternity.

God, I thought to myself, this kind of thinking must stop. Better had I stayed at the residence with its skeletal staff, cleaned my own room, and eaten at Cultures, Murrays, or Swiss Chalet, going to the occasional movie at Manulife. Going back to Davenport was a step into the past: murky, chilling, and isolating—except for Mutti's dinners and perhaps Carl. But then there was Ma. And I felt a certain veneer of confidence from my time in Toronto, a shimmer of glamour that made Davenport, and its inhabitants, even more loathsome.

It was four-thirty when the bus rattled into the Davenport Bus Terminal. It was already becoming dark and the snow, which had been floating down like white feathers all day, was increasing. I was the final passenger and I stood waiting by the door, a bag in each hand, with Ma's coat in its plastic bag thrown over my shoulder.

"Sure you can manage all that?" the bus driver asked. "I could've dropped you off nearer your place. It's gonna get worse an' I gotta head back as soon as I have a butt an' a piss. Where you get a coffee an' a doughnut near here? Or do they even have a Tim Hortons?"

"Davenport's even going to have a McDonald's," I

laughed. "But it's going to be at the new shopping mall. There's a Timmy's close to where I live. But it's the Snow Belt, remember, so don't delay too long."

We trudged along together after I gratefully surrendered one of my bags, the one with the books.

"College girl, eh? Wish I didn't drop out in Grade 10. Worse thing I ever done. Now I spend my life shuttling a bunch of losers from Toronto to Northern Ontario. Not even a decent pension when I do quit, an' my old lady hates the hours."

The snow was getting heavier, stinging my face and soaking my duffle coat. Above us the streetlights were smudged miniature suns. I waved goodbye to the driver at Tim Hortons, only a block from the apartment. He was without a doubt one of the vast army of humanity marching toward the grave. As a fellow traveller I felt sympathy, but little kinship.

Ma was home. Standing outside the door I could smell the smoke. It was a Friday and she'd probably just arrived from her house-cleaning and was bracing herself for the office-cleaning at seven. I would not use my key but surprise her, let her answer and see me standing there. I knocked lightly at the door but everything was silent. No one ever visited, so Ma was probably in shock. I knocked again, a more demanding knock. The security chain rattled, the door opened a few inches, and then fully.

"Sonja, you should have told me. I would have had something for you to eat."

Ma was pleased, it was obvious. Not that she kissed

or embraced me; that was not her way. Seeing her I felt a surge of sadness. Always small, she seemed to have shrunken more, and her face was as puffy as usual, her hair still in its sparse grey knot. Only her green eyes, looking out from their swollen purple sockets, had life.

"We can go out and eat. I'm not leaving 'til New Year's and I'll get some groceries tomorrow. Can you take the night off?"

Ma nodded thoughtfully. "I'll have to work Sunday night to make up for it, but that's all right. It's good to have you here."

It was strange to hear the Ukrainian after three months.

"I bought you a present, a great little coat, really expensive."

I opened the bag from Holt's with the same flourish used when producing my expensive essays. Showmanship, I thought. Who'd have ever thought it: a marketer of tainted goods, selling essays to the student plagiarists and now a secondhand coat to Ma. *Good as new*, a voice in my head mocked, *good enough for a non-English-speaking immigrant cleaning woman.*

"It beautiful, majestic," Ma crowed in Ukrainian, unbuttoning the top hook and gasping at the price tag. "How you get money like this?"

The question was accusatory and in English. With me gone, Ma had been forced to speak English, and her thoughts were obvious. There was only one way such money could be obtained. Her studious daughter had become a hooker. I stifled the urge to laugh, but I knew I had better straighten this out immediately. I explained the source of the funds several times, describing it as a second job, something like I did for the Helbigs. Ma listened carefully, nodding her head.

"But, Sonja, these people, they use your work like it their own. You think that good?"

I was shocked—a morality check from my little cleaning woman mother. Incredible. I would never have believed or expected it.

"Better than what you were thinking."

This time I did laugh and diverted her by forcing her to model the coat—a perfect fit, but inappropriately elegant, the fur collar overwhelming.

"Too grand for me?"

"No, Ma, not at all. You look wonderful. You just need a fox hat to balance it off and some new boots."

Ma sat, the coat across her knees, caressing the collar as if petting some silent, sedated cat. She smiled at me, a rare happening.

Later we drove together through the snow in Ma's crumbling freezing car to the dining room of the Sinclair Hotel, where Ma had her first meal out since her arrival in Davenport twenty years before. She was, I thought, very happy, and except for a couple complaining of her chain-smoking, it seemed to be one of the high points of her life.

Ma sat, her fur-collared coat on her shoulders, clumsily eating slices of lamb with mint jelly, canned peas, and mashed potatoes, sipping her glass of Niagara Sauvignon

Blanc, just pausing long enough to look over at me and produce a tremulous smile. Later that night she patted my cheek with a hand rough as sandpaper and smelling of soap and smoke.

"You good girl, Sonja," she said in English. Then again switching to Ukrainian, "And I'm happy you go to school. You right, I wrong."

LATER I HEARD Ma hacking into her pillow and then smelled her cigarette. More of the same, I thought cynically.

"People aren't smoking so much anymore now, Ma. I heard you coughing last night. You should try to stop."

I waited for her usual speech on smoking being her sole pleasure and as such essential, but it didn't come.

"I will try, at least cut down."

Apparently gifted coats and dinners out opened new doors, perhaps with more yet to come.

I slipped into a routine. The refrigerator was empty save for the usual pumpernickel curling in its plastic, the jar of Bubbie's Pickles, and luncheon meat, a candidate for ptomaine poison, turning a suspicious shade of green. I purchased eggs, fruit, chicken legs, fresh rye bread, tomatoes and milk, even a few baking potatoes with some butter and sour cream. When Ma arrived home from her cleaning I would have something prepared before she went to the office.

On the first night Ma arrived home, she smelled the chicken legs roasting and saw the table set with her sparse cutlery. She sat down at the table, head in her hands, her shoulders shaking.

"You shouldn't have to do this for me," she sobbed in Ukrainian.

"Oh Ma, cut it out. I have to eat too, you know, and you work so hard."

I placed my hands on her tiny shoulders, which felt like skeletal birds, so fragile they would crush under pressure. I had never seen Ma cry before, not even at Pops' death, which had merely made her silent and withdrawn, and now her wrenching sobs filled me with guilt. I had been a real pig, so ashamed of her, treating her like a workhorse, sharing Pops' intellectual disdain; well, I would make it up to her. I bent over, hugging and rocking her, which only increased the sobs.

"If you don't stop, Ma, I'll throw it all out and make you live on pickles again," I threatened. The sobs finally subsided.

6

THE CHRISTMAS PARTY

I T WAS NOON ON CHRISTMAS Eve when the call came.
Carl was home and Mutti was having her little party for
him that night. "Sonja must come . . . she family. Carl, he
ask for you."

I accepted.

"Ma, Gerda Helbig phoned. She's giving a party for Carl
tonight and she wants me to come."

"You got clothes?" Ma's few English phrases impressed
me. Necessity, the mother of invention, I thought.

I brought in the black dress hanging in the almost-empty closet. "On sale, half-price, you like?"

Ma shook her small head with enthusiasm. "Boo-tee-ful. You want drive?"

"No, no." To be deposited via Ma's decrepit vehicle would ruin my entrance. "They're picking me up," I lied.

Ma had been ordered to go to the office building to clean up after the pre-Christmas parties. They usually left her an extra hundred, a Christmas gift and a bonus for ruining her Christmas Eve, not that it was ever celebrated by the Danychuks.

My hair needed help. The shower in the new apartment was no better than that of the old one and Michelle's Beauty Salon was at the corner.

"Do you know what day this is, and can you read?" exploded Michelle.

There was a sign on the door that said CLOSED.

"I reckon the fact that my kids won't get no Christmas presents ain't no skin off your back."

Another clod from the army of humanity marching toward the grave, but I'd learned the value of a dollar, especially to the Michelles of Davenport.

"I've got a big date tonight—Carl Helbig the hockey player—and you won't have to put me under the dryer, just use the extra-large rollers and I'll dry it at home. I'll give you an extra fifty toward the kids' Christmas gifts." A huge tip, when Michelle's usual charge for a wash and set was $25.

Michelle's face was a study: money or time?

"The stores are open until six," I reminded her gently, "and they sell everything half-price after four."

Money won. And I even got fifteen minutes under the dryer, not long enough to dry my thick bush of hair but enough to circumvent meningitis. Going out with wet hair in a Davenport winter would do it.

"I WANT TO see you in your dress before I leave." Ma was sitting in Pops' chair, sipping on her pre-work Camel, a smile of anticipation on her small, puffy face.

I had now forged a relationship with Ma: the coat, some baked chicken legs, and the meals out had started it. Sky-high marks and academic success meant nothing; what really mattered was food and clothes. But at least I was making Ma happy, a feat never before accomplished, and I was taking her out on Christmas Day to the Sinclair Hotel for their Christmas Day Turkey special, four courses at $19.95 a person. Ma would be ecstatic.

I brushed out my thick black hair, enhanced by the borrowed rollers into a wild bouffant, outlined my mouth with fierce red lipstick, labelled HELLION, and shaped my eyebrows with my thumb and index finger. My black eyes, I decided, looking into the stained bathroom mirror, were almost Asian—Slavic eyes, I thought, with my usual disgust—and my cheeks were too full for a sculptured effect, but the overall product was exotic, even arresting. I left the bathroom panty-hosed and spike-heeled, my full breasts spilling from the low square neck, my skin—and there appeared to be yards of it—as white and unblemished as milk.

"Well?"

Ma sat transfixed.

I laughed. "You like?"

"Boo-tee-ful, a movie star, every man there will be in love with you." There was no mistaking the sincerity of her comments, uttered in a mangled mixture of English and Ukrainian.

"Let's hope not, Ma. There's no one there I want to be in love with me. I just want to show them I'm not the geeky dork of Davenport High anymore." But Ma was not listening, and if so she didn't understand, the words *geeky dork* not translating well.

"I was pretty as a girl, Sonja, not with all this." She placed her hands on her non-existent breasts and jiggled. "But blond and tiny. I would sit on your father's knee like a little doll, and for a while I used to look so young a few times they'd ask your father if I was his daughter, he was so heavy and stout. Then one day I looked in the mirror and I was old. It was all gone."

I paused and looked at Ma for a minute, and my throat swelled in sympathy.

She got up reluctantly and offered her services again. "I drive you?"

"No, Ma, I told you they were picking me up. We'll have a nice Christmas dinner together tomorrow. Good we're going out: too depressing to cook a Christmas dinner with just the two of us."

Ma nodded in agreement. "Have fun with the Germans."

At least she didn't say Nazis.

"YOU'RE NOT FROM here?" asked the cab driver after we'd driven halfway.

"No," I lied. Neither was he, I thought; he was probably in Davenport hiding from the police.

"I can always tell the locals, knew right away you were a city girl."

I tipped him more than I'd intended: the last remark was worth the cash. It occurred to me that I was going through my money too fast. After the exams I'd have to step up my business, no reason I couldn't have enough to pay next year's living expenses, and maybe make a down payment on a car, although I doubted whether in my officially unemployed state I could get credit.

Mutti's bungalow—I always thought of it as Mutti's; Carl Sr. and Carl Jr. were mere appendages—dazzled with dozens of Christmas lights. The lights covered the trimmed hedge and hung from the snowy eaves, mixing with the artificial icicles. Santa in his sleigh was illuminated, and Rudolph, a large red bulb glowing from his nose, pranced in metallic glory on the front lawn. A little much, I thought, but unmistakably festive.

"Some folks really go in for this Christmas crap," commented the cab driver, pocketing his fare plus tip and then adding, his mouth curled in disdain, "Whatever turns you on."

Ah, a sergeant among the marching army, and apparently as cynical and jaundiced as I sometimes was.

I touched the bell once and it promptly chimed, "Oh Come All Ye Faithful." The door opened and Mutti appeared, a Santa hat perched jauntily on the side of her head.

"It's Sonja," she shrilled. "Ant she's gorgeous."

They surrounded me, the members of The Helbig Choir, Candace Stewart, Jerry Henley, Sophie Gallo, Gwen Andrews, all of them, as if I were a long lost-buddy. I smiled at Candace, whose red miniskirt displayed knobby knees and whose low-necked top displayed very little, and who was totally eclipsed by my own pneumatic splendour.

Carl stood in front of the blazing fireplace looking much the same except for two band-aids on his left temple. Clinging to him was a black-haired girl who looked borderline anorexic, but tanned and toned, with a wide Hollywood-white capped smile and two breasts, twin golden balls, blatantly synthetic, intruding into her plunging neckline. Not only was she clinging to Carl's large upper arm, but I noticed she had entwined a muscled leg around his calf and was moving it up and down as they both stood together, giving him what I was sure she considered a seductive calf massage.

I felt an inward scratch of jealousy, even anger, but my smile never faltered.

"Oh my God," she squealed in that sexy-baby voice I always found so repelling on the rare occasion that I watched the Red Carpet broadcasts and various talk shows. "This can't be Sonja. She's not one bit like you said. Not one bit."

Carl looked embarrassed, disentangled himself, and

walked over and kissed me on the cheek. I smelled the Aqua Velva and Irish Spring soap and felt the sting of long-remembered affection.

"Really glad you came," he said. "I was afraid you wouldn't. Mutti said you might stay in Toronto. This is Tula. She's trying to break into the movie industry in LA, but right now she's a personal trainer."

"I was a backup dancer in *Evita* and *Chicago*," Tula pouted, defending herself. "Tell it right, Carlie."

The Choir exchanged glances. No wonder I had been welcomed with such enthusiasm: a Davenport alternative to Tula, with real breasts making a rare outing.

IN THE GUEST bedroom I was touching up with Candace Stewart, who was studying social work at Laurentian University and who had suddenly become my new best friend.

"Can you imagine his bringing home a cheap cunt like that for Christmas?" she hissed. "No respect at all for his friends and family. I'm shocked and disappointed."

"She's obviously what he goes for," I replied.

I was more shocked at hearing the c-word come from this future social worker than by Tula herself, who'd I'd mentally characterized as a type—a type I detested—but I nodded in agreement with Candace. No need to alienate my new best friend. At this point, the object of our discussion appeared, the muscles of her tanned arms and legs rippling, as firm as the two golden balls that appeared glued to her chest.

"She must live on a tanning bed," muttered Candace, "or on some other bed."

But Candace had long been dismissed. Tula turned to what I suspected she saw as the real competition. "I don't mean to be rude, Sonja, but do you know what I thought you'd be like? A frump—a real dog. Carlie was always talking about how smart you was, but never about what you looked like."

"Sorry to disappoint you. Maybe he was just speaking of my inner bow-wow?"

Was this Carl's choice in women? I had been right to reject his kiss.

Candace crowed her appreciation. It was apparent she couldn't wait to rejoin The Choir and relate the latest conversation.

"Carl used to spend a lot of time with Sonja," Candace added. "In fact, I used to get jealous 'cause Carl and me, we were close, really close."

Tula shrugged and made for the en suite bathroom, hips swaying, golden calf muscles taut as steel. "He never mentioned you," she tossed over her shoulder. "Guess he grew up."

Candace uttered the c-word again, this time more audibly. Tula dismissed us both with a harsh stream of urine.

MUTTI'S CHRISTMAS EVE spread was everything I'd anticipated: slices of ham and turkey on large platters, bowls of huge pink shrimp with pungent seafood sauce on the side, an assortment of salads and breads, and on the dessert table, apple strudel, custard, and bowls of fruits and berries.

"Guess you heard about Carl's concussion. It almost put him out of the game against the Wings, but he got right back on the ice, like always. Didn't want anythin' to fuck up that contract: one mil a year for three years, plus his signing bonus. Best rookie scorer in the league." Jerry Henley, piling up his plate with turkey, ham, and potato salad, was still basking in Hel's reflected glory.

So it had been a concussion, not just the little bumps described by Mutti. I felt concern, lessened by the presence of the slithering Tula, whose flesh-pressing antics I attempted, but failed, to stop staring at.

"What are you doing?" I had little interest but was trying to be polite.

"Apprentice electrician, good money later on, nothin' like Carl, but good money. And you're at U of T, Carl said. He always talks about you, says you're the smartest girl he ever knew. You're lookin' good too. Never even knew you when you walked through the door. Guess you gotta lotta guys hittin' on you in Toronto?"

I merely smiled. Jerry was no doubt gathering information for Carl. In the background, Eartha Kitt gasped "Santa Baby" and everyone was talking at once. I took a glass of wine from the buffet and sipped it—Riesling, Mutti's favourite. I looked across the room. Tula had discontinued her leg massage and was rubbing Carl's back and upper arms, but he was looking directly at me. I looked back and smiled. For a moment our eyes met.

He did not smile back but just kept looking at me.

At eleven I approached Mutti. The crowd was getting louder and I noticed Carl adding a bottle of rum to the bowl of eggnog. I had three glasses of wine, more than I was used to, and my head was aching, although I had enjoyed Mutti's buffet. The Choir all urged me to stay. It was gratifying. I remembered the "you don't do normal" remark from my new best friend, who now wanted me to "do lunch," an invitation I avoided. I was not interested in a cat session concerning the toned and tanned Tula and Carl's bad taste. Candace irritated me, although I appreciated my new acceptance from the rest of the crew.

"I'll drive you home." It was Carl.

"What is this!" squealed Tula.

"She's right," said Mutti. "It your party ant a host can't leave. You drink too much. I drive her, it like old times, Sonja, yah?"

In spite of my protests, Jerry Henley's offer, and that of a fellow Bruin who'd been hovering nearby, Mutti prevailed, as always.

"What you think of my *wunderbar* Carl now, Sonja?"

"I don't know what you mean, Mrs. Helbig," I said, knowing full well what was meant.

"Sonja." Mutti sighed, negotiating Carl Sr.'s Mercedes like a sea captain, her Santa cap flopping over one ear. "You so smart, you know what I say: my Carl bring home trash to his Mutti for Christmas. I cannot blame Carl; men are veek, so veek. Girls like that use their veggies to get their man, and the men, they give in. Last night, I give this trash her own room. I think she show respect under my roof, but no, I hear her going to Carl's room and she stay there one hour, maybe two. A shameless huzzie, this Tula, why she not with her family at Christmas, tell me dat?"

Bringing her "veggies" to Carl instead, I thought, stifling an urge to giggle.

"Tell me, Sonja, you like Carl?"

"Of course I like Carl."

"Sonja, I mean, really like Carl."

"I haven't thought of him in that way."

I was lying. I not only thought of Carl "in that way" but felt a mixture of jealousy, anger, and guilt that my rejection of him may have propelled him into the hands of a crass hands-on masseuse like Tula.

"Well," ordered Mutti, "start thinking of him in that way. Carl really like you and you decent girl. Carl Helbig is for you. You think about it, Sonja."

I thought about it, and would think about it more that night.

Of one thing, however, I was certain: in the Helbig household, Mutti ruled.

Tula was toast.

7

CHRISTMAS DINNER WITH MA

"THIS IS SO NICE," WHISPERED Ma in Ukrainian as she started on the tossed salad and tomatoes, the first course of the four-course Christmas dinner at the Sinclair Hotel dining room.

Looking at her, I thought she looked . . . presentable. On Christmas Eve she had purchased a soft velour tam, which matched her blue coat and covered her sparse hair, and small fake pearl clip-on earrings from Zellers. I decided I would purchase her new footwear at Easter, at which time I felt confident my bank account would be substantial. I was glad I had returned for Christmas as I felt a closeness to Ma never before realized.

I smiled at her and gently pushed a strand of grey hair under the velour tam.

Ma stopped eating and asked in English, "I all right?"

"You look really good, Ma, really nice, in your hat, coat, and earrings. You could go anywhere."

Ma beamed her appreciation, showing her small, tobacco-stained teeth. "I make you proud, Sonja," she said. "I learn English and stop smoking." This was said in English with great effort, an erratic, accented effort obviously the result of some practice but worthy of praise.

"That's wonderful, Ma," I said with sincere surprise, "Just keep it up. I want you to be smoke-free and speaking English when I come home at Easter. Maybe we'll take a little holiday together this summer."

Ma nodded seriously, wiping her mouth free of salad dressing with the linen serviette that carried the Sinclair crest. The Sinclairs, who had been Davenport's first family, had owned the large brick building as their personal residence prior to its sale to the Holiday Inn hotel chain, which was making some effort to keep the Sinclair ambiance.

"Last night, you enjoy yourself?"

"It was great, Ma. Everyone made a big deal over me, kids I'd never bothered with before. Carl was there with a girl from Los Angeles. His mother didn't like her, said she was using her 'veggies' to get Carl. She meant her vagina, I believe."

Ma shook with silent and appreciative laughter, so much so she choked on her tomato soup with rice.

Nothing, I thought, like someone who struggles with English, making fun of someone who makes an occasional mistake—although this time a big one.

"I believe Mrs. Helbig would like me to get together with Carl. She said I should think about it."

The laughter suddenly stopped. "You love Carl?"

"Of course not, Ma, I was only his tutor. He's making a lot of money now and has a lot of girls after him. He may like me, or I used to think so."

Ma nodded her head thoughtfully. "About love, Sonja, perhaps it's not so important like you think. I loved your father when I married him, loved him so much I was crazy for him, but look what happen. In some countries, they arrange marriages, the parents. Sometimes you fall in love later, or just one person love. Other things matter—a nice life is important."

I sat stunned, my mouth open. The last thing I expected was a lecture on the limitations of love from Ma, and an intelligent and personal lecture at that.

"I'll remember, Ma," I finally said.

Ma smiled. "I'll really miss you, Sonja," she said. "I never thought we'd talk like this."

CANDACE STEWART PHONED the day before I left for Toronto. Carl had left early with Tula.

"I bet Mutti told them to leave," she giggled. "You could tell she was really pissed off after she drove you home from the party. Everyone had a lot to drink after you guys left. She didn't even speak to Carl or the wannabe star for the rest of the night."

"Can't say I blame her," I replied, "Tula's a vacuous sleaze."

I surprised myself—this was not the way I usually talked. Candace hooted her appreciation, and we laughed, and even bonded briefly over Carl's dubious choices in women, conveniently ignoring that in the past we had both been chosen—but for very different reasons.

ON NEW YEAR'S Eve, I went with Ma to the local Greek Orthodox Church on the edge of town. I took her hand as we walked up the wet stone pathway cleared of the snow now lining it. I towered above her. There was a sign on the door: the church was closing in the New Year. The congregation had moved from Davenport to be nearer to Toronto, and there was no one left to support the church.

Inside, the air was thick with incense, and the last remaining light of the declining day pushed through the stained-glass windows. There was only a handful of parishioners, all women with covered heads, kneeling in the weathered pews. The priest was saying Mass and in front candles flickered, each one sending a prayer upward. Ma bowed, went to the front, and lit a candle, her blurred green eyes fixed on the orange flame, her rough hands clasped.

I sat awkwardly, looking at a statue of a benevolent Christ, and then at the priest in his ornate gown, cream with broad strips of gold, and strange bulky headgear. I took no sense of comfort as it lacked familiarity, but I loved any sort of dramatic pageantry—the flickering candles, stained-glass windows, and perfumed incense. I even formed an inconsequential prayer in my mind: *Please God, make things all right.* Nothing specific or demanding. God could make of it what he wished, but he would know, if he were there at all, that I was not badgering him unduly.

All day long, while Ma was gone, I studied for my future exams. Then, in the late evening, I prepared dinner for us both or we went out together, usually to Swiss Chalet.

When it was time for me to leave for Toronto, Ma sat, tears trekking down her mottled, puffy cheeks, looking as beaten as after Pops' death.

"C'mon, Ma, I'll be home for Easter, and then again in May, and we'll go on a little trip. I'll rent a car and we'll go to Kingston, and then to the Thousand Islands by boat. Wouldn't you like that? You'll get some nice sun and good food. Take a week off from your cleaning—tell them you're taking a trip with your daughter. Two things: I've got you some English tapes and a transcriber; you'll play them every night. And the smokes have to go. I know you've got filters, but they're still killers."

Ma did not reply, but the crying stopped, leaving only rivers of tears drying on her full but shrivelled cheeks.

"I get lonely," she said in halting but definite English.

"It won't be for long. I'll phone you. Watch the television. Good for your English too."

I hugged her briefly, marvelling at the fragility of her

arms and shoulders—a scrap, yet a scrap that could clean yards of house and office floors each day. There was a new closeness, based on much more than clothes and food: perhaps Ma was merely waiting for me to show her little kindness, and I was waiting for some praise, or it was Pops' death, but for whatever reason, our relationship was transformed.

"ENJOY YOUR CHRISTMAS?" asked the same bus driver I'd had many days earlier.

"Very much, and you?"

"Not bad, but the kids were all sick. I had to take Virginia to Sick Kids on Christmas Eve for croup, but aside from that it passed okay. We had a good dinner, the wife had her mother and her third husband over, the one with the bucks, so it was top of the line. She'd never cook like that for me, not in a million years."

I gave a light laugh of commiseration. Strange how relationships change: I thought of Ma and our meals out and what had become shared confidences. Soon the bus would start to fill up and he would be forced to keep quiet. I opened my textbook on medieval literature, but my mind kept wandering. I was ready for my midterms, the ten-day hiatus was just what I needed, and after that I would push my business into high gear. There was no reason I couldn't do four essays a week, which would come to between $800 and $1,200 in total, depending on their length and complexity. Next year I'd get a computer and do my research by accessing search engines and databases.

It would cut down on some of my time-consuming library visits. If things went as planned, I could look forward to five thousand a month, even this year. And next year I'd have a car to drive to and from Davenport. The possibilities were endless.

Janet Murdock had spent Christmas in the Caribbean with her family, and Jo, the future mining engineer, had gone to Palm Springs, alone, right after Christmas—a romantic liaison perhaps? They both looked at me with some sympathy after my Davenport Christmas, but it didn't last.

"There was a great Christmas party for Carl," I said, "but he's getting much too serious. I have to get my degree before even thinking of marriage. He's signed a three-mil, three-year contract with the Bruins, not surprising for the top rookie scorer."

"Plus signing bonus," said Jo, who was up on all the sports.

"Yes, I didn't mention that, you'd think I was bragging."

They laughed in unison, thinking exactly that.

"He took quite a hit against the Wings in the last game. Everyone thought he was concussed, but he got up after a minute as if nothing happened," said Jo.

Jo didn't miss a game. I bet she wished she were a defenceman; God knows what hits she'd inflict.

"He had two band-aids on his temple," I said, "but he didn't talk about it. His mother told me he'd gotten 'a little bump.'"

"Hell-oo, little bump," crowed Jo. "He was flat on

his back for two minutes, got up and sat on the bench for another two, and then went back to the game. Bad stuff. Bet he had a concussion."

I nodded, remembering my conversation with Jerry Henley: Carl had been hurt and Mutti was underplaying the problem, as she had before. My concern came back, but then I remembered Tula. My Christmas plans for us had been unfulfilled, partly because of my earlier rejection. But it was obvious that Carl had gotten on with his life, and I would do the same.

8
COMEUPPANCE

THERE WERE FOUR EXAMS, TWO of which were finals. I did well, probably as a result of my Christmas studying. Not even a challenge, I thought. Then there were four new requests for essays. "Certainly," I told them, taking the hundred and fifty each down payment, "but you'll have to wait until I finish my exams."

Then at one o'clock, after I finished my last exam, a note came. It was placed on my desk by the presiding monitor. Professor Latham, dean of English and special lecturer on Shakespearean studies, for whose class essay I'd received an A+ and one of the "original thought" comments, wished to see me in his study at two o'clock. Professor Latham had written a three-book series on Shakespeare's tragedies. They had, for academic works of non-fiction, been enthusiastically received; in fact, you could not even profess to critique a Shakespearean tragedy without referring to the Latham trilogy.

Did he, I wondered, want me as the only student with an A+ to apply for the special Shakespearean student award of $1,500? But then I reconsidered. No application would be required; such an award would be at the discretion of the English Department, with definitive input from Professor Latham.

In the cafeteria I saw one of my buyers, a plump blond girl from Vancouver. I threw her a smile. It was good to have a friendly relationship with your customers; nothing better than repeat business. We had a friendly chat when I had produced her term paper and she'd seemed pleased, chirping a "really appreciate this." Now she turned away. Strange, I thought. Was she now embarrassed by the whole thing?

Professor Latham was in his late fifties, tall and stooped, with thinning light-brown hair and small gold-rimmed glasses pulled so far down on his aquiline nose that they were obviously just used for reading. So much for bifocals, I thought. When he looked up from his chair behind his large walnut desk, his eyes were a cold enamelled blue, the sea on a frigid day, contrasting with his hair and pallor.

I wished I looked better, although I had squished tap water through my teeth, combed my hair, and applied lipstick. My black jeans, pullover, and down-stuffed duffle were so ordinary. Better not to smile with teeth full of tomato sandwich and anemic lips. But as it turned out, there was nothing to smile about.

"So this," said Professor Latham, not even getting up, "is the famous, or should I say infamous, Sonja Danychuk." He had an upper-class British accent, either authentic or adopted from a few years at Oxford.

No one, I thought, depending on my well-read list of British authors, could do nasty better than the Brits, especially Brits of a certain class.

"You don't know why you're here, do you, Miss Danychuk? You probably think you're here for me to render congratulations on your term paper or recent exam, which I retrieved from my associate and read prior to this visit—an excellent analysis of *Macbeth* and a second-to-none analysis of *King Lear*. My, it appears you could recite *Lear* from beginning to end. But I'm sure you must expect this is not the reason for your visit. In fact, in spite of your considerable gifts, and they are considerable, Miss Danychuk, I've been pondering whether I should be recommending to the dean that you be expelled forthwith from this university."

I felt myself choking.

"But why?" I gasped, already knowing the answer.

"It's your sideline, your plagiarism business. Surely you didn't think those little dolts you've been producing for—and who've been paying you handsomely, I under-stand—would show you any loyalty when they were fingered for submitting your work as their own? Most of them didn't change a word, and they confessed as readily as most shoplifters caught in the act, pointing directly at you and placing the blame directly on you, as if any one of them were capable of these erudite essays in your unmis-takable style. I must confess, I'm surprised you made no effort to simplify matters. The work done was absolutely yours, the only addition the name of the false author.

"Amazing that they think their teaching associates are stupid enough not to detect your fine hand in this. One chap—from France, I understand—produced a work of art on Macbeth that he insisted was his own, although I understand he found writing one sentence in English much too challenging. It bore a marked resemblance to your Macbeth exam answer. Needless to say, they've all been awarded a zero mark and will doubtless be demanding their money back from you. Don't give it to them."

"I merely gave them outlines—suggestions—they were to expand them with their own ideas."

"Balderdash," scoffed Professor Latham. "These were finished productions on your part, apparently, according to your customers, produced with pride and enthusiasm."

I placed my head in my hands. Not only was I facing expulsion, but all my future monies were gone, monies I was to use to buy a car, to meet next year's residence fees, and to take Ma—whom I had only recently made happy—out to eat and to dress with second-hand clothes. I might,

I thought with horror, have to return to Davenport and stand behind the wicket of the Toronto-Dominion Bank or, even worse, waitress at Swiss Chalet. My only out, I realized, was a shameless bid for sympathy and mercy.

"You don't understand, Professor Latham," I sobbed. "I'm here on an Imperial Oil Scholarship, which only covers my fees. I tutored all last year—twenty hours a week—to meet residence costs and if I can't make money, I can't come back. I'm not rich, not like some of the students here. My mother cleans homes and offices and my father's dead. This was a great way for me to make money and I didn't think of the implications."

The latter statement was, of course, untrue. I had been well aware of the implications, even Ma had mentioned them, but I had been confident of lack of detection. Professor Latham did not appear moved but eyed me with little compassion—more moved, I suspected, by academic expertise rather than by histrionics.

"Danychuk . . . What's its origin? Russian?"

"Ukrainian."

"Oh, an agricultural people. I don't know where you fit in. The Russians had some great writers. They wrote powerful, moody stuff. What do you intend to do?"

"Teach high school."

"Sorry about that, it's a bit of a waste. If you must be an academic, it should be at the university level. You should have tried some critical essays on your own behalf. Don't bother with Shakespeare, I've got that pretty well covered."

He smiled at me and I felt relieved, but my relief did not last as Professor Latham continued.

"You must, of course, put a stop to your plagiarism business as of now. If you have any retainers, which I understand you take, give them back. As I've said, don't return money to those awarded a zero mark. Your essays were phenomenal, indeed much too much so.

"I have little choice but to consider expulsion, which traditionally involves me, as department head, together with two members of the administrative board. Apparently your case has been seized upon by the papers and you've achieved considerable notoriety on campus. I find your defective judgment strange, considering your intellectual reputation."

He sat back, his cold blue eyes fixed on me above the gold-rimmed glasses.

"You are suspended from your classes for a thirty-day period until a decision regarding your expulsion is made. The decision must be unanimous. You will notify the Scholarship Board of Imperial Oil as to your suspension and possible expulsion unless you'd prefer we take responsibility for that. I wouldn't be unduly optimistic; your actions have shown a shameless disregard for the academic integrity of our university."

My recently eaten tomato sandwich was pushing against my throat. "I'll notify Imperial Oil," I croaked.

"Do that," said Professor Latham with a tight smile, "and you may remain in the residence for thirty days pending the expulsion decision, but as I've warned you, don't be unduly optimistic. In fact, in your position, I'd make alternative plans."

He nodded toward the door and I bolted out, tearing down the corridor to the men's washroom, which was the most accessible, and puking up my tomato sandwich in the nearest urinal.

I spent the next few days huddled under my bedclothes, not sleeping or eating. Janet, who I suspected had heard the rumours, came knocking at the door with fruit and yogurt from the cafeteria. I thanked her but couldn't eat. Finally, I forced myself out of bed and set out to find my customers. I returned the retainers I had collected, apologizing to them and explaining that I lacked both the time and inclination to produce further work. Some had already heard of my forced retirement and possible expulsion as there had been an article in the *Varsity* complaining of the rampant plagiarism and cheating on campus, a cause that had been taken up by the *Toronto Star*. The *Star* proclaimed that this insidious plagiarism was indicative of the lowering of moral standards of today's university students and that an absence of integrity had become the new normal. Both newspapers called for severe penalties. As such, my explanation as to my voluntary withdrawal was met with knowing smiles, even laughter.

Those students who had been caught, who had given evidence against me, and who subsequently received zero grades, were furious with me, several informing me that they found my continuing presence on campus "perplexing, considering everything." I was, after all, a serial offender. It was, I thought, highly ironic, but then what was to be expected from individuals who were willing to pay up to $500 for someone else to produce a top-grade paper for them and then turn out to be revolting snitches. As per Professor Latham's advice, I refused to pay damages, telling them I at least expected them to modify my papers to their personal specifications and to have the decency to refrain from informing any investigator as to their source. It all made me feel as if I'd been selling street drugs. My smoke-soaked friend Jean Pierre had disappeared from the campus, becoming the Christmas graduate he'd feared he'd become.

The fact was the money could not be returned, even had I been so inclined. It was gone. I could, I thought bitterly but not seriously, auction off my virginity. I had not kept it for any lofty conception of morality but simply because I had not yet met anyone I was even remotely interested in sleeping with, although Carl Helbig had crossed my mind at times. God knows how much some mad individual would pay for this privilege. I had missed the sexual revolution of the sixties, and now at the start of a new century, I was out of step as usual, tossing off a flippant prayer in the dying Greek Orthodox Church in Davenport for God to make things all right, which He or She assuredly had not. I suspected that asking Him or Her to promote plagiarism might be taking unfair advantage. In any event, save for some unforeseen happening, it appeared that my academic career would come to a close in thirty days.

9
ALTERNATIVE EMPLOYMENT

I WROTE TO THE CHAIRMAN OF the Imperial Oil
Scholarship Committee—so much better that the letter
came from me rather than the disgruntled university
administration. I would, I decided, put a spin on the situation. At this point, there seemed to be little to lose.

Dear Sirs,
Update and Notification regarding Sonja
Danychuk: Recipient of Year 2000 Imperial
Oil Scholarship Award.

As you are aware, I have been the grateful recipient of a four-year scholarship award covering my tuition at the University of Toronto. I am writing to update you on my progress and of an unfortunate incident that has resulted in my suspension from classes for a 30-day period. I am disclosing this to you in the spirit of candour with the hope that this will not in any way impede my scholarship monies on which I am completely reliant.

Academic Update: Throughout last term I have maintained an "A" average, and I understand that my winter term's final marks are on an equivalent level. My grades have been throughout above the eighty percent criteria upon which my scholarship depends.

Suspension Rationale: Last term, through a surplus of generosity, I helped several less academically inclined students develop their term papers. Unfortunately, they were overzealous and some of their work closely mirrored mine. As a result, I have fallen into disfavour with the university and I am currently under a 30-day suspension. I would appreciate your assurance that my compassionate acts will not in any way stop the receipt of your scholarship funds upon which I am so dependent and grateful.

In anticipation of a prompt and favourable response,

Yours truly,
Sonja Danychuk

A reply to the letter, delivered by courier to the residence, was prompt but hardly favourable.

Dear Ms. Danychuk,
Your rather unusual letter prompted us to con- tact the university and make an inquiry behind the situation as described by you in your letter of January 15th, 2001. You have, as you are no doubt aware, distorted and misrepresented the facts behind your current suspension. You were, I am informed, not motivated by what you designate as "a surplus of generosity" but have been running a highly successful plagiarism business from the residence of the university, benefitting handsomely from your so-called "compassionate acts."

It is more than disappointing, in fact, fraud- ulent, that you would so blatantly misrepresent the actual situation to us. Our scholarship holders are held not only to high academic standards but are presumed to act with the highest personal integrity. This is manifestly not the case here.

Your scholarship funds are terminated as of this date. You are indeed fortunate that we are not demanding a rebate in view of your ongoing deception.

Yours truly,
J. Saunders, on behalf of P. Ryan, Committee Chairman.

Shot with a ball of my own shit. I had heard a member of The Choir utter this hideous maxim against a member of the opposing team at the hockey finals, and it seemed particularly apt. I threw myself on my creased bed and howled into my rumpled pillow. I was finished. I would not tell Ma. Why worry her? So fortunate that I'd paid the residence fees, but there were still the academic fees for the spring term, fees that would no longer be covered by the scholarship. But why worry about that when it seemed certain that I would not be here. I would be an expelled student, seeking a job in Toronto or back in Davenport.

I had not eaten for three days, except for a few bites from Janet's donated apple. Her yogurt had grown a green beard when finally opened, and the half-eaten apple was gnawed rust. I saw myself in the bathroom mirror: my black hair a tangled mop framing my ashen face, and my dark eyes cupped by violet smudges, a far cry from the guest of honour at the Helbig Christmas party with her hellion lipstick and gleaming pearl arms and bosom.

I had to eat, pointless to hibernate in my warm, air-less room like some terminal cancer patient. I could not go to the cafeteria. They would all know and despise or pity me, the latter worse than the former. I would walk to Bloor and pick up some food at Cultures, which made much of its organic products—something loathsome but healthy, like a salad of iron-filled spinach with hard-cooked eggs.

Outside it was so cold that my teeth pained, and there was steam from my mouth when I gulped the air. But not as cold as Davenport. I pulled the hood of my duffle tight around my face to prevent the icy air from leaking in and trudged up University to Bloor. Cultures was closed, so I started walking to The Steak and Burger. To hell with calories and health—I needed comfort food.

Matheson's was not high-end like many of the restaurants in nearby Yorkville but specialized in cater-ing to tourists who wanted a cheap meal in the summer months, office workers and salesgirls for lunch, and, at this time of the year, to those who had come to the city to take advantage of the greatly reduced prices from the remnants of the Boxing Day sales. College and university students, some teaching assistants, even an occasional professor ate—rather than dined—at Matheson's. In the corner of the large window was a small, gold-edged HELP WANTED sign.

I would, I decided, go in and order a bowl of soup and take advantage of their bread basket, although I noticed, shown with the displayed menu on the side of the glass window, a separate sheet announcing "Tonight's Three Course Special." I thought of the Sinclair Hotel and poor Ma, whose future new Easter boots had been flushed away with the collapse of my plagiarism business.

A gaunt, grey-haired woman with a tight, unsmiling mouth, and a name tag declaring her to be Mrs. Greenley, showed me to a corner table and handed me a menu and a printed sheet with "Tonight's Specials." Within two minutes a beaming waitress appeared. She was little more than five feet tall, with unexpectedly broad shoulders and thick, short arms, her pink uniform sleeves reaching to her elbows. Her legs were noticeably bowed, and her bunched calf muscles were worthy of a marathon runner. Her short fair hair, showing white throughout, was brushed back from her square face, which had pronounced lines around her eyes and mouth. Her left lateral incisor, exposed by the smile, was chipped, and I felt a surge of empathy, thinking of past struggles to pay dental bills.

"I'll just have the night's special soup," I said apologetically. "I'm not that hungry."

Her smile never wavered. "A great choice," she said, "I had some at five. It's very rich, full of beans and lentils with tomato base, it remind me of Hungarian goulash."

She had a slight accent, and I glanced at her name tag, which said MAGDA. A Hungarian Canadian, perhaps, brought here as a child to escape the Communists.

As I sipped my soup, I watched her clean and reset the tables, moving from table to table, never losing her smile. Before I knew it, my bread basket was replaced, together with a new butter dish. I was appreciative, but before I could say "thank you" she was gone, on to another table. She was, I marvelled, a powerhouse of a waitress, but there was no doubt they were understaffed. Even the Olympian-muscle-packed Magda could not service the demand.

I pushed a $1.50 tip under my plate before I got up to leave, a ridiculous tip for a soup-only order, especially considering my circumstances, but I really liked her and appreciated the extras.

"You're short-staffed?" I asked. It was more a statement than a question.

"You got it. Ginger and our sous chef took off for that new restaurant on Adelaide yesterday, and our dishwasher's sick, or hungover, or whatever. You interested?"

I heard Pops' cautionary voice, as if he were standing next to me: *You must not end up like us.*

But I said, "Yes."

"AS YOU'VE ALREADY noticed, no doubt," said Mrs. Greenley, brushing the flat chest of her grey tailored suit with a shriveled but manicured hand, "we're short of staff. Ginger and Carlos disappeared yesterday without the decency of an hour's notice, and Alistair's probably lying in a snowbank somewhere insulated from freezing by his usual blanket of Scotch. There's no work ethic among these new Canadians—except for Magda, of course. I've got to get some information, but it's just a formality. To be frank, I'd hire anything without a tail on the spot."

She was so wrong about new Canadians, and I thought

of Ma, but I was not about to argue with Mrs. Greenley, who obviously had the power to hire and fire. I saw her frown when I identified myself as Sonja Danychuk, no doubt classifying me as another new Canadian without a work ethic. I felt like telling her that I'd been born right here at St. Mike's, some two miles away, but didn't.

"You can help Zoltan clean up the kitchen, and then we'll see if we've a uniform to fit for tomorrow. You're not small by any means, but Ginger was also well endowed, in every area but her brain."

"Any experience?"

"Not as a waitress. I'm a university dropout. Money problems."

Mrs. Greenley's parchment-like face soured even more. "Academics are a spaced-out crew. My former husband had a BA and never held a job for more than a week. Just watch Magda, she's the best when it comes to waitressing. Our cook Edmund's a Brit, which doesn't say much for his cooking, and Peter mixes the cocktails and fills the wine glasses and carafes with house white or red; Coors is on tap. We've no demand for bottles of expensive wine.

"Peter's Irish, with Alistair's problem, only his drink of choice is whiskey. I keep thinking they'll dig him out of the same snowbank some day. He drinks more than he makes—and serves. Push the alcohol, there's a good markup there, and be agreeable if it kills you. If anyone complains, offer to substitute or if you really have to, deduct the item off the bill. They'll probably make it up to you in tips. You'll get seven an hour, plus tips. The size of the tips are up to you. Customers tip according to service, or they're supposed to. Questions?"

"Zoltan?"

"Magda's son. I let him come here after school and he gets the night's special. He's a clever boy, sixteen, although you'd never know it. He lacks his mother's muscle tone, which is unfortunate. He studies at the kitchen table and leaves at night with his mother. He helps clean up at times of emergency, like today. I only allow this because of Magda. Don't think I'd let anyone else take this kind of advantage: Magda's very useful to the business."

Zoly was Magda's reason for living. "He could be," she confided, "a world-famous surgeon or scientist." Almost every cent she made went into the nearby Toronto-Dominion Bank for his future education. He sat in his isolated corner of the kitchen every day from four to nine, absorbed in his books for his last year of high school.

He was a short, slight boy with narrow pale hands and long, tapered fingers, round steel-framed glasses over large green eyes, and hair cut in a sugar-bowl fashion with blond bangs covering his forehead. Magda told me she cut it herself to save money. I feared that this, among other things, could have been the source of his constant and relentless bullying at Jarvis Collegiate.

"They call me Ratzo," he said sadly to me one evening, just as they were leaving for the night, "and they push me. I don't push back 'cause they're bigger."

"Bad little bastards," I muttered. "Don't worry, you'll have the last laugh. You'll be a famous doctor, and they'll be driving hack or washing dishes like Alistair."

Zoly smiled wanly, not fully taking in the possibilities. "I just want to buy a house for Mama, a big stone one, with a garden out front with flowers."

"And I'm sure you will," I said, blinking hard and trying to sound convincing.

"He does all excellent but the English," complained Magda. "He hate it, but it important for grade average."

"How do you like *Hamlet*?" I asked, seeing his paperback textbook on the table one slow, stormy evening.

"I hate it. He can't make up his mind to kill his uncle for murdering his father. Such a jerk. Just sitting around making speeches about whether he'll do it or kill himself instead."

"Some critics say he was secretively in love with his mother, so his uncle only did what he'd been wanting to do, so it made it difficult for Hamlet to kill him."

"Wow," he said, "that's really awesome—and awful. I love my Mom, but not in that way."

"I could," I said, "write your Grade 12 term paper on Hamlet. I sucked at math, but I used to do really well in Shakespeare. I was supposed to be 'highly original,' whatever that means." It was a safe offer, news of the notorious Sonja Danychuk had hardly reached Jarvis Collegiate.

"That would be truly amazing, Sonja, but I can't let you do that."

"Why not?" I asked, already knowing the answer.

"Because it wouldn't be my work, it would be yours. And you can't pass something so valuable onto someone else."

I looked away and heard Ma say, "But, Sonja, they make your work like their own. You think that good?"

I was shamed by Ma, who I hadn't listened to, and now by a bullied high school student from Jarvis Collegiate whose sense of morality was so much superior to mine. It had more of an impact on me than anything Professor Latham said, or all the articles in the *Toronto Star*, or the letter from Imperial Oil.

I pushed aside his yellow bangs and looked into his solemn green eyes shining behind the thick glasses.

"You're a wonderful boy, Zoly," I whispered, "and ignore those other little creeps. They couldn't stand me in high school either, they thought I was a fat smartass fart."

We laughed together about that and many other things. We really liked each other. He was like the little brother I wished I'd had.

"You're a lousy waitress, the world's worst," sputtered Peter after he'd watched me clean up the spill I'd made pouring coffee, which had followed on my tipping over one of his vodka martini masterpieces the night before. "Not of the ilk, not one iota of competency, clumsy as a cow. Find something else, girl, for the love of Jesus."

I gave a sigh of resignation. He was right. I was clumsy and slow, unable to mimic Magda's brisk efficiency. And I found it difficult to be sunny and ingratiating, taking the diners' criticisms of the food, which were often warranted, much too personally.

"What crawled up her ass and died?" asked a swollen fellow to Magda. He had an East Coast accent and bulged from a turtleneck sweater. He'd made some crack about my possible bra size and the possibility of my dropping one boob into his glass of draft, and instead of the expected smile, I'd frozen him with a glare.

"She a college student, real clever, they have different sense of humour," said Magda. "I serve you. My boobs no laughing matter."

Before I knew it, they were laughing together. All so demeaning, I thought, but I liked Magda and I knew she meant well, trying to be a buffer between me and some of Matheson's raw-mouthed customers.

"I can't eat this gah-bage," drawled a well-dressed lady with a New England accent after tasting Edmund's soup. She was, I thought, probably here visiting one of her kids at university.

"Can I offer a substitute?" I asked, thinking of the joy of pouring it over her obviously freshly done hair, although Edmund's soups were on a downward trend.

"Anything would be an improvement," she sighed.

"Customer says she can't eat your garbage soup and wants a substitute," I told Edmund, knowing it would incite him into an entertaining outburst.

"Open a tin of cream of mushroom, luv, and add a cup of coffee cream, and stir the hell out of it, and we'll give her a bowl of rare homemade soup right from the can. But not before I clear my throat and christen it with a big fat gob of snot."

"I can't let you do that, Edmund," I hissed, clearly alarmed although enjoying the prospect.

But Edmund had just started. "Do you know what Luther Olmstead used to do at Jake's Steakhouse when they'd send back their steak? He'd whip out his wanger and piddle all over it before he'd put it back on the grill. Then they'd ooh and aah about how much better it tasted and ask what he'd done to it. Nothing like a stream of piss to improve a tenderloin. These people aren't gourmets, luv, or they wouldn't be coming here."

I would, I decided, never return food when eating out.

A little later, the soup gourmet cooed, "Tell the chef he really excelled with the cream of mushroom. I'd love the recipe if he'd part with it."

"I'll tell him you enjoyed it," I said, "and you won't be charged for the substitution."

"Aren't you a darling," she replied, and I looked forward to an extra tip, hopefully in American dollars.

I kept my tips in a large glass jar under my bed in the residence but refused to count them. It was all degrading enough. I was living my worst nightmare, but at least I had Magda and Zoly as friends, and Edmund and Peter for comic relief.

It was week three and Zoly had been moping all week, refusing his dinners and coughing a lot. His condition was thought to be typical of a winter cold, or a flu bug, prevalent at this time of year. He did not turn up on Wednesday afternoon at four o'clock as usual.

"Where's Zoly?" I asked Magda.

"Home. He say he feel sick this morning, and his head was hot. Would you do a big favour? Bring him over a bowl of Edmund's soup, it not bad today and a plate of the lunch special. I pay for the cab, and, no offence, I be missed more than you if I leave."

"Oh, you really know how to hurt a girl," I mewed. "Are you saying you're a better waitress than me?"

A smiling Magda didn't even answer.

I OPENED THE door of one of the few brick duplexes on Huron Street that had escaped gentrification and headed downstairs to the basement, as Magda had instructed. The house was cold and airless, with the stifling stench of damp carpet and stale urine. I opened the door with number 8 on front with the second key. The room had two narrow beds, a small fridge, a hot plate, a rickety wooden table, and no television. Through an open door I glimpsed a sink and toilet. There were no windows, and the air was as putrid as that of the rest of the house. The walls, covered by what had originally been cream paint, were stained, moist, and peeling.

Zoly was lying on one of the narrow beds and seemed to be gasping for air. He coughed from what sounded like a phlegm-packed chest, and I noticed that the mucous-soaked toilet paper lying by his pillow was an ugly dark green. I went over and pushed back his bangs with my hand. His forehead was a furnace.

"Zoly," I murmured, "You're very sick. I'm taking you to Emergency at Sick Kids."

"What will Mama say?"

"She'll be fine with it."

There was actually a phone in the room and I dialled Matheson's. Greenley answered and I asked for Magda.

"No Magda for you—we've a filled-up dining room and one waitress. Nice of you to sneak off with no notice to anyone."

"Tell her Zoly's very sick and I'm taking him to Sick Kids."

Greenley banged up the receiver. I knew I should have told her I was leaving, but I knew she would see it as yet another opportunity for me to dodge work, like the lazy new Canadian I was.

I ordered a taxi and helped Zoly get dressed in his threadbare jeans, down jacket, and wool cap, noticing again his thinness. As we drove down University, I reached for his slight hand and it burned in mine. My heart thudded with concern. Was this, I asked myself, what it was like to be a parent? And why was Magda living with Zoly in an airless mildewed dump in a basement tenement on Huron Street?

He was admitted, diagnosed with double pneumonia after an X-ray, and placed in the intensive care ward on a course of antibiotics.

"You won't leave me?"

"No, I won't leave you."

Three weeks, and I was closer to him than I'd ever felt to anyone, except perhaps Miss Steinbrink, Ma, and Carl.

The hours ticked by, he drowsed, and when he woke up I gave him sips of juice through a straw. A doctor came and administered a shot of penicillin to the cheek of his small white bum, the sight of which made me want to cry. He should be bigger, I thought, my mind clouded with concern.

It was nine-thirty when Magda finally arrived.

"The bitch waited until nine to tell me," she hissed. "She could have closed, said it was a staff emergency."

I shook my head and didn't answer. I hated Greenley, and I knew Magda was frantic with concern and guilt.

Later, while Zoly slept, we sat close together in the cafeteria.

"Why," I blurted out, "are you living in a mould-ridden dump like that? No wonder Zoly got sick. I lived in the worst apartment in Davenport, but it's a palace compared to yours."

"It only four hundred dollars a month," she stammered and then bit her lower lip and I saw the chipped tooth.

"Four hundred too much."

We both sat silent.

"You could have lost him. That beautiful bright little guy."

But I didn't continue as she'd burst into tears.

"Magda," I said, my love for Zoly making me bold, "you can't go back there. Zoly can't go to medical school if he's dead. You have to get a decent apartment. How much do you have in the bank? I'd offer to share one, but I'm broke."

She pulled a tattered tissue from her purse and blew her nose loudly before answering and again bit her lower lip. I smelled her breath. It was as brown and as tired as her filmed eyes.

"Twenty-five thousand," she whispered, "for university and medical school. It was all for Zoly."

I was so angry I was speechless, but it didn't last. She meant so well.

"Then you have more than enough for a one-bedroom, that's what I share with Ma, and you can buy oranges and oatmeal for Zoly for breakfast. You can even get him to a barber: looking like Little Lord Fauntleroy doesn't help the bullying."

For the first time a smile flickered across her face.

"Oh Sonja," she said, "you so funny."

She sounded like Ma.

"And tell Greenley you want more than seven dollars an hour; you want at least ten. You carry that damn restaurant, but for you she'd be stuck with the waitress of the year, like me."

She leaned over and took my hand in hers. I felt its harshness, and I saw her arm muscles move beneath her long-sleeved black T-shirt.

"You save him, Sonja, you know that. I do what you say."

She would stay with Zoly for the night, and I would cover for her the next morning.

"Tell Greenley if she fire you, I leave," were her parting words.

THE SNOW HAD started, small silvery scales swimming around the street lights, floating down and disappearing on my black duffle and on the pavement. It was eleven, so the traffic was now light. I trudged toward the residence, breathing in the grey cool, thinking of Zoly, with his phlegm-packed lungs, soon to be vacuumed out by the dedicated efforts of the staff at Sick Kids. And then I thought of my future. It had been three weeks and in another week the administration would give its verdict on my expulsion. It had to be unanimous, but there was no doubt as to the result. I would be expelled. There had been too much publicity to ignore. And what if there was a holdout? With my scholarship gone, I couldn't continue anyway. And Greenley was just waiting to fire me from Matheson's, notwithstanding Magda's support.

I entered the residence, signed in, and went to my room. I reached under my bed, pulled out my tip jar, and poured its contents on the bed. I counted every quarter, loonie, toonie, and crumpled bill. One hundred and forty-three dollars and sixty-three cents, for three weeks of being the worst waitress in Toronto, just slightly more than seven hours of payment for tutoring Carl Helbig.

Tomorrow, I would get up at seven and trudge to Matheson's. There I'd attempt to paste a plastic smile on my tired face as I served the early morning crowd over-easy fried or scrambled eggs with sausages or bacon, and with what had been concentrated fresh frozen orange juice, now well diluted, together with white toast. And keep topping up cups of Timmy's Java to those as comatose as myself, but without the plastic smile and only the occasional muttered "thanks."

But Zoly would get better, and that made my heart sing.

10

BERTIE AND PRISCILLA

IT WAS NEARING THE END of my fourth week at Matheson's and my waitressing had improved, possibly because of Magda's constant mentoring. She feared my dismissal as Greenley had not yet forgiven me for my unauthorized departure on Zoly's sick day.

It was the third week of February, and there was no promise of spring. The days were short, and frozen rain poured, or fat flakes of snow drifted, from the low-hanging mottled grey skies. Matheson's was doing badly, with Edmund's luncheon specials failing to lure the usual luncheon crowd. He had been attempting both Thai and Italian, but his Thai was tasteless and his pasta a soggy mess, far from the desired *al dente*. And there were restaurants serving much better Thai and Italian within blocks.

"Try omelettes," I advised, "you can't do much harm with an egg."

"Cheeky young tart," he muttered. "Such nerve from someone who can't fill a glass of water without flooding the table."

I merely smiled. We were friends, as I was with Peter, who offered me a shot every night at nine, which I reluctantly refused, thinking of Ma's warning. Even Alistair, the dishwasher, called me "lass" and offered me a swig of Scotch from his mickey, hidden in his filthy apron, which was easier to turn down. We were all united in our hatred of Greenley. Edmund spoke of her under his breath as a yet-to-be-exposed murderess, by cyanide, of her first and only husband. This information had been relayed to him by a "perfectly reliable source," whose identity he had sworn not to divulge.

"But why?" I finally asked.

"He had a BA," he rasped, which left me more perplexed than ever.

Then, on a Tuesday evening, our slowest night, a couple appeared, oozing drab respectability. Both wore head coverings: the man, large leather Russian-style headwear, with ear flaps tied to the top; the woman, a snug navy cloche; and their bulky overcoats made them look as if they were heading for an arctic expedition. Greenley hung up the man's coat and hat and the woman's coat, but the woman wished to keep wearing her cloche. She seated them directly by the front window to show that not only was the empty restaurant being patronized, but its patrons were respectable and not dishevelled louts from questionable—possibly immigrant—backgrounds.

"They're all yours, Sonja," she said, her voice tinged with regret that she had let Magda, who was moving into an apartment in North Toronto, leave. I hardly inspired confidence.

I approached the table, menu in hand. The woman looked English, if there is such a thing. The fitted cloche covered all but some escaped tufts of mud-brown hair and framed a face with pale eyes, very close together, a long nose, and a narrow chin: a face that bore a close, almost startling, resemblance to a sheep. When she smiled, she exposed an uneven overbite, not because, I felt sure, her family could not afford the services of an orthodontist, but because an emphasis on such things was thought to be superficial—even American.

Sitting across from her was a familiar stooped figure, scrutinizing the menu with gold-rimmed glasses worn low on his nose. I inwardly gasped. It was my nemesis, the head of the English Department of the University of Toronto: Professor Albert Latham.

It was suck-up time.

"Would you like a cocktail?" I inquired. "Our bartender, Peter, makes an outstanding Manhattan."

Peter was at the moment barely able to stand, weaving behind the small wooden corner bar, but he could always make a drink: years of habit, I presumed, like being able to always ride a bicycle once you'd learned.

"How perfectly lovely," trilled the woman in the most British upper-class accent. "It's a Manhattan night, don't you agree, Bertie? One needs strong drink to propel one through Canada's dastardly winters."

But "Bertie" was otherwise occupied, looking at me.

"Is that you, Sonja?" he asked.

"It is," I answered, wondering if my month of angst and turmoil had drastically changed my appearance.

"Sonja," he explained carefully to the woman who I presumed was his wife, "was one of my more promising students, quite a talent for interpreting Shakespeare."

"Delve into something else, Sonja," said the woman, smiling away, and I noticed a ridge of misplaced lipstick smudged across her uneven top teeth. "Bertie's trilogy has the final say on The Bard, which he reminds me of on a daily basis. You can't imagine how vain it's made him, he can hardly get his head in the door." She threw her head back and gave an open-mouthed bleat of laughter.

"I'm Priscilla Myers-Lewis, by the way," she said, extending a slim, cool hand. "I kept my name. It's more significant than Latham back home."

"Since our arrival, Priss has managed to acquire the American tendency to depreciate others, quite openly, unfortunately," commented Professor Latham dryly. "She specializes in denigration clothed in humour."

"Oh Lord," brayed Priscilla. "You've become so insufferably pompous, Bertie, we're going to have to cross the pond and parachute you back to Derbyshire to bring you down to earth. I do hope he's treating you well, Sonja. As women we must stand united. When we're undermined, I think of Margaret Thatcher, the very best of our prime ministers. She actually had Ronald Reagan take notes of international meetings like a schoolboy. She was unfortunately destroyed by her greasy male underlings."

"Professor Latham's been very fair," I said, feeling a rush of affection for Priscilla Myers-Lewis, whom I loved from her sheep-like face and crooked teeth to what I felt sure were her thick ankles.

"Bertie will have a Manhattan as well," said Priscilla. "He likes to play with gin-laden martinis, as dry as dust, but this is a night for a robust Manhattan. You say your bartender makes a fine one?"

"He's very robust with liquor," I assured her, taking a quick glance at the unsteady Peter.

"Where's the chef from?"

"He's British, near London, I believe."

"Rather unfortunate," sniffed Priscilla, "but I hope he'll rise to the occasion when he learns we share his heritage. What do you say to some overcooked mutton chops with mash and undercooked Brussels sprouts? It'll make us homesick, even bangers and mash will do it. Of course, we'll have to wash it all down with some fine French Chardonnay—nothing from Niagara, please."

Professor Latham merely grunted. Priscilla reminded me of a British version of Mutti.

Bertie didn't have a chance.

"The strongest and biggest Manhattan you can muster," I instructed Peter, who reached under the counter and produced an unopened bottle of Crown Royal, which he used to fill up his largest cocktail glasses, merely adding a dribble of sweet vermouth to each and two cherries.

"These are on the house," I said, keeping my voice low enough to bypass Greenley's acute hearing and attempting to avoid my usual inept spill caused from my serving anything remotely liquid.

"How absolutely dear of you, Sonja," sang my new friend Priscilla. "Bertie, you can't be kind enough to this girl, remember that."

Edmund hustled up the desired typical English meal, even thawing out a frozen fruit pudding by boiling it in sugared water, and Peter produced a long-forgotten bottle of Chardonnay, far superior to our house white.

At the end of the meal, as they stood up and got ready to leave, Priscilla addressed me.

"Bertie tells me you found yourself in some difficulty as a result of your talent and entrepreneurial nature. Don't let this dissuade you from your goal, Sonja. As women we are programmed to prevail, remember that."

In my mind I heard the distant playing of "Hail Britannia" interspersed with "I Am Woman." My eyes met Professor Latham's. Then we both smiled.

THE NOTE WAS left in my mail slot at the end of the last week of February: Professor Latham would see me at four regarding a personal matter. I knew it was the expulsion ruling. I phoned Greenley and told her that I might be an hour late, and she hung up in my ear after snarling that they might just manage to limp along without me. I was surviving there, I knew, solely because of Magda's support.

Professor Latham was sitting behind his desk as usual and did not get up to open the door, merely thundering, "Enter" to my hesitant knock.

"Sit down, Sonja," he ordered.

"I've been hearing about you on a daily basis from Priscilla, who's taken up your cause as a feminist rather than a moral issue, typical of these types, I fear. So unfortunate that superb complimentary Manhattan loosened my tongue."

He leaned back in his chair and fixed me with his cold, enamelled eyes, much as he had during our previous office meeting. "I'd ask that you keep this conversation confidential, although you've already been made privy to some of Priscilla's somewhat cringe-making propaganda. Her background may clarify matters. She's the daughter of Lord Myers-Lewis, who, although living in a decrepit mansion burdened by debts and taxes, and demented beyond belief, is still considered British aristocracy. She attended Roedean, a private school for girls akin to Eton for boys, but she didn't make Oxford or Cambridge. You've heard the adage 'a little learning . . .' I'm sure.

"Two years ago, she self-published a volume of poetry known as *The Convoluted Toad*. I knew nothing of her plans or the poems. If I had, I would have attempted to stop her. The volume lacked one original symbol, image, or thought, the poems inadvertent doggerel. It was an abysmal and humiliating effort, and she was at a loss to explain the title, which might be just as well. She sent copies to every member of the English Department, and saw that it was carried by the University Bookstore. It's become a matter of hilarity among the staff, and many a faculty luncheon has been brightened up by a rib-tickling discussion of Latham's wife's *The Convoluted Toad*. Suffice it to say I'm still attempting to live it down among my colleagues. Luckily I can bask in the success of the trilogy, which incidentally she very much resents, seeing herself as my literary competitor and combatant—short-sighted and ridiculous in the extreme." Professor Latham sat back and closed his eyes, as if to attempt to erase the entire situation from his mind.

I would not, I decided, disclose to Professor Latham under any circumstances my affection for Priscilla. It would be seen as yet another indication of my bad judgment, worse even than promoting plagiarism.

"I'm telling you this so you'll realize Priscilla has no influence on any decision I'm taking part in when considering your expulsion."

I looked at him and our eyes met. I did not believe a word he said. The wretched poetess Priscilla was still Lord Myers-Lewis's daughter, a bastion of British nobility, and a product of one of Britain's most prestigious private schools. He was still Bertie Latham from Derbyshire, with what I suspected was an acquired accent from Oxford, where he had probably attended by means of a scholarship.

I had much more in common with Bertie Latham than I had with Priscilla Myers-Lewis, yet I liked her so much more. And of course he listened to Lord Myers-Lewis's daughter.

"I understand, Professor Latham," I lied. "It never occurred to me that you'd be influenced."

"Actually," he said, "I had a cursory meeting with the other two board members of the advisory board at the beginning, and we'd tentatively agreed that you were to be made an example for bringing shame—even notoriety—on the university. But then, when I saw you in your pink waitress uniform at Matheson's, carrying out your clumsy duties, I must admit to a swelling of compassion. It saddened me."

"I'm a terrible waitress," I muttered.

He nodded in agreement.

"I even read over your Shakespeare exam and term paper yet again—not your plagiarized creations, but your own work. You may not be as brilliant as some others, including yourself, I fear, think, but you do have a unique turn of phrase and interpretive talent that I find sad to be wasted."

I sat waiting. I felt little of the panic I'd felt before. I felt almost . . . flat. The scholarship was gone, and that placed a financial burden on me, making an academic future difficult, if not impossible. But I did not want to be expelled from the university. It was a disgrace I could never live down.

"To get to the point," said Professor Latham, suddenly

becoming enlivened, "I argued against expulsion. I was the sole dissenter. They're all angry with me, and perhaps rightly so. You can dedicate your first literary effort to me, it's the least you can do." He gave me a rare smile and I noticed his teeth were much straighter than Priscilla's.

"I'm very grateful," I said. "I've given it all a lot of thought and I'm ashamed of what I did. I was sick of being poor and I let making money override everything else. It's probably all futile in any event as Imperial Oil has cancelled my scholarship."

"Yes, I saw that," he said. "We received both your letter and their reply—sanctimonious bastards with their billions in profits. Your letter, of course, was duplicitous in the extreme, euphemistically saying you'd helped others out of a surplus of academic generosity rather than committing to line your own pockets. It shocked the other committee members. You have, I fear, Sonja, a streak of the fraudster, which surfaces at opportune times. You must attempt to curb it."

I did not answer, and we sat silent; there was nothing to be heard but a group of students chatting and exiting a far-off classroom.

"I admit I tried to put a spin on it, but being honest wouldn't have helped, it would have been even worse. But I appreciate the advice. As it is, I may not be back next term, let alone next year, and my reputation is ruined."

"I wouldn't fret too much about your reputation, Sonja. People are largely self-absorbed, and things pass and become distorted with time. Plagiarism and *The*

Convoluted Toad will fade into the background with the success of other things. You have only to write a literary masterpiece, and all will be forgiven and forgotten, like winning an Academy Award after being convicted of grand larceny."

Professor Latham got to his feet and smiled again. I suspected he was glad to end the interview, but at least he could report its favourable outcome to Priscilla.

"And as for continuing your education, don't cancel it out, Sonja," he said. "You're a very resourceful girl. Perhaps you should try tutoring."

I RETURNED TO Matheson's at six, feeling relieved but not happy. Everyone was there and Zoly was back, sitting at the corner table looking paler than ever, but cough- and pneumonia-free.

We were having a rare busy night, probably because Edmund had advertised a new series of "The Cheapest Meals in Town" in the window. Tonight's monstrosity was an esoteric combination of onions, hamburger meat, Hamburger Helper, kidney beans, tomato soup, the remnants of the week's leftover soups, and tablespoons full of chili pepper and garlic powder, with Minute Rice on the side.

At nine, when the last diner left, I went over to Greenley, who was checking cash receipts.

"You always complain of lack of notice, so I'm giving you three days. I'm returning to university as of next Monday."

"Wrong," she spat. "You're leaving as of now; you're

the most incompetent moron of a waitress God ever made. You've been here by the grace of Magda, nothing else."

"Fine," I answered dully.

But I did not want to leave. I went to the kitchen to say goodbye to Edmund, Alistair, and, most importantly, Zoly. He was gone from the table, and Edmond nodded toward the small staff toilet with a sad shake of his head. Greenley's ultimatum had reached the kitchen before I had. I went to the door and heard muffled sobs from the inside. I opened the door and we hugged, my little boyfriend of five-foot-two and one hundred pounds. I was his sole friend, and he'd been the man in my life for four weeks.

"I'll take you out once a week for hamburger and fries and you'll tell me everything that's happening," I whispered against his wet cheek. Magna had taken him to a barber, and I missed the bangs but had assured him he looked much more mature.

Magda and I embraced, and she lifted me off the floor with her mighty arms. Edmund patted me on the back, and Peter offered me a shot, which I accepted, choking down the last of the Crown Royal that he'd been nipping since the Latham dinner. Alistair wished me well and called me "a good lass."

I felt sad leaving them all, although I knew I'd keep in touch with Magda and Zoly. They were like family and I felt much more comfortable with them than I did with anyone at the University of Toronto, or at Davenport High, for that matter. This said many things, as they were all members of the marching army.

There was a month's work to catch up on, and I accepted Janet Murdock's kind offer of class notes. Janet had turned out to be a real friend. I'd missed the turn-in date on two term papers, and I'd attempt to get extensions. I'd spend the weekend working, just surfacing for meals. If I were forced to leave, at least I'd go on a passing, if not high, note.

11

THE HOCKEY PATIENT

"SONJA."

It was Mutti's assertive voice, taking no prisoners on a freezing morning in early March. The bare black branches of the maples were ensconced in tubes of ice and a neon sun cut through the chill, causing the icicles rimming the eaves of the grey-bricked student residence to bleed crystal globules. Two people crossed my mind: Ma and Carl.

Mutti was staying at the Sutton Place Hotel. "How soon can I see you?"

"My last class ends at four."

"Then I must wait until then," muttered Mutti.

They were serving High Tea in the Sutton Place dining room, with warm scones, dishes of various jams, together with whipped butter and clotted cream. The thin, flowered porcelain cups were filled periodically with steaming tea, poured from large embossed sterling urns that looked like English or Scottish heirlooms. Mutti sat, her face rigid with irritation. Or was it fear? She wore a mink tam, which was a similar colour to her light-brown mink coat. Away from Davenport, her affluent aura was less, and she looked more like a reasonably well-off housewife in the city for a brief visit, perhaps to see an old friend or relative.

"You have heard of Carl?"

I hesitated before answering. I had been so busy at Matheson's and then at doing catch-ups. I never read the sports sections of the daily newspapers, and always turned off any sports coverage after the nightly news, but it would not do to show my lack of interest to Mutti.

"I've been writing exams and studying, so I haven't been watching anything lately. As I recall, Carl always goes back to the ice."

"Of course he goes back," snapped Mutti. "Our Carl is not one to give in, never, especially now he sign contract with the big bonus. He let no one down. Not our Carl."

I sat silently, waiting.

"Two nights ago, he hit again. Leafs enforcer blindside him and knock his helmet off. He stay on the ice. Doctors say he must not play again until he better. One doctor say he must not play—never again. He is at the Toronto General in what they call trauma unit. He much depressed. He asks for you."

I sat shocked by this information. Mutti was obviously immersed in the hockey culture with words like *hit*, *blindside*, and *enforcer* tumbling easily from her mouth. I placed my fingers against my temples and rubbed them as if to wipe out the thought of Carl lying in the trauma unit. "Guess it's Hollywood or the military," he had once said when I had explained the prevalence of dyslexia among movie stars and five-star generals. But then he had added, "Good I can skate."

It was about five when we left Sutton Place, Mutti insisting that I finish at least two of the buttered scones before our departure. Outside, the traffic on Bay Street was heavy, and after fruitlessly attempting to hail several cabs, we trotted, bent against the wind, across Gerrard to University. Mutti clutched my arm as I towered above her. The icy air was smudged with the oncoming darkness, and the hunched figures surrounding us, carrying briefcases or backpacks, shuffled quickly. Above, bees of snow encircled the lights of the street lamps.

"I should have brought car," complained Mutti, "but Carl's father say he drive me. After he see Carl, he go back to Davenport."

I kept quiet, my mind on Carl and what Mutti saw as my role in all of this. We climbed the steps of the Toronto General together and then took the elevator to the trauma unit. Carl was in room six. Mutti introduced me to the ward nurse as "Carl's girlfriend" and the nurse gave me a nod of acknowledgement. I accepted the label. It was, after all, what I'd been promoting to my two university friends all year. But outside the door of room six I felt a sense of nostalgia, and then a reluctance to go further. Sonja and her little hammer primed to fix the damage. But this time it was different.

The room was dark, with only a small lamp at the corner giving light. "Light hurt his eyes," whispered Mutti.

I softly approached the sleeping figure. He looked so young, so vulnerable, lying there, his short fair hair showing too much pale scalp, his ears, as usual, pink like the inside of seashells. On his right temple was a festering brown crab. It had no right there: an ugly interloper. I felt a wave of tenderness and concern.

"That where head hit ice," whispered Mutti, pointing a stubby finger at Carl's temple. "They let air get to it . . . for healing. He cannot get up . . . he dizzy. Yesterday he said head and neck give much pain. He must be very quiet and still, that's what doctor say . . . he not ready to be moved."

Then, in a loud voice contradicting all her whispered information, "Carl, Sonja, she come to see you."

His lips formed a very faint smile.

I took his large, warm hand in both of mine and moved it gently back and forth. "No need for formalities," I whispered in a strained attempt at humour, "I'll forgive you if you don't get up."

The smile broadened.

"See," crowed Mutti, "the first time he smile since hit ice. We need you, Sonja. You help us get through this."

I sat by his side holding his hand while Mutti obsessively cleaned all available surfaces with a washcloth and soap she'd resurrected from the adjoining bathroom.

Carl seemed to be sleeping again, so after an hour I carefully released his hand and started to leave. To my surprise I heard the word "Tomorrow?"

"Yes," I assured him. "I'll come again tomorrow, for sure."

"*Bitte* you talk to the doctors, Sonja," instructed Mutti as we rode back together in a taxi. "One doctor say Carl never play hockey again. Not to play kill Carl. You tell them it important he play hockey. I tell them soon you will be Carl's wife, then they listen."

Mutti, irrational and stubborn as ever, and Sonja, unveiled plagiarist and future impoverished dropout, with her little hammer and screwdriver, was to cure what well could be found to be incurable.

But I went, timing my visits before or after classes, and saw some improvement. The anti-swelling medication for the brain was stopped, the painkillers decreased, and his vision improved—or so he said. He still, however, could not stand without dizziness.

On the sixth day, Mutti decided that Carl Sr. should come and drive her back to Davenport.

"You in charge, you better than me with doctors," she instructed, even leaving a signed authorization from Carl and herself at the nursing station that gave Sonja

Danychuk decision-making and access to information from any tests and specialists.

This new power frightened me, and I was shocked that Mutti would leave Carl, abandoning him to me. I kept visiting, not wanting to disappoint this recovering wounded warrior who I now felt was my responsibility. I even watched the hockey games at the residence at Carl's request and read the sports section out loud to him. Watching the games I recoiled against the unrestrained roughness, the high-sticking, slashing, and cross-checking.

"It's a horrible game," I informed him late one afternoon, after a defeat for the Bruins I'd watched the night before. "They're worse than Roman gladiators. And Le Blanc only got a two-game suspension for your hit. What a bunch of bastards."

He smiled at me, obviously delighted by my knowledge and recent interest. "Don't knock it, I'm going back soon. No one else is gonna pay me the big bucks to get my head bashed in. I'm just waiting for clearance . . . they had a guy in here this afternoon asking me a battery of questions, and the Bruins have paid for a top guy from Boston, a specialist in head injuries, to come tomorrow. Then as soon as he gives his okay, I'm back. But I'm not letting you go again."

He grinned at me, those square white teeth of his glistening, but I saw only the brown crab now fraying about the edges, still sitting on his right temple—waiting.

I smiled back but felt uneasy and scared. Why the questions and the "top guy" from Boston? And of course he was letting me go; he'd never had me anyway. He'd made that choice at Christmas, flaunting his tanned and toned masseuse, while I made myself ridiculous in my revealing black dress. Once he was cleared, I would be gone, back to my studies and worries about my last term and second-year expenses. He would be all right. I was sure there were more Tulas in the wings, although no.other birds had surfaced.

A nurse informed me, "Dr. Folkes sent a message. He wants to see Carl Helbig's next of kin at four tomorrow afternoon. He's been emailed the questionnaire results and he's coming for more tests in the morning. Looks like you're elected."

Pamela Scott, who gave me the information, and who showed a special concern for Carl, was an attractive blonde located at the nursing station. She would be a better choice than Tula by far.

I would miss my special tutorial class on Chaucer at four, but I would explain my absence: a sick relative and I was the family spokesperson. Or why not tell a partial truth: my boyfriend, Carl Helbig of the Boston Bruins, had a head injury, and I had been asked to speak with a specialist who had come from Boston. It would give me some sympathy, even prestige, this being Canada.

"You tell doctor how much hockey mean to Carl," ordered Mutti when I phoned her that night to tell her of the meeting. It was odd she wasn't here. I felt the same annoyance and powerlessness I had felt when ordered to fix the dyslexia and ensure Carl's high school graduation. The woman was an irrational fool with much too much power, who, however, cooked great dinners.

"I'll be the one receiving the information, Mrs. Helbig, not giving it, but I'll tell him anything I feel is important."

A normal person would respond to the irritation in my voice, but not Mutti, who said, "I count on you," which made the situation so much worse.

AT FOUR O'CLOCK I was sitting in a small office off the trauma unit facing Dr. Dennis Folkes, who, as I saw from the card he gave me, was not only an MD but also a neurologist and surgeon. He lacked the cadaverous, almost emaciated look of the surgeons I'd seen since I'd visited the hospital, and was a man of considerable heft—an ex-athlete, I guessed, just before he told me he'd been a professional football player many years before.

"And you, Ms. Danychuk?"

"I'm a student at the University of Toronto."

"Pre-med?"

"No, English."

"Then I'll try to make it as simple as possible. What do you know about concussions?"

"Very little."

Dr. Folkes sighed and started. "Well, the brain does not fit snugly in the skull; it's set off by intracranial space, so that the skull and brain don't move together. If, for some reason, the head in motion stops suddenly—a blow or fall could cause it—the brain compresses into the skull and is jolted again as it rebounds. This causes swelling and damage, leading to classic concussion symptoms:

headache, vomiting, dizziness, balance problems, sensitivity to light and noise, confusion, even amnesia.

"A player with these problems may be benched for a period of time. A player whose brain has been jolted at a sub-concussive level is more likely to stay on or return to the ice. The damage can then become deadly. Kids who began playing at a young age, and Carl tells me he played hockey at seven, can receive cumulative damage to young brain tissue, but not enough to cause immediate symptoms. It's what we call a 'dose response' and eventually, after a certain number of hits, the damage starts to show."

I felt sick. "Could it cause learning problems like dyslexia? Carl is dyslexic."

"It could," replied Folkes. "Learning requires considerable metabolic activity. If the brain's impaired, that metabolic activity will be reduced.

"Then there's the CTE factor, chronic traumatic encephalopathy, that appears to occur varying years into the play. This phenomenon was known to occur with boxers but is now being studied on the brains of other athletes during autopsies. The brain becomes flecked with tau proteins, which are linked to brain damage. Tau protein is one of the main materials of brain tissue. Shake the brain too hard, the nerve fibres are torn, and the tau gets out. The brain tries to clean it up and given time it could, but if the hits keep coming, the tau simply accumulates like flecks of porridge. This sludge, this porridge, has been recently found in the brains of some players, mostly football players, who have committed suicide or have died violent deaths.

"The disease starts at a young age and progresses. Players who return to the field or the ice too soon may suffer malignant brain swell or second impact syndrome, where another blow could lead to a second episode of brain bleeding.

"From the information given to me by your Carl, I suspect that two days before he sustained his latest concussion—and that's what he has: a complex, grade-three concussion of which he has no memory—he experienced a first concussion, or sub-concussion. During the first concussion I suspect he was unconscious, if only briefly, at which time he retired to the bench, assured everyone he was fine, and returned to the play. He was still suffering from its effects when he experienced his second hit and this time he succumbed. Had he admitted to his first concussion, his coach hopefully would not have permitted his return to the ice."

"Before Christmas I was told there'd been a hit, and he'd followed the same pattern. He'd appeared to be unconscious, retired to the bench, and then returned to the play," I said.

Dr. Folkes sighed again, this time more heavily. "I suspect Carl Helbig has experienced a series of concussions throughout his playing career but out of some misguided—I could say stupid—sense of being macho or invincible has refused to admit to them and has played through them."

"He felt he had no alternative," I interjected, but Dr. Folkes ignored me and continued.

"He's been given an MRS: magnetic resonance spectroscopy. His brain's metabolism denotes brain injury, as does the resting MRI, which shows damage to its underlying activity. In other words, Ms. Danychuk, Carl suffered a second concussion during his critical recovery period from the first and his symptoms could last for months. He's lucky. He could have died.

"Now I suspect he may be suffering from post-concussion syndrome. He has the usual problems with headache, balance, vision, sensitivity to light, although he only admits to those that are obvious to third parties, the dizziness, blurred vision, and his wish for darkness.

"He may become depressed, even angry. I suspect he is already both. He became upset with me this morning. If he's not exhibiting these symptoms now, be assured they'll reappear if he attempts to return to the Bruins and resume strenuous activity.

"Remember, the more concussions an individual experiences, the more likely he is to have more and the longer it takes to recover. And at some point the symptoms become irreversible and permanent. Carl Helbig should never skate again."

"This will be an awful tragedy for him," I murmured. "It's been his whole life and because of his dyslexia other choices are limited."

Dr. Folkes ignored me and continued, his voice softer and less professorial. "I had my first football concussion in high school. I kept playing and experienced another at university, where I was attending on a football scholarship.

Unlike Carl, I had recovery time. My third was during my first season with the NFL. I stopped and became a doctor. I quit. You can't continue with something that'll result in brain damage or frontal lobe dementia—unless you're a suicidal idiot."

"It's so ironic," I mused, "Carl probably became dyslexic because of hockey injuries and then continued to play because he believed his dyslexia gave him no alternative. As well he loves the game, and the money and adulation that goes with it. Now, if he can't continue, he'll feel he's got nothing else."

"No doubt," said Dr. Folkes, his voice becoming almost gentle. "He'll be depressed, but remember, Ms. Danychuk, he has you."

I did not acknowledge the compliment. Carl did not even have me.

IT WAS AFTER five when I went into room six. Carl's nurse Pamela was spooning a pasta dish into his obediently opening mouth. His upper body was now elevated, indicating some improvement. Pamela appeared flustered at my entrance, as if she owed me an explanation.

"This is usually left to the nursing assistants, not an RN, but I wanted to be able to tell my son that I helped Carl Helbig of the Boston Bruins eat his dinner."

"Too bad she's married," I said after she left.

"Single mom," he mumbled.

"You asked?"

"She told me . . . it doesn't matter."

We sat silently together in the darkened room.

"I'm gonna try to take a piss."

Before I could stop him, he was on his feet but then just as abruptly staggered back on the elevated bed.

"I'm so fuckin' dizzy. You spoke to Folkes?"

"Yes. He's not going to give you clearance. He believes you've had a complex concussion and may be suffering from post-concussion syndrome. You have the symptoms and they could last for some time. Even if they disappear they may come back if you start strenuous activity again. He suspects you've had a long history of brain injuries. They could have caused your dyslexia."

But he was no longer listening and in the dim light I saw that his eyes glistened as he looked straight ahead.

"What the fuck am I supposed to do? Get a job drivin' hack? Or maybe I could teach Shakespeare—I'm an expert on King Lear. I can't read or spell and only made it through high school with your help. What the fuck am I supposed to do?"

"Try not to think about it; perhaps he's wrong. Doctors aren't always right. You're getting yourself all upset. I was too frank."

"Fuckin' right he's wrong. And since when haven't you been frank? 'Say it like it is, Sonja,' the Davenport diplomat, who didn't have a decent meal until she started tutoring Carl Helbig but who was always too good for a dyslexic hockey player. Well, I'm goin' back, absolutely goin' back. I signed a three-million, three-year contract, with a half-mil signing bonus up front an' I'm goin' to give 'em their money's worth. Christ, they're not going to make me rookie of the year if I cave with a concussion in the second half."

I left the room and went to the nursing station where Pamela Scott was making notations on charts. "Can you give Carl some sedation?"

Pamela gave me a hard look. Strange, I thought, how some women take instant dislikes to others, like Candace Stewart to Tula, and Pamela to me—an instinctive emotional recoil. I used to view most people as types or even specimens to be seen and analyzed under glass. It all came from not being a thread of humanity's fabric. Not only being undiplomatic but isolated. But since then there'd been Magda and Zoly. And now Carl. Of course, looking back there'd always been Carl, ever since the tutoring.

"He shouldn't be stressed in his condition," lectured Pamela. "His test results were concerning and he had an outburst at Dr. Folkes. You've obviously made things worse. Only light topics should be discussed."

"I understand. I'm sorry. I answered his questions. He tried to get up and couldn't and that upset him as well."

"He has to be kept quiet," she offered over her shoulder.

I followed her as she entered the room. "Some medication for you, Carl," she carolled. "We have to keep you nice and quiet so you'll be better soon. Open wide."

She placed two capsules on his tongue and he gulped them down with water.

"Why not bring 'em all? I may need more later."

"You know better than that, Carl. Would you like to empty your bladder? Ms. Danychuk can wait outside until you urinate and I'll make you comfortable for the night."

The perfect touch, I thought. Treat your patient like a recalcitrant and backward child: be kind but firm. Carl needed a Pamela Scott so much more than a Tula, a Candace Stewart, or certainly a Sonja Danychuk.

"Don't go," he pleaded when I came back, "I'm sorry I said those things. I wouldn't have passed high school without you."

"It's all right, no apologies necessary. I'm too out-spoken and you're right, I never did have a decent meal until Mutti's dinners, and you forgot, my mother doesn't even speak English. But you're wrong about my thinking I'm too good for you. It's just that we're different, with different interests and tastes. You're an athlete and I'm an egghead, a geek. But we can still be best friends."

"Not enough," he said slowly, "not nearly enough."

We were silent for a moment.

"Tomorrow?" he asked.

"After class. I still have to pass my year."

"But you'll still come?"

"Of course."

I sat by the bed holding his large, warm hand in the darkness until his breathing became even. Outside, cars sped along the wet surface of University Avenue and bitter chill clawed every face. Yet here I was, thinking of econo-mizing by walking back to the residence rather than taking a taxi while holding the hand of a hockey player who, only six months before, had signed a contract with a $500,000 signing bonus.

IT WAS TEN more days before Carl would be released from the trauma unit and transported back to Davenport, where his routine of rest and medication were to continue. Before that time, there were visitors. Two members of the Bruins playing in Toronto came one afternoon and urged him to "get off his ass and get back to the team." It was part of the Code that the Warriors, the tough guys, played through their injuries.

The only visitor I appreciated was Howard Keefe, who had stopped playing for Dallas after his eighth concussion. "You don't understand 'til you've been there," he said, sitting with Carl and me two days before discharge. "None of the guys understood. They thought it was some sort of cop-out—that I'd bailed, let the club down. And all the time I wanted to kill myself. Every day I thought about it. I'd be driving a car and there'd be a tractor-trailer on the other side, and I'd think, What if I turned the wheel and rammed right into that sucker? There'd be no more head-aches, no more depression, it'd all be over. But I didn't do it. I told my wife and she got me a therapist. I went on antidepressants, and after a few months I stopped staying in my room where it was dark and safe, and I started seeing some light again. Now I'm coaching one of the Junior teams and taking business courses. There's life after the NHL, yuh hear me, Helbig? You gotta believe that. Sonja here, she'll help you. Won't you, Sonja?"

"I hope you listened to Howard," I said later, "instead of the Goon Squad."

Carl looked straight ahead and didn't reply.

During one of my visits I told him of the threatened expulsion and loss of the scholarship. He'd shaken his head but said nothing.

The day before he was scheduled to return to Davenport, he was sitting in a chair, finally with the blinds up, and looking at me. I felt a sense of sadness yet relief. There would be no more visits, and I would finally be able to concentrate on my studies again. Yet I knew I'd miss him: his joy at seeing me, holding his hand as he drifted into sleep, even giving the back of his hand small soft kisses before I left. We had developed a closeness, rich and undeniable, which neither of us could ignore.

When he spoke his voice was husky, and I knew he'd been going over what he'd say for several days:

"I want to marry you and I want you to think about marrying me. I know you don't love me—not like I love you—and you think I'm a dummy and now it's worse. Now I'm a fucked-up dummy. But I can give you a good life, make everything easier for you. I know you want a great education and I'll see that you get it. I'll see that you get everything you want. There's a clause in my contract in case of injury, and I remember that, because I knew I'd had concussions before I signed the contract, that I'd be paid for the entire year, and there'd be no rebate on any signing bonus. We're talking about a little less than one and a half mil, nothing like the three I was getting if I played for three years but enough for us to get a really nice house—sorry, but it'll be in Davenport—a couple of cars, and for you to get an apartment here in Toronto and finish your courses. You can even help your mother. Maybe she can stop cleaning houses; that's worse than getting your brains bashed in chasing a puck around the ice. There's no one cheering after you clean a house. I'm going to try to go back, you know that, but if I can't, at least I'll have you."

It was a long speech, coming out of all the pain, depression, and anger. I asked myself if I had encouraged this proposal by my regular visits and by confiding my money problems. I didn't think so. I was not merely a viable alternative: I was a Hail Mary pass. His proposal was generous. He wanted to share his money with me, money he had acquired by mutilating his brain, and he even suggested helping my mother.

I was not a crier. My last and only outbursts occurred when I feared that I would be expelled from university and when I lost my scholarship. But now I felt my eyes burn. Carl was reaching out. It was bribery, of course, but bribery of the sweetest kind.

"I'll really think about it," I said, my voice thick.

"I'll," he said softly, "ask you when you come home for Easter, then I'll never ask you again. I don't want to be a pest. I'm not a great catch. Not for someone like you."

"You are a great catch. Look at your stable of girlfriends: Candace, Tulas by the dozen, even Pamela Scott's a potential."

"They don't matter," he said.

And I knew he was right.

There was only me.

12
MARRYING CARL

AFTER CARL LEFT THE HOSPITAL, I missed him. I had become used to seeing him every day. My spring midterms were coming, then there would be Easter. My exams went well, no distracting papers for plagiarists or hospital visits to interfere with my studies. My social life consisted of hamburgers and fries with Zoly once a week.

"Your guy recovering?" inquired Jo, after we had settled into our usual seats in the cafeteria. "Horrible thing to happen after he signed that big three-year contract. Wonder if it's got an escape clause?"

"I wouldn't know," I replied stiffly. "Anyway, he's improving."

But she continued. "These guys sometimes have ongoing damage, the football players more than the hockey players. They get their brains curdled and a few end up killing themselves or being zombies." This was all contributed without missing a chewing beat.

Insensitive bitch, I thought, and asked myself why I hung out with her. Perhaps, I thought, because she always gave me a dose of reality, unpleasant but at times necessary.

At night, unwelcome thoughts plagued me. All my life I'd been lonely and yearned for communication with someone who'd appreciate and share in my love of books and passion for literature. Now I was contemplating throwing away my aspirations and settling for a companion who could only read with difficulty and who would never ever read anything I'd written or admired. True, he wanted to pay for my education, and he would be proud of my achievements, but he'd be a detached observer. We could, I thought, never enjoy a Shakespearian production together unless I explained the plot first—unless it was *King Lear*. And if I met my aspirations—and I was no longer limiting myself to high school teaching—and actually produced an original work of criticism, how would he be introduced or accepted by the academic community? Would I say, "Here's my husband, the former Bruins player, don't discuss anything remotely intellectual or he'll leave or sleep, take your choice. He's not stupid, just not interested. He's read nothing, not a thing, so limit yourself to ordinary topics, preferably those found in the sports section of the evening news." And he even wanted to live in Davenport . . .

Then I was ashamed of my own arrogance. He was not a Priscilla, writing doggerel and competing with, and embarrassing, an academic spouse. He was encouraging and supportive of my achievements. And he'd always wanted to make me happy. And who else ever had?

THE DAVENPORT GREYHOUND had a new driver. I inquired about my old friend as we approached the town, turning off the highway and up the pot-holed road to the terminal. I was the only passenger left.

"They gassed him. His ol' lady's mother married some rich guy an' she persuaded the wife to leave him. Not good enough for her anymore, an' then they cut him off from the kids, guess he weren't good enough for them either, so he started to drink, an' had a little accident, nothin' serious, but he got charged for blowin' over. And that ended it."

"Too bad," I said, remembering how he'd taken one of his kids to emergency for croup at Christmas.

"You from here?"

"Yes." I did not want to become familiar with another bus driver.

"The armpit of Ontario. I hate the place. A girl said to her dude, 'Kiss me somewhere dirty,' so he took her to Davenport. Heard that one?"

I didn't reply but then said, "It's got a good sports arena."

"Yeah, Carl Helbig of the Bruins comes from here. Know him?"

"No."

I walked from the terminal, down Main Street, and toward our apartment building. It got dark later now, but there was no sign of an early spring in Davenport. It was damp and cold and I passed a packed Tim Hortons and O'Dare's Bar, equally crowded, thinking that the Dare family had business in Davenport tied up. I sniffed the sour of beer as two locals lurched out, most likely celebrating the holiday weekend. Dull and depressing, I thought, comparing Main Street Davenport with Bloor Street West. And unlike Christmas, I didn't come bearing gifts but did have my black dress.

"Welcome home," sang Ma in English upon opening the door. She looked even smaller than usual, shrunken, and when I hugged her bird-like frame her fragility gave me a lump in my throat.

"Good to see you, Ma, and to hear you speaking English."

I would, I decided, tell Ma about my threatened expulsion, loss of scholarship, and about Carl, whom I was seeing the next day. It would all be conveyed in Ukrainian, as it was much too important to be lost in translation. Ma had surprised me last Christmas and might well again.

"They have Swiss Chalet up the street. We go. I pay."

"I can still buy you a dark quarter, fries, and even a

glass of white, Ma, but things aren't as good as they were."

We walked slowly up the street, Ma drowning in her coat with the large fur collar and wearing her matching tam and boat-like boots. She was holding my hand. Large child takes small mother for a walk, I thought with affection.

"I'm not cleaning tonight," she whispered happily. "Tonight, just you and me."

We were shown to the last booth available in the large dining room with the smell of barbecued chicken and spicy sauce heavy in the air. I was reluctant to approach the first topic, waiting until our glasses of house white arrived.

"Ma, there are two things, really serious things that have happened. I got caught doing essays for other students and I had to stop. Then I was suspended for thirty days and almost expelled. And I've lost my scholarship."

Ma covered her face with her grained hands and rocked back and forth with despair. "I worry of that Sonja, when you tell me at Christmas, really worry, but you not care."

"I didn't think they'd catch me, Ma. It seemed like such a good way to make money at the time, but it was wrong and I should have listened to you. Losing the scholarship is really serious. I had some great plans for both of us, but they'll have to wait. It's finished, so now there are money worries again."

The dark quarters, fries, and pungent sauce sat untouched, but the wine had disappeared.

"Two more glasses."

The waitress smiled, "A celebration?"

"Of sorts," I replied.

Once she left the table, I continued. "That's the bad news. Now, there's other news, it could be good or bad and I haven't made up my mind. It's not all good or all bad. Carl Helbig's asked me to marry him. He's been hurt and may not play hockey again. It's a brain injury and it's serious. I saw him every day at the hospital. He signed a contract with the Bruins, and even if he can't complete it he'll have over a million dollars. He wants me to finish university. He wants to buy a house here—unfortunately—and two cars. In other words, he's offering me a future. He knows I'm not in love with him in the usual sense, he even said so, but he really cares for me. This brain injury, it sometimes makes him very emotional, angry and depressed, and that's a concern. What do you think, Ma?"

Ma frowned into her chicken, massaging her lined forehead rumpled under her blue tam.

"Sonja, you say you don't love him, but you do like him, yes? It's not just the money, no?"

"Ma, he's so clean, physically—and I like that. And I don't love anyone else, that's important. I'm a virgin, Ma, isn't that crazy? There are no virgins around anymore and I didn't even try to be one. I'm not religious or very moral, for that matter. It's just that I've never met anyone I've wanted to have sex with, unless perhaps Carl."

Ma had stopped rubbing her forehead and was sitting up straight looking at me, and then she started to laugh, showing a mouth full of tiny, sharp brown teeth, like a little cat.

"Sonja, you so funny," she said in English, and then in Ukrainian. "Perhaps in time you'll care for him."

"I'm way smarter than he is, Ma"

"Not worry," replied Ma, still smiling. "You're smarter than everyone. Sometimes that's not so bad."

CARL TELEPHONED THE next morning. He sounded better, his voice more vibrant. Was I coming over? Mutti was preparing lunch and then we'd take a drive "around beautiful lakeside Davenport in my new black Challenger," he laughed. "I'd pick you up, but they don't want me driving by myself, though the dizziness is gone . . . for good, I hope."

I could hardly wear my good black dress showing yards of skin and cleavage: it had already made its Christmas impact. It was only lunch, but a special occasion. I was, however, left with only my black pants, sweater, and cropped leather jacket. Although it was Saturday, Ma had already left for her cleaning job, and I did not smell the usual stench of smoke. I had asked her about the smoking, but she did not reply. Perhaps she had stopped, although I doubted it, picturing her manoeuvring her rickety car through Davenport's chilly streets, her morning Camel steaming between her lips.

I had my usual struggle with the shower, and finally settled on washing in the bathroom sink. I remembered Ma, when I was very young, perhaps six, administering one of her "split baths." "You go up as far as possible, down as far as possible, then you wash possible." Said with a chuckle, it was one of Ma's rare attempts at humour and even funnier in Ukrainian.

It would be so good to have my own bathroom with a bathtub filled with gallons of steaming water, instead of a shower with a lukewarm dribble. I would lie there and luxuriate in the scented foam, or even better a Jacuzzi, with piercing hot jets massaging me into oblivion. I shouldn't think this way, I thought. Surely I wasn't considering marriage so I could have a good bathroom. Or was I? It was, I admitted to myself, unfortunately a consideration, as was the car. Never to take the bus again, but to speed along, the radio booming, feeling the power of the engine pulsate through my fingertips, would be a joy. There was no doubt that these amenities—more than amenities, luxuries—were swaying my judgment.

Was I selling out? I had produced term papers for the academically limited, now it was a luxury bathroom and a car—perhaps even a Holt's credit card. There were, of course, the absolutely commendable goals of educating myself and helping Ma. Surely, there was nothing wrong with any of that. I wasn't a cheap gold-digger, my goals were much more lofty. Besides, he needed me, needed me to straighten out his tangled life, to try to protect his mangled brain from future damage. Didn't he say I was his final option, his sanctuary? And I did care for him, more than I'd acknowledged to Ma. In fact, looking back I always had, ever since the tutoring.

We hadn't even kissed, let alone shared intimacies. What if we had no chemistry? There were, of course, no comparisons. He was big, taller than I was, and well muscled. And his ears shone pink, his teeth glistened, and he smelled of Aqua Velva shaving lotion and Irish Spring soap. These were plusses, and I thought of the way he'd looked at me in my black Christmas dress and the wave of affection I'd felt just seeing him again. His hands were large with their square nails, and rough and warm. I had held them in the hospital room. Perhaps he would hold my breasts in those large hands. I was finally appreciative of my full breasts that I had kept so well hidden until their outing at the Helbig Christmas party.

What if I turned out to be a disappointment? Athletic and toned girls like Tula, who worked out for hours, were no doubt capable of twisting and contorting themselves into all sorts of titillating positions, positions that I'd never experienced, and could excite a man in all sorts of ways, ways I'd only read about, and then only briefly. Was my attraction only that I understood his limitations? It was all very worrisome.

I hated my hair and decided to go to Michelle's Beauty Salon. It was only eleven and lunch was not until twelve-thirty. Michelle greeted me like a revered client, remembering the $50 Christmas tip, and produced a startling creation that I quickly brushed out at home, pulling my hair behind my ears to show the diamond earrings, which would remind Mutti and Carl of the successful high school tutoring.

My thoughts were running wild as the silent taxi made its way up Main Street, then I had an inspiration. I would present Mutti with an Easter bouquet, some daffodils and lilies—so un-Tula like. It would be gracious and somehow commemorative.

"Could you stop here?" I asked the driver in front of Davenport's only flower shop.

"I'll keep the meter runnin'."

"I'm aware that's the usual practice," I snapped, my nerves getting the better of me.

Back in the taxi, with the bouquet in hand, we travelled through Davenport's streets, past the red-brick rooming houses, row houses, small bungalows, then the better homes, finally reaching Knightsbridge, with its picturesque bungalows. The grass lawns were grey and the trees bare, the sky pale as milk, all seen through a cool April mist.

Carl stood at the door, smiling in his usual V-necked sweater, fresh shirt and jeans, his blond hair longer than usual. He hugged me, something I was not used to, and I smelled the soap bracing as an ocean breeze. I enjoyed the closeness. Mutti appeared from the kitchen, taking off her apron as she walked toward me. She was pleased over the flowers. "Such a thoughtful girl," she said, darting an accusing glance at Carl.

Mutti served baked sole, a crisp salad, and chilled Riesling, and toasted us.

"To Sonja and Carl, and to Carl's return to the Bruins."

I felt the chill of two-fold trepidation. It was not just the joining of us both as in a wedding toast, but it was the fact that Mutti had accepted, perhaps even encouraged,

Carl's return to hockey. She had refused to listen to the information I'd received from Dr. Folkes. It was a repeat of her failure to recognize the dyslexia for so many years. But this was so much more serious than a learning disability. This was a potentially deadly decision.

I looked sideways at Carl. He did not lose his smile and I saw the scar, no longer a scabbed crab, but brightly pink on his right temple. I would argue with Mutti later, now was not the time. He had told Mutti of his future proposal, and Mutti as usual had not only predicted my acceptance but was congratulating us both, no doubt taking full credit. I took a long swallow of the Riesling, but nothing helped the tightening in my throat.

Mutti kept getting up from the table, topping up our glasses of Reisling and serving Carl extra sole. On occasion she rubbed my shoulder, as if I'd met, and would continue to meet, her approval and expectations. Finally Carl and I finished lunch, and after bidding a beaming Mutti good-bye, we drove down the street in Carl's recent purchase.

"Like it?" he asked as he revved the engine of the new Challenger, engaging in a playful burst of speed. "You can go 180 clicks an hour in this car."

"Not with me in it, you can't," I said lightly, my mind on other things, boring things, like permanent brain damage and tau protein scattered porridge-like through the brain in a future autopsy.

"Why are you going back? Why didn't you listen to me? I told you and Mutti about Dr. Folkes' recommendations. He said anyone who insisted on playing in spite of the chance of future brain damage was a suicidal idiot. I can't understand them taking you back. Dr. Folkes wouldn't give you clearance."

"I'll pass the ImPACT test. Can we change the subject?" His voice had an edge. "This was supposed to be about something really important, remember?" He revved the engine again and the Challenger roared like a lion.

We were heading toward that part of the lake where the original port had been some fifty years ago. It was fringed by a forest of spruce, from which an occasional Davenport resident would illegally cut a small Christmas tree, and there was a crumbling wharf that broke the waves. It was a good choice, the only part of Davenport I liked, isolated, with the smell of spruce and the muddy water from the lake sucking boisterous against the rough rocks on a cold day in early spring.

As we drew near the lake we were both silent, and remained so as Carl expertly parked the car as close to the water as possible.

"April is the cruellest month," I murmured.

"Nothing cruel about being proposed to."

He displayed the ring with a proud smile.

It was a beautiful ring, with a large square diamond, at least two carats, I estimated, set in smaller diamonds with a platinum band.

"It's gorgeous."

"Picked it out myself, I went to Tiffany's in Toronto last week. I had Jerry wait in the car. There was nothing good enough for you in Davenport. Try it on."

I tried it. It was a little tight, but that was good. It was not a ring that should be lost.

"You haven't asked me."

"You didn't say no."

It reminded me of the comment I'd made to Ma. "I don't love anyone else." It was all being done by default.

"If I say yes, will you consider not going back to the Bruins?"

"You're ruining everything," he said, obviously annoyed. "I always told you I was going back. And you'll say 'yes' anyway."

He kissed me gently. It was my first kiss. I had never been on a date, even with the kiss giver. I loved it, the softness of his lips, the scent of soap and shaving lotion, the smell of the car's new leather seats all blanketing me. He was sealing our future with a kiss, and while I craved the closeness, it frightened me. I could no longer hide in my literary world, and I was aware now I'd been hiding but would be exposing myself to the rawness of life, pledging myself to an uncertain future at nineteen. By marrying Carl, I was taking a bizarre and wild risk. I could feel my heart beating, and it was difficult to breathe.

"I may be having a panic attack," I whispered as I saw him watching me as I struggled for air.

He took my hands, cold and tremulous, in his large rough warm ones and drew me close. I felt his warmth and smell and it cocooned me as he cradled me in his arms. My heart returned to normal and I started to breathe as if falling into a deep slumber, but through the drowsiness other parts of me were coming alive.

"No need to panic, I'll always be there for you."

It was then that I knew I'd marry him and would try not to question what I knew was a risk-laden decision. I felt full of hope. I placed my arms around his neck and kissed him, but after a moment he drew back.

"We'll wait. I want it to be really special . . . with us. June's a good month. You'll be finished with your exams and the season's over."

"Perhaps," I said, "I don't appeal to you . . . in that way."

He kissed me again, this time less gently. "You appeal to me too much," he said. "That's why I want to wait. You'll see."

THAT NIGHT AFTER he had dropped me off, kissing me goodnight and cupping my breasts in his hands, I lay in bed. I was naked, my usual flannel pyjamas in a twisted heap on the floor. I explored my body, holding my breasts where minutes before I had felt his hands warm through the wool of my sweater. I massaged them, feeling their sponge-like heat overflow in my hands while my nipples hardened. I rubbed my hands against the elastic flesh of my hips, and then clasped the harsh nest of my crotch, pushing into the warmth inside, and feeling it pulse against my fingers. I felt a longing, searing in its newness, that caused my throat to tighten, and I wanted Carl. My urge for intimacy, so long repressed, had become compelling. Carl had said, "It sets me free, hockey does." Now perhaps sex would do it for me. And he said he'd always be there for me.

THE WEEK OF the Easter break was full: an engagement party in my black dress, Jerry Henley crowing his approval, Candace Stewart purring her congratulations with her eyes never leaving my ring. Dwarfed in a large chair, Ma actually swinging her legs, showing her new shoes and wearing a new dress and hairdo, courtesy of my fast-diminishing bank account. Ma smiled and nodded her head, pretending to understand what must have seemed to her a torrent of animated babble.

Carl was solicitous of Ma, with her occasional English phrase, actually kissing the tiny chafed hands upon introduction and escorting her from the Challenger, gently removing her coat, hanging it up, and fetching her a glass of wine, with a plate of Mutti's hors d'oeuvres. Ma was obviously thrilled and smitten, chirping a "Dank yoh" after every gesture.

His kindness to Ma touched me more than anything else he'd ever done. I had underestimated him.

"Thanks for being so good to my mother," I whispered that night, parked in front of the apartment, hugging and kissing him in the car—but still not inviting him in.

"It was a pleasure," he said, seeming surprised that a thank you was necessary, and with such sincerity that I hugged him even more. He seemed aroused but he held back, and I wanted more.

"Oh Sonja," gasped Ma when I entered, "how come you

not love a man like that? Soo bootiful. Soo sweet. If I had man like that, I eat him with a spoon."

"Perhaps you should be marrying him yourself, Ma," I laughed, but I was pleased.

Apparently having Carl Helbig for a son-in-law much surpassed blue coats with fox collars and Christmas dinners at the Sinclair Hotel.

"YOU'LL LIKE MY sisters, Helga and Anna," Carl said the day after he gave me the ring. We sat looking at the lake again, watching as the lusty wind blew tangled fingers of foam against the brown rocks. "They're both living out of province. Anna's in Vancouver and Helga's in Calgary: their husband's career choices. They've got some European hausfrau in them, following their men, in spite of their own careers, or perhaps getting away from Mutti, or all of the above."

We both laughed.

"They were great to me when I was young. I was their little plump brother with white frizzy hair and eyes like blue saucers, and they could never say no to me. I was a junior artist, always scrawling over Mutti's nice clean walls with Magic Markers. It drove her crazy, and she'd go on one of her wooden spoon rampages. They'd hide me under their beds and lie for me, and it always worked. By the time she'd find me she'd cooled off, and settled the score by telling me there'd be no dessert for a week, and calling me a naughty boy: a *schlimmer finger*, which would always get a laugh from the girls. I knew I could always count on them to sneak me some of their dessert anyway."

"Was she a good mom?"

"You could say that. The thing I remember most was that she was a clean freak. I was the cleanest little kid in kindergarten. I was scoured morning and night, and she'd even call me in from playing in the backyard so she could wipe 'my filthy hands' with a cloth soaked with dish detergent. It was a pain in the ass; show me any kid who doesn't get his hands dirty when he's playing with his trucks in the backyard dirt. She loved routine, study hours, bedtime hours, and TV hours—a real Kraut. My sisters fought her on it, but by the time I was in my teens, they were off to university and she'd loosened up. She encouraged the hockey. She and my dad attended all the games, and she drove me to hockey camp in the summers. My dad's a great guy. He hates confrontation so he always let Mutti run things, but he always had my back."

He leaned back and watched the restless water with half-closed eyes. "I remember my first concussion: I was seven and it was my first summer at hockey camp. I was speeding like a crazy little dynamo when I crashed into another kid and hit my head on the side of the rink. Everything went black and I couldn't remember the rest of the game. My buddies said I lay there for a few minutes, sat on the bench for another minute, and then started again. I went back the next day, and no one was upset. The couch told Mutti I'd had 'a little tumble.' It became a pattern for me: I'd always get up and keep playing even if at times I couldn't remember what had happened. Mutti thought it was great and called me her 'little warrior,' and so did the coach. And then when my grades took a nosedive I'd be even more of a warrior—you gotta be great at something—and with me it was hockey. I never made the connection that maybe getting my head whacked on a weekly basis wasn't helping my brain."

"Terrible," I murmured, "just awful."

"Let's look at the upside," he said, smiling, "Everyone loves a hockey star, especially girls. It makes you a sex magnet, and you might say I took advantage of that, but not unfair advantage."

"You should take advantage of me." Said with a complaining pout, it only increased his smile, and he didn't answer. "Did you care for any of them?"

"I liked them: I appreciated their co-operation and the fact that they liked me. I treated them well. Mutti was hot on manners, so I was a door-opener, and never rough, or rude, or too forceful, and because of that some of them thought I cared for them more than I did."

He smiled at the turbulent lake where the windswept water reflected the white incandescent sun, barely visible behind the sheer grey clouds.

"Did you ever really care for any of them?" I was insistent: it was important to me.

"No, not really, you see, they didn't know about my reading, or the lack of it. And I'd never tell them, I was too ashamed, and that drove a wedge between us right away.

I'd always think, 'What if she knew I was such a clueless bastard that reading a book was like Chinese water torture?' Then you found out and it was such a relief."

Was that my attraction—that I knew so much?

"Glad I was a help," I said, smiling, but not inside.

He continued, his voice low and serious, "I used to watch and listen to you in class when I wasn't cutting up, distracting everyone, and being the class dickhead. I used to marvel at you. You always knew the answer to every question, and you answered in that high, clear voice of yours, and I thought that was really great, and I wished I was half as smart." He leaned back, rubbing the wheel of the Challenger, and a smile hovered around his mouth at the memory.

"I'd look at you when I thought you wouldn't notice, with all that black hair scooped back from your awesome little white face, so different from everyone else's. But you'd never look at me, and I'd think, she doesn't even want to look at an idiot like me, shows what great taste she's got. Then I finally got up the nerve to ask you to a movie, and you said no. And that was it: I knew for sure you had great taste." He looked at me, and his smile deepened.

I placed my face in my hands. "I thought you asked me so you could make fun of me later . . . to your choir buddies."

"Why would I do that?" He was obviously shocked. "The worst I ever did was the period question, which was really bad, and what's this about choir buddies? None of those guys go to church, even the Catholics. Let's get out, I want to feel the wind on my face, it reminds me of hockey."

He got out and came over to my side of the car and opened the car door, but I shook my head so he walked toward the lake. I watched him standing on a rock, his black bomber jacket and square shoulders silhouetted against the cream-coloured sky, his golden hair blowing in the wind. I left the car, walked up behind him, and put my arms around his waist.

"I'd like to freeze this moment, and then when we're old we can say, 'Remember that afternoon at the lake, with the wind blowing against us?'"

"I was thinking about our kids, you don't mind having kids, do you? I love kids, love the way they're so eager about everything because it's all new and shiny. We can have our own hockey team, and one little girl with black curls, who'll sit on my knee and smell nice."

"Girls have their father's brains, boys their mother's. Psychologists are saying that now."

"All the more reason to have six boys. And we'll have a nanny so you can go to university forever."

"As long as the nanny's not too good-looking. Some fathers sleep with their kids' nannies when the wife's away; I've read instances of that."

"That's terrible. Why would I do that when I've got you?" He sounded genuinely astounded.

"Just kidding," I said. "I forgot about how moral you were about the adultery in *Gatsby*."

"You know when I decided I wanted to marry you? When you almost broke down reciting Lear's speech after Cordelia died. You frightened the hell out of me, and I thought to myself, if this girl can get this worked up about some play written hundreds of years ago, think of how she'd be if something exciting really happened to her in the present."

"Like?"

"Like our getting really close."

"You were gauging my orgasm potential, right?"

"That's not a very delicate way to put it."

But I continued, "Which you won't know about for months, which is your choice, as we both know."

We both laughed into the wind and he turned and placed his arms around me, and we stood swaying together on the rock with the harsh wind blowing against us and all the time I smelled the tang of spruce, mixed with his Irish Spring and Aqua Velva, and my heart swelled with love for him, but I didn't say so. I don't know why I didn't.

CARL'S SISTER HELGA arrived from Calgary for her yearly visit with her boys three days before I left for university. She was a tall woman, who looked like Carl with a blond wig. I admired her: she seemed so serene and capable. Carl saw me watching her and whispered, "She's a large animal vet. She can handle anything, rambunctious boys, me, and even Mutti."

Her three little boys were full of joy and energy, bouncing off everything, including Mutti's newly upholstered brocade sofa; the Royal Doultons, I noticed, had disappeared. Three-year-old, yellow-haired Brad was first. He stood waiting until Carl, smiling broadly, scooped him up and placed him on his shoulders, holding his sturdy thighs with his large hands. Brad placed two small grubby hands over Carl's eyes and the now-blind Carl staggered around the room, bumping into walls, while Brad shrieked with delight.

"Enough," ordered Helga after a few minutes, and a protesting Brad was deposited gently on Mutti's waxed floor.

"You promised," said five-year-old Max, and off they went to the brown grass of Mutti's backyard where a game of catch took place. Here Carl slowly threw underhanded pitches with a bruised baseball and praised a beaming Max after every successful catch.

From the concrete steps, eight-year-old Lewis sat and waited, then finally called, "We got Lego, Uncle Carl, don't forget."

They sat at Mutti's shiny dining room table, where protective newspapers had been placed, and focused on assembling the Lego purchased by Carl to celebrate Lewis' visit. Carl sat, head bent foreword, fair hair falling over his forehead, frowning in concentration; Lewis, having finished putting a truck together, stood beside him, a slight hand on his arm, smiling as if they shared some private secret.

Watching them, I felt choked up with tenderness. I would protect Carl from all harm, such as bangs to the head suffered as he rushed to the net in pursuit of a goal.

Brad, holding out his arms, howled with fury when

we prepared to leave, fat tears pouring down his flushed full cheeks.

"If you're bat like this, Uncle Carl won't play with you no more," warned Mutti with an ominous pout, but Carl knelt down and, taking the small, hot clenched fists in his hands, gently explained he'd be back soon, and even sooner if he stopped crying.

"Take care of my little brother," whispered Helga at the door. "He loves you so much and now I know why, and even Mutti approves." I felt part of the family and I loved it.

"You must have run a daycare in your previous life or spent it coaching Little Leaguers," I said as he drove me home.

He laughed. "I coached Little Leaguers in this life. There's nothing like kids, they really just want to please, some people don't realize that."

"And then they become teenagers, and only want to please themselves."

We both laughed, not that far from our own teenaged years.

"My worst time with Mutti," he said, "was when she gave away my shepherd. I loved that dog, he used to sleep at the foot of my bed, and I took good care of him, used to walk him every day, feed him, and brush him down, and he'd be all over me when I came in the door. Then I came home from school one day and he was gone. He'd been shedding fur over her damn rugs and furniture and she'd given him away to some tradesman who'd come to fix the kitchen sink. I freaked out, told her I hated her, and even my dad got angry with her. And he never got angry. It took us weeks to track him down, and then the guy told us that he'd been killed by a car, trying to run away. I cried all the way home. I was about twelve at the time, and I remember my dad patting me on the shoulder and saying, 'Your mother's too much for the clean house. But you've got to forgive her.'"

"Did you forgive her?"

"Of course not. I didn't speak to her for weeks. I still haven't forgiven her."

"Did she apologize?"

"Not Mutti. Just kept mumbling about some people being happy to live in 'dirt and filth,' which was crazy, absolutely nuts. His name was Lucky, which he wasn't. They say you should never call a dog Lucky—he ends up never being that way."

"We'll have a dog for our six boys and one little girl," I said, keeping my voice light and playful, "and we'll call him 'Carson,' a combination of both our names. And he'll be very lucky."

"So will I." He smiled, reached over, and took my hand.

We drove on through the chilled streets of Davenport, with its leafless trees and starless sky, a comfortable silence between us. I cared for him, I knew that now, and it had nothing to do with hockey contracts that would pave my way through university. I cared for his essence, a vulnerable boyishness and sensitivity, and his lack of literacy meant nothing.

"I guess I'll be invited in as usual."

His voice was bantering but with an undertone of irritation.

"You must understand," I said, attempting to keep a self-conscious hostility from creeping into my voice. "Some people don't live like your family does. Some people don't have shiny mahogany tables, Royal Doultons, and newly upholstered furniture. Some people have surroundings that are ugly and drab, that smack of poverty. No need to expose you to that." I was thinking, of course, of my own exposure.

He kissed me gently on the lips. "It wouldn't make any difference in the way I feel about you; you must know that. What kind of snob do you think I am?"

But he'd see me in a different light, an impoverished lower-class light. And even worse, he might feel sorry for me.

"Perhaps someday," I lied, knowing it would never happen.

THEN THERE WAS a dinner at the Helbigs, with Ma as a guest, and a double date with Jerry Henley and his girlfriend, Pattie Beaumont, who seemed much more interested in Carl.

"Carl won't have sex," I complained to Jerry, watching with narrowed eyes as Pattie gyrated on the dance floor, grinding into a grinning Carl, who she'd almost pulled out of his seat. "It makes me wonder what my attraction—or lack of it—is. We make out, and then he stops."

I wouldn't have said it if I hadn't been drinking and watching Pattie make such an obvious play for Carl. And Jerry was, after all, Carl's best friend.

"Silly bugger," scoffed Jerry, "he's got you that high on a pedestal that he's afraid to risk it, afraid somethin' may go wrong, and you won't go through with the wedding. Never thought he'd be such a nutter. He wants you two to be special. But he loves you, no doubt about that."

"So ridiculous," I stormed. "What could go wrong? It's not rocket science, it's pretty basic stuff. It's not as if he hasn't had experience. Perhaps I don't compare to Tula and the many others."

"Naw, that's not it. Too much respect for you, Sonja, you're such an intellect. It's not that he don't want to, he was on about you in the black dress that night after the party, I couldn't shut him up. But he doesn't want to lose you—or 'spoil things,' he says. Want me to talk to him?"

"Never. Promise me you won't."

Jerry shrugged. "Perhaps you should come on to him really strong . . ."

But Carl and a smiling Pattie had returned to the table.

On the way back to Davenport my anger surfaced. "Not nice, not nice at all, you grinning away at Pattie Beaumont doing a bump and grind against you in front of your best friend, who she's supposed to be dating, and of course me—although we both know I don't really count."

"You're jealous," he said, obviously delighted.

"Not really, just disappointed with your lack of sensitivity."

He paused before he spoke and sighed, driving with one hand and reaching for me with the other. "Pattie, she's a certain kind of girl; I've met a number of them.

They're into professional jocks, and they don't discrim-
inate. They'll go from football to hockey to basketball.
It's got nothing to do with sex, though it's a preliminary.
They like the money, but mostly the glitz. Jerry won't last;
she'd never want anything permanent with an electrician.
I love the guy, and I don't want him hurt. He'll be lucky to
be rid of her. They're not in our category. You can't compare yourself with her. You're not on the same planet."

"No, she's the kind of girl you'd have sex with," I
observed sourly.

"Right. And it wouldn't mean sweet fuck all," he replied.

"I'VE OPENED AN account for you at the Commerce
on Bloor," Carl said casually, handing me a debit card as
we were driving back to Toronto. "It's a debit account.
You'll need some money for a wedding dress, perhaps a
car, and other stuff. I don't want you embarrassed about
money. The trouble you got into at the university really
bothered me."

I shouldn't have told him I was embarrassed about
money. And then when I saw the $100,000 he had placed
in the bank account, even more so. He was giving me a
portion of his signing bonus.

"I can't take this," I gasped. "This is outrageous."

"I wanted to be sure you wouldn't change your mind,"
he laughed, clearly pleased by my reaction.

I finally kept it. Bought and paid for as usual, I thought
as I kissed him with a renewed passion only money,
together with my own soaring longings, could buy.

We were standing close together in the cool mist in the student parking lot outside the residence, and I could hear the sound of the tires of the passing cars as they travelled on the damp asphalt of University Avenue. I had my arms inside his leather jacket, and my fingers rubbed the soft skin of his lower back as I felt him hard against me.

"Come upstairs," I whispered into his warm neck. "My roommate's never there. We won't do anything: I just want you to hold me. I promise I won't have a panic attack."

I was lying. I had much more in mind.

"It's only another two months. It'd be too hard on me just to hold you . . . it's not a good idea."

"Can't I even show my appreciation for your generosity?"

I was trying to keep it light by being playful, but it didn't help. In fact, it bothered him.

"Do you ever listen to yourself?" he said, removing my arms from inside his jacket. "Connecting my giving you money with our making love." And then, aping my speech after our double date with Jerry and Pattie, "Not nice, not nice at all. I'm surprised at your lack of sensitivity."

I gave a forced laugh. It wasn't as if I were charging for my services. But at least he had listened to me, a good omen for the future. I placed my arms around his waist again and pressed against what had been his erection. I was becoming so bold. "Are you sure?"

At least he hesitated before he said yes.

LATER, I SECLUDED myself in my room, grateful for the absence of my roommate. Lying on the bed, I made a mental to-do list: Ma needed a dentist with a good hygienist for cleaning or, as a last resort, veneers; a wedding outfit for Ma. I would, I decided, give her ten thousand for her own bank account. Then there was my own wedding dress, and honeymoon clothes, but what kind? We'd never even talked about our honeymoon. I needed a BlackBerry, a Mac computer, a printer, and some spring clothes. Carl would be visiting, and I had promised to return to Davenport once more before school ended. I would make a car purchase, nothing too showy, a Honda perhaps or a Toyota, even a demo with a few miles on it. If I took driving lessons, it would cut down on the insurance. I needed top-of-the-line hair styling, nothing too radical—he liked my hair. I would make arrangements for a September apartment, with two months' rent in advance. I would lose weight, just a piece of fruit for dinner should do it. And I would get some birth control pills, no babies yet. I had to get my degree first; he was supporting me in that. But we would have children, he would be too good a dad to go to waste. The irony of a virgin obtaining birth control pills didn't escape me, especially a virgin now becoming ever more anxious each day not to be one. I clasped my pillow and buried my face in it, giddy with excitement. I couldn't remember ever feeling that happy, and it was all because of Carl.

The hockey season was now almost over. I hoped he wouldn't insist on returning before next October. I would have that long to persuade him to retire altogether, and I was now convinced that he'd listen.

"Quite the rock you've got there," said Jo at dinner that

night. "Guess he's going to try to go back. Hard to carry on without the big bucks and the big rush, and with these guys it's been their whole lives. Nothing else matters. Did you hear about Clive Anderson? He quit the Penguins after five concussions. He just got killed in Montreal, a car accident, blood alcohol four times over. His wife wants them to examine his brain. She says he never stopped complaining of headaches and he was living on booze and painkillers. He didn't know his ass from his elbow and he was twenty-eight with three kids. His wife said he couldn't even remember their names."

"Thanks, I really needed that, so kind of you to keep me up to date on every casualty in the NHL." My voice was edged with sarcasm, but I felt nauseated and pushed my plate away.

"I think that's really insensitive, Johanna," fumed Janet, "really inappropriate talk when Sonja's just gotten engaged and we're eating dinner."

"Shit happens." Jo shrugged, cutting into a piece of steak with a crimson gash in the middle and depositing it in her large, lipstick-free mouth. "You have to be realistic, that's the chance you take with these guys. The big bucks don't come without a price."

I had, I decided, had enough of Jo and her clichés. No more shared meals; it was time for me to start my diet, with my apple or pear and a grapefruit as replacement for dinner. I left the table without another word.

Doubts still plagued me at times. Was I selling out at only nineteen? Perhaps not in the millions like a professional athlete but for a comfortable lifestyle with all the fringe benefits, for me and Ma, all contributed to by a smiling hockey player with a history of concussions that I'd be insane to ignore. Women didn't marry this young anymore, and I wanted a career, now as a university professor rather than as a high school teacher. I had listened to Professor Latham, who had recommended it. Carl would encourage me: he was like that, not a bit jealous or controlling. And I would escape the rigid nine-to-five schedule of high school. But still . . .

THE FINALS WERE in May, but life had already become busy apart from academia. I gave Magda $2,000 toward Zoly's university applications after checking with Carl. I took driving lessons and received my ninety-day permit, and put a deposit on a last year's model Toyota at a discount, after discussing it with Carl on my new cellphone.

"You should have gotten something better, with more class," he insisted.

"Not appropriate," I replied, but he merely laughed.

This time, I thought, I would drive back to Davenport free from the army of humanity and chatty bus drivers.

The wedding dress, plain white satin with long sleeves and a plunging neckline, was selling off at a store on Spadina. It was not the strapless version so currently popular.

"I bought my dress," I informed him.

"Great," he said, and the eagerness in his voice made my heart lurch.

A few days following the last exam I received written notification that I was the recipient of the Shakespeare

Award of $1,500. Professor Latham had come through in spite of the plagiarized essays and the criticisms he'd face. Or was it Priscilla again? I had, I thought wryly, after all, produced more Shakespearean work than anyone else, although in a less than orthodox way.

The week before I was leaving I secured my new apartment at the Manulife Centre on Bloor. It was a small apartment with reasonable rent, and I decided to only purchase a sparse amount of furniture, a bed, a computer desk, and a set of table and chairs for my three-year stay. It was pointless to duplicate furniture that we would be buying for the Davenport house. My one exception was a large television set, which dwarfed the wall of the bedroom from where Carl could watch sports.

I felt sure that following our marriage I could convince Carl not to return to hockey. We could, I told myself, live in Toronto during the week and Carl could attend a community college. I had helped him before and would do so again. He could become a real estate salesman, one of the many options I'd persuade him to consider. Who in Davenport would not buy or sell a house from hockey hero Helbig? And I could help with any purchase and sale agreements.

I deliberately chose the Manulife Building, which I'd visited in the past. The building had its own self-contained little world. Downstairs there were dozens of specialty shops and the flagship of Chapters, a bookstore that carried thousands of books. There was even a movie theatre with six current films that I'd visited during first year, and across the street was Holt's, made accessible by an underground walkway. And it was near enough to the university so I could walk to classes, and Carl to an assortment of colleges. Matheson's was across the street, just in case Magda and Zoly were still around.

The wedding was June 10, and Mutti was masterminding everything. "All you have to do iss show up mit your dress." I was to submit a guest list, but there was only Magda, Zoly, Janet Murdock, and Jo, whom I had not yet completely forgiven. Both Janet and Jo were out of town. Then I remembered my two high school luncheon companions and gave their names to Mutti. I had no maid of honour. I had thought of Miss Steinbrink, my former favourite teacher, but feared she would be shocked by the mismatching of her favourite student and Carl Helbig. I was sure he was still memorable for his disruption and lack of academic interest, but I would invite her as a guest.

"Perhaps Carl's sister Helga could serve as matron of honour," I suggested.

"Gut idea," agreed Mutti with enthusiasm.

Encouraged, I continued, pleased that the entire conversation was by telephone. "I really only want a very small wedding," I explained carefully, "just a family wedding would be fine—and I don't believe Carl cares."

There was a deafening silence. "*Nein*," sputtered Mutti, "Carl has many friends. It would be insult not to invite them. This is big important wedding."

"Can you control your mother?" I pleaded with Carl that night. "I really only want a little family wedding. I will still wear my white dress, which is unfortunately very appropriate. I have very few friends and I have always thought of a wedding as an intimate exchange of vows. I never wanted a walk-down-the-aisle effect, with a shower of rice or confetti. It's just not me at all. Can't we simply elope?"

The voice on the cellphone laughed. He would try, but there was the problem of upsetting Mutti. He would attempt to keep the list down to a few dozen, but there were no guarantees. Jerry Henley would be best man. "Would you like Candace Stewart as a bridesmaid?" he asked. "Or Tula as maid of honour?"

"Hardly, too close to the groom, unless you want a ménage à trois following the wedding."

"What?" He sounded shocked.

Too bad that his literacy and knowledge of French were as lacking as his sense of humour.

"Are you mad?" I asked, feigning indignation. "We are probably the only engaged couple in Davenport, perhaps even in all of Canada, who haven't had sex. I'd hardly be suggesting a threesome after the ceremony."

IT WAS A thirty-minute ceremony at the Lutheran Church, then an endless reception line and a sit-down five-course dinner at the Davenport Golf Club, with at least one hundred and eighty guests, and Ma's new veneers chattering with nervousness. A toast to the bride celebrating her scholastic achievements, including her recent Shakespeare Award, was made by Carl, who addressed the guests and confessed to them that he did not know what such a brilliant girl was doing with a klutz like him. A row of Bruins applauded, while I hoped he wasn't right and longed to be elsewhere. But the deed was done. My bridal bouquet was aimed directly into the waiting arms of Candace Stewart.

The next day there it was, right on the front page of the *Davenport Guardian*, "Davenport Hockey Hero Weds Local University Student," together with a picture of the two of us, slicing into a three-tiered cake, with a hockey figure standing close to his bride on top. The honeymoon, the *Guardian* stated, was to take place at "an undisclosed locality in Europe."

We left at ten before the serious drinking from the open bar started, both limp with exhaustion and with throbbing champagne headaches.

"Surprise tomorrow," Carl murmured. "We're going to Paris for a week."

Somewhere, sometime ago, I had mentioned to him I'd love to visit Paris, and he had booked a first-class Air France flight leaving at six the following night from the Lester B. Pearson International Airport in Toronto.

"Oh God," I said, shaking my head.

"Disappointed?" he asked, obviously anxious not to disappoint.

"No, of course not, how could anyone be disappointed seeing Paris? But I wish you'd told me. I don't know if I've got the clothes."

"Where did you think we'd be going?"

"Jamaica, Florida, anywhere ordinary, but not Paris."

"You're tired out. Maybe we both should just take some Tylenol and sleep."

I couldn't believe what I was hearing.

"No. We'll go change at the Sinclair, walk to the drugstore, get some Tylenol and spearmint gum, then walk back."

I had waited long enough.

IT WAS A cool early June night and we walked briskly to the Drug Mart wearing jeans and light jackets. The silvery orb of a moon seemed as near as the street lights, and there was the barest sprinkle of stars, bright but so far away. The cool air was pleasant and I sniffed the new grass growing on the front lawn of the Sinclair. Carl took my hand and I felt a tingle—anticipation or the foreshadowing of new intimacy, I wondered.

"Sonja Helbig—do you like that?"

I didn't. It was a hideous Russian-German combination. I'd stick to the Danychuk, but this was the wrong time to tell him. We bought the gum, Tylenol, and small, icy bottles of water from the corner machine and by the time we returned to the Sinclair our headaches were clearing.

I sat on the side of the bed and smiled, undoing the upsweep that Michelle had spent hours perfecting that morning, and shaking my thick black hair that bounced off my shoulders. Carl stood by the bed, looking down at me, big, blond, and muscled, frowning his concern.

"What's your experience with virgins? That's what this long wait's been about, isn't it? To keep me as the Virgin Queen looking down from her throne."

"I knew you were, but Jerry Henley said no after he saw you in the black dress at the Christmas party."

"Nice to have you discuss my virginity with Jerry Henley, who wouldn't know a virgin if he saw one. I'm sure my panic attack after my first kiss convinced you, although I've been trying to have sex with you ever since." But I kept smiling, he was so obviously worried.

"You haven't answered me. What's your experience with virgins?"

"Never had one."

"Not even Candace Stewart?"

"She was no virgin."

"When I got my birth control pills, I told the doctor. He was suitably impressed and wanted to make a little cut, just to make things easier for you. But I told him I thought you'd be up to the task—all those pucks you put into the net."

He didn't smile; in fact, his frown deepened.

"Let's wash," I said. "It was a sweaty wedding."

I LAY IMMERSED in the frothy bath water, watching him behind the glassed-in shower. As long as I could remember I had longed for the luxury of a steaming bath, and now I was lulled by the bliss of having the lavender foam creep slowly up and cover my legs and belly. He was finished before I was and I kept watching him, drowsy from the heated water, as he rubbed himself vigorously, his now grown-out hair falling damp over his forehead. I liked it longer, so much better than the military brush cut he had when he was playing hockey. He was not, I decided, as heavy as I had thought. His arms were well muscled but not large, his stomach flat, and I estimated his weight to be little more than 210 pounds. A 260-pound enforcer could and had inflicted serious damage. His arms and legs were covered with golden fuzz, but his chest was smooth. I wanted to see the rest, but he had tied a towel around his waist.

He brushed his teeth with the intensity he had used when drying himself with a towel. Would he, I wondered, take me with the same intensity—once he stopped worrying?

"Help me dry." It was a seductive request, almost a plea, certainly not a demand. He rubbed my back and then cupped my breasts in his hands.

"You have," he said, as if giving a benediction, "great breasts." He didn't say "tits" or "boobs." It was as if my breasts had acquired a majesty, a unique life of their own. "You'd never need implants."

No doubt many of the puck bunnies had implants.

"I've packed a nightgown," I said, "a black satin one. I was going to make an entrance, but it seems silly now. I want you to feel my skin and I want to feel yours."

We lay down together under the crisp sheet. I felt his hands, warm and rough-skinned, exploring my ears, breasts, hips, and then I felt his index finger, with its square, well-clipped nail, one of the nails I used to watch during our tutoring days, tentatively penetrate my vagina and then withdraw. Checking for size, I presumed. I thought of Mutti and her veggies and felt his penis, rock hard against my hip.

"It's okay," I whispered.

I felt him pushing against the tight wet cushions holding him back.

"Tell me if I'm hurting you." His voice was hoarse with concern.

"I'm fine," I yelped in pain. He was tearing me apart. I felt blood, warm between my inner thighs, but now he wouldn't or couldn't stop. As he drove into me the pain was replaced by a musical sensation, and the melody flowed over me and entered my very core.

"THERE'S BLOOD ON the bed." He sounded contrite.

"I guess we should soak the sheet in cold water," I answered drowsily. "No need to inform the cleaning staff at the Sinclair." I fought the urge to laugh and continued, "If you were in the Middle East, you'd be waving the sheet from the window. You must tell Mutti, then she'll know I'm not a girl who gets a man with her veggies."

"It's none of Mutti's damn business."

"It'll make her happy. She sort of recruited me, you know, and this will validate her choice. I really liked it. It's good we didn't do it before. God knows what I would have been up to in Toronto."

I felt him stiffen against me and mutter, "Jesus."

My stupid mouth: the Davenport Diplomat strikes again. "Carl, lighten up. No one in the world smells like you, has your pink shiny ears," I reached out in the darkness, touching his forehead, "and your pink shiny scar. I never, ever, wanted to have sex with anyone else; you must know that."

I clasped my arms around him, pushed my breasts into his back, and felt his warmth. He turned and held me. And we slept.

13
THE HONEYMOON

"DID YOU KNOW THAT GENERAL von Choltitz was told by Hitler to destroy all the beautiful monuments in Paris when Germany was losing the war? But he wouldn't do it, so now we can see them all."

We were sitting in first class and I was reading from one of the three tourist books on Paris I had picked up at the airport while waiting for the Air France flight. We had finished one of the best dinners I'd ever had, complete with white and red wine. I was nineteen and was on my way to Paris with a husband who smelled of soap and who had felt apologetic for taking my virginity, for which I not only forgave him but was appreciative, even enthusiastic.

"It's called The City of Light, know why?"

"'Cause it's all lit up."

"That and the fact that it was a place of enlightenment way back when, with lots of intellectuals and new ideas."

He reached over and rubbed my leg.

"Tired?" I asked. I would keep the reading to myself and merely tell him each morning where we were heading.

"If you hadn't been so secretive about the honeymoon, I could have brushed up on my French and listened to some tapes. But it should come back to me."

I picked up his hand, studied the pink clipped nails, and then bit his index finger gently.

"Why did you insert it the way you did last night? Checking the fit?"

Being playful didn't work. "Read your books," he ordered, "then you can plan our week."

"Didn't you want to go to Paris?"

"Not really. I don't speak French, but you wanted it—and that's what mattered."

"So you're just along for the ride."

"What's wrong with that, me wanting you happy?"

"Nothing, I guess." So much for the sharing of ideas and enthusiasms, but he did want me happy and that was something—and I loved the sex.

We stayed at the Hôtel du Louvre, across from the Musée du Louvre. "Really convenient," I said with enthusiasm, "we can just nip across the street and spend hours looking at the art." The travel agent had chosen the locality after he had told her, "My wife's really into art and all that stuff."

We lay down briefly to combat the creeping jet lag but had sex instead.

"I never thought you'd be like this," he said thoughtfully afterwards, "deep down sexy. I'm really lucky. It's something I'm good at and it makes you happy."

I could have been flippant and made some remark about the puck bunnies, but I decided against it. It was obvious that he was very serious and had given the subject considerable thought.

That day we strolled through the streets of Paris and finally in late afternoon took a taxi to Notre Dame Cathedral. "Isn't it magnificent," I breathed, "those soaring ceilings and the stained-glass rose window?"

He nodded solemnly but stood behind, waiting at the back while I roamed through the church.

"You're not participating," I chided.

"Doesn't turn me on like it does you, but I like watching you enjoy it."

I would, I decided, restrict the churches, or see the Église de la Madeleine on my own.

The travel agent had booked a dinner for two at the Tour d'Argent. "It's really high-end and very expensive," I cautioned. "No need for us to spend money like this."

"I told her I wanted to take you somewhere very special for our first night."

I wore my black dress and he learned to ask for the bill.

"L'addition, s'il vous plait."

"That's all you really have to know," I joked, "that will serve you well everywhere we go."

We were satiated with eating duck done in four different ways, a bottle of wine, and a rich dessert, so we decided against having sex after what seemed like walking miles back to the hotel. Then we went out onto the small balcony to look at the city. I put my arms around him, and we decided we'd have sex anyway.

"Tomorrow," I whispered afterwards, "we'll be like the French. We'll have a croissant and café au lait for breakfast and go to a nice family restaurant at night."

"I can take you shopping. The travel agent said I had to take you shopping."

"I thought you'd never ask. You must be sick of seeing me in my black dress with my boobs hanging out." This time he at least laughed.

So we walked the Champs Élysees, visited the Galeries Lafayette, and even dropped in on Givenchy and Dior on the Avenue Montaigne.

"Too much money and I've got too much T and A," I said, dismissing much of the merchandise.

He did, I noticed, pay much more attention to my wardrobe choices than to the historical monuments and buildings, sitting solemnly, arms crossed, while I modelled an assortment of dresses, suits, and coats, with Carl pronouncing them to be "not for you" or "perfect."

"Too expensive and dressy," I complained about one of his "perfect" choices. "Where'll I wear it? Going to classes on the U of T campus, or slinking around Tim Hortons in Davenport?" But he insisted.

"You have," I pronounced finally, "wonderful taste in women's clothes. You lean toward nice, clean, basic lines, really classic. You're a hidden Armani. If you hadn't been a hockey player, you could have been a woman's clothes designer or at least a buyer. Even the saleslady said, 'He's got great taste for a German.'"

"Is that what you two were giggling about?" he said, but I could tell he was pleased. "They caved in soon enough to the Krauts in the Second World War."

"I defended you, reminded her of Karl Lagerfeld, but it seems she doesn't like him either. Apparently your taste's much better."

He did, however, admire the Arc de Triomphe, standing and looking at it with narrowed eyes for several minutes.

"Approve?"

"More than approve."

We climbed the Eiffel Tour, bypassing the layers of tourist shops, and when we reached the top exhausted, I gasped and said with breathless gusto, arms outstretched, "Now we own Paris."

Then we kissed.

"Like in a movie," he said.

Rigoletto at the Opera Garnier was a mistake: Carl slept after Act One.

"Tired or bored?" I inquired.

"Both," he answered. At least he was honest.

So the next night we attended a jazz concert at The

New Morning, which we both enjoyed, and afterwards visited the Deux Magots for a glass of wine. "This was an intellectual meeting place," I explained. "Simone de Beauvoir used to come here with Jean-Paul Sartre. They believed in existentialism, that you made your own life decisions, regardless of religion or current morality, important life-or-death decisions. De Beauvoir was an early feminist."

"Are you a feminist?"

"I suppose I am, although I'm not as independent as I should be. I really enjoy you buying me things. Maybe if my parents had been rich I'd be a much stronger feminist. Feminists, after all, just want to be treated on an equal basis with men. Besides, I only want to be an English professor, not take on the world."

"I never think," he said, "of a feminist having big boobs and loving sex like you do. You're not my idea of a feminist at all."

"Your mother is more of a feminist?"

"Mutti is a sergeant major, but she has nothing to do with being a feminist. She doesn't even know the meaning of the word."

"She doesn't need to, Carl. She's a natural leader, not always right, in fact at times very wrong, but she's got all the right instincts, way beyond equality."

We both laughed, thinking back to how she controlled our wedding.

On the fourth day I woke early. I watched Carl as he slept, his brows slightly drawn, his scar shining pink against his forehead, which had acquired a slight tan. What was he dreaming of, I wondered, a missed goal or never going back to the Bruins? He was tired out. Was it all the sex or the residue of the last concussion? I felt a wave of tenderness, an urge to protect him. The day before we had walked the entire Rive Gauche, or Left Bank, and ended up at a neighbourhood restaurant that was family owned. We shared a bottle of hypnotic Beaujolais and beefsteak and frites.

"No lovin' tonight," I insisted as we took the lift to the tenth floor.

"Dixième étage," he said.

"There you are," I sang, "you can not only order a restaurant tab, but you know our floor in French. In one more year you'd be parlez vous-ing away like a true Frenchman."

In spite of my voiced prohibition, the lovemaking started in the bathroom, continued on the balcony, and ended in a feverish finish on the bed, which was not made for two quite large individuals, by French standards.

Exhausted, I thought affectionately, watching him take a deep breath and continue his dreams, dreams that made him frown.

I DECIDED TO visit the Louvre. It opened early and it would be exciting to experience Paris on my own, if only briefly. I would be back in two hours. I placed the *Occupée* card on the doorknob and left.

Although it was early, there was a lineup for the Louvre.

Once inside, I moved quickly from exhibit to exhibit, savouring my independence. Someday, I would come back and spend an entire week visiting the Louvre and the other museums, especially to see Renoir and the Impressionists. My interest could not be stifled by Carl's inability to relate, although his artistry and clothes sense—women's clothes sense—was surprising.

It was eleven when I returned. Carl was up and dressed and angry. Why didn't I wake him? He was concerned. He'd been awake for hours, worried. Why would I sneak off without him?

"You could have gone downstairs and had breakfast."

"You know I can't speak French."

"The staff here will all speak English."

I found his insecurity unsettling, bothersome. I had enjoyed my time alone, but now he had ruined it.

"Were you worried about me, or about yourself, or because you were alone?"

"What are you trying to prove? I was worried about you."

Both, I thought, but I knew he did not want to be alone.

"I should have left a note. It was inconsiderate, but you're over-reacting, really you are."

"Sorry. I'm an asshole."

"No, you're not. You're great. I really thought you were tired. I was thinking of you."

We were both liars, but it had gone on long enough.

"Let's have lunch. We'll go downstairs, and later I want to visit the Sorbonne, that's where I always wanted to attend university. Then we can take the Metro; there are 384 stops. We can get off anywhere it looks interesting."

I SMILED AT him over my café au lait, watching him cut into his omelette.

"Did you know you scowl in your sleep? I was watching you this morning before I left."

"What were you doing that for?" It was apparently an invasion of privacy.

"It's not as if you were snoring with your mouth open; you look cute when you sleep—just not peaceful." Then as an afterthought, "We haven't seen the Court at Versailles, or any of the Gardens."

"I'll take a pass."

"Not interested in Louis XIV? Kings in those days made a ritual of going to the loo; apparently having a daily bowel movement in front of their courtiers was expected and complied with." This would at least catch his attention.

"Gross."

"I bet you'd never forgive Steve Jobs for soaking his feet in Apple's toilet to chill out."

"Double gross."

"You're so hygienic, but I appreciate it."

Finally a smile. But I would not leave him alone again.

IT WAS RAINING. A Parisian drizzle is not unusual in mid-June, and we were in a French-style chocolate bar, only about fifty feet from Notre Dame, which soared through the mist. We were sipping rich hot chocolate and nibbling flaky croissants, where yet more chocolate had been poured and solidified. It was our last day. Tomorrow it was the Orly Airport at noon.

"I don't want to leave; it's been a dream. We'll come back again someday, won't we?"

He was frowning again, not listening.

"I'll be going to training camp in August."

I held my breath. "You're not serious, you can't be serious. It's only been four months. You still have headaches. I know you do, even though you never tell me. Doesn't it mean anything to you that Dr. Folkes said your brain was damaged and that you should never play again? Never. He said you'd be a suicidal idiot to play again. Remember?"

My voice had taken on a raw and grating edge and was too loud. Several of the patrons glanced at us and then looked away quickly. Outbursts never bothered the French, I thought. They understood passion.

"I never told you I'd stop. Where do you think all the money came from, for the big wedding, your Toyota, your bank account, the restaurants, our hotel, and your new designer clothes? There's no other way I'd earn the big bucks, no way, a mil a year for the next three years. And it makes me feel good, hearing the crowd and doing somethin' I'm great at."

I felt my face burning and suppressed a desire to burst into tears, not from sorrow but from rage and frustration and the unfairness and futility of the argument.

"I never asked you for any of this. I didn't want a big wedding, high-end restaurants, and two-thousand-dollar gowns. The wedding was all Mutti's idea, not mine, and I asked you to stop it. I didn't want luxury at the price of your damaged brain. You thought you were buying me with a hundred-thousand-dollar bank account. You really underestimated me. I only wanted to pay for my education and to try to stop my mother from cleaning buildings and yes, I wanted a bathtub with hot water and to stop worrying about money. You're stupid, and it's got nothing to do with being dyslexic. You're stupid about feelings and what matters, really matters."

It was then that I realized how much I cared for him, how much I loved him, and not by default.

Perhaps it was the sex, or his kindness to Ma, even his taste in women's clothes, but it was there, raw and unyielding, as tears poured down my burning cheeks, unchecked, as testament to my hurt and rage—and love.

The entire bar sat transfixed, apparently ready to applaud. In five minutes, I thought, looking back on it on our way home, I had reversed their entire perception of the unemotional North American.

"Ask for your damn 'addition, s'il vous plait.' I'll be outside."

Once outside we strode together into the mist, walking down cobbled streets and smooth treed boulevards, heads down in silence. Then the mists cleared, and we passed the Parisians on their way home from work and the occasional tourist looking for a cheap café. We kept walking the wet sidewalks shining under the street lights, and when we saw the bright sign of the Hôtel du Louvre we had been walking for hours, never speaking, clutching our respective hurts against our hearts.

Carl lay on the bed, his face buried in a pillow.

I sat by him on the bed and rubbed his shoulder, damp from the evening's mist, my voice finally soft and plaintive. "We have enough for a great start when you get your money for the first year, and you'll get it regardless. It'll buy us a wonderful house, pay for my Toronto apartment and school fees, and we'll have a cushion for the future. I don't have to be an English professor. Wiley Wheaton told me when I got the scholarship that I was right up there at the top two percent in the standardized testing and that I could be anything I wanted. If it's the money that's worrying you, I'll transfer into commerce and become a hedge fund manager."

A muttered "Christ" came from the pillow. I was making things worse, shredding his self-esteem by my frankness. I was being arrogant and insensitive. He took pride in being my provider, making me happy, but now I was throwing it all away as if of no consequence.

"The playoffs are this month," he said.

"So bloody what?" I replied.

What was he thinking? I thought.

I started to pack, quietly, for both of us. There was not enough room for the new wardrobe and another suitcase was necessary. I'd get one tomorrow. I watched him closely. He was asleep. He tired so easily. Was it the remnants of the concussion combined with the stress of our altercation? I wondered. I should not have been so combative, but it was because now I loved him so much. Ma had been right—if you love, then the hurt begins. I went out to the balcony. Before me was the beauty of the Louvre and around me Paris winked. I longed to take a final lingering look at the city, but I could not leave him. The summer, a summer of intimacy and closeness, lay ahead. I would convince him not to return.

"I've packed for you," I said the next morning.

"Thanks."

There was silence all through breakfast, even while we purchased the extra suitcase and until we were settled in our first-class seats for the trip home. Finally I could stand it no longer. He was sitting looking straight ahead, his fair hair dipping over his forehead and his dark blue eyes looking into the distance. What did he see? Was it a crowded stadium? Did he hear the roar of the fans intermingled with the growling engine of our soon-to-depart plane?

I reached over and took his hand. "Let's make up. I'll stop. If I didn't love you so much, I wouldn't care."

I had never told him I loved him before: it had always been his line. He squeezed my hand hard and started to smile, and the smile remained, a faint vestige of it, even when he dozed during the flight. Unlike Carl, I couldn't sleep. Inside my head lurked the dark intruders of dementia and death. But I kept, and would keep, these thoughts to myself.

14

THE END OF SUMMER

THE NEW HOUSE WAS LARGE, stately, and only two streets north of Mutti's bungalow. And there were four bathrooms. We took back a small mortgage, which would be paid off in six months from Carl's hockey money. The house, down payment, and new furniture, shipped from the Art Shoppe in Toronto, finished off the shrinking signing bonus.

"I love the bathrooms. You do know I married you for hot water and a big tub and shower?"

He laughed. He was more relaxed since our Paris fight

and my use of the word *love* on the plane. Perhaps, I thought, some things have to be said. I avoided voicing my concerns until late August, a week before he said he was leaving for training camp. I approached the subject tentatively, having already exhausted my efforts to get Mutti to intervene. She was worse than Carl.

"I don't want us to fight," I murmured.

My timing was good. We had made love and my skin smelled of him, a diffuse smell of soap and sweat. He had taken longer than usual and I felt drained and satiated but was still throbbing with the intensity of our shared climax. I rubbed his back and my hand was wet from his thin layer of sweat. Outside the open window of this warm August night the moon appeared tangled in the branches of a giant maple, and the air breathing through the window was rich with the ripe, sweet smell of the grasses of late summer.

"It's just," I continued, "I want you to know you've got options. They're looking for a coach for the Junior hockey team and you'd be perfect. The kids would all think you were Jesus Christ incarnate and if that doesn't move you we can go to Toronto together. You can go to community college and take a course in design, advertising, real estate sales, anything you like. We'd be together every day and make awesome steamy love every night, and I'd tutor you, just like in the old days."

He was very still and I thought for a moment he was sleeping.

"Finished?" he asked briskly. "Didn't we visit all this two months ago?"

"Would you consider going with me to Boston to see Dr. Folkes, to redo the tests?"

"No way. They'll be checking me out at training camp. They have their own doctors."

"But Dr. Folkes is famous . . . and independent."

"End of story."

"It's never the end of the story."

But there was no reply.

IN LATE AUGUST, Carl drove to the Toronto airport. I sat in front with Carl, and Mutti and Carl Sr. were in the back seat. I wished they had taken their own car as now he was leaving I was jealous of the time remaining and inwardly irritated by Mutti's stream of upbeat comments meant to encourage everyone, especially me.

I looked at his profile, his hair tousled over his forehead where the pink scar still shone, the dark glasses, and the slight smile playing around his mouth. He was obviously happy—a mindless euphoria, I thought, trying not to think "suicidal idiot." I took his hand and he easily navigated with one. He could have been a pilot—anything but a hockey player.

He would phone me every night, he promised, as we hugged our goodbyes. I would come down for the first game against the Penguins in October, and we would celebrate my twentieth birthday together. On hearing this, I buried my face in his neck and shook with worry.

"Sonja, this is not way you treat my son," scolded Mutti, her mouth tightening into a rosy knot of disapproval. "He go to win games, not go to war. You make him feel bat."

Not quite true, I thought, when I composed myself. Carl smiled, and when I whispered I loved him, his smile broadened. As I had learned after our week in Paris, Carl needed to be told. Loving glances were not enough.

"Don't know what I'll do without you," he whispered.

"Nothing, I hope," I whispered back and we both laughed.

Perhaps, I thought, Dr. Folkes was wrong and all will be well. My love has made me over-anxious and neurotic. Doctors make mistakes. In the back seat Mutti for once kept quiet and Carl Sr. slept. Next week I'd be back at university and moving to the new apartment, but nothing would be the same.

"MA, I WANT you to move in. No one will be here until Christmas. Just promise me you'll smoke outside or, better, not at all."

It was the day after Carl left and I was taking Ma for a final meal at the Sinclair, a hotel I now thought of with even greater affection because of my honeymoon night.

"I'll keep paying the rent on your apartment, but it'll be a break for you living in a house like ours and you'll keep it safe."

Ma nodded but appeared concerned. "So much money, living in one place and paying rent in another."

"Not really, Ma. We may want the house back at any time. I tried to stop Carl from going. I didn't want any more head injuries, but I couldn't stop him."

The waitress bought us two glasses of the house white. Ma looked at me thoughtfully. "I watch you, Sonja, together with Carl, and when you speak of him. I believe now you love him. Remember what I say before: sometimes things change, for better or worse. You different now, Sonja, not so high up, and I not say this 'cause I get money. You are a little more soft. Usually a woman get like this when she has baby, but with you, I believe it Carl."

"He's my baby, Ma."

Ma looked into her wineglass in silence before saying anything. "It's then when you care that you get hurt. That's why at the beginning, I glad you not love him. Love open you up."

I smiled at Ma, the Ukrainian philosopher cleaning woman, who, although she had money in the bank and no longer held her night job, kept working, "for independence."

"Not much I can do about it, Ma: good sex, a new house, and a Paris wardrobe, it'll do it every time."

My flippant reply did not work and Ma didn't return my smile. "It more than that, Sonja," was all she said.

I WAS PLEASED with my second-year courses, especially the history of the novel and nineteenth-century poetry. I settled into the small apartment in the Manulife Centre and spoke to Carl every night. "Things," he said, his voice upbeat, "are going great." Once his neck was stiff after an accidental brush against a buddy, but he took some Vicodin and the next day he was fine. I had worried for nothing. He had passed his ImPACT test and the team doctor had given him clearance. He missed me "somethin' awful" and could not wait to see me for my birthday in October when I came to Boston to see them take on the Penguins.

I had been, I told myself, much too morbid. Things were going well, and for my birthday I'd have Carl.

At times out of loneliness I ate in the old cafeteria. Jo and Janet both said they were sorry to have missed the wedding. Jo was noticeably circumspect over Carl's return to the Bruins, stating only that she hoped he had fully recovered.

Magda and Zoly were moving to Montreal, as Zoly had received a scholarship from McGill. Magda had given her notice, and had already secured a job at one of the better restaurants in Old Montreal, and Zoly was staying in residence. Greenley gave me a look of pure hatred, as if I were to blame for Magda's leaving, when I went to pick up Zoly for our final hamburger and fries. He looked healthier, I thought, his face fuller, and Magda had purchased more sophisticated horn-rimmed glasses for him in place of the silver ones.

Edmond gave me a grin and a wink when I snaked my head around the kitchen door and asked me if I was considering re-applying for my old job, and a smiling Alistair was still drying dishes. Peter was gone and there was a younger replacement. It was rumoured he'd passed out in Allen Gardens and had been the victim of an untargeted killing, but no one really knew. No body had been found. The rumour probably came from the same "reliable source" that had assured Edmund of Greenley's cyanide-killing of her husband.

"Carl's playing hockey again," Zoly said with enthusiasm as we settled ourselves in a booth at The Steak and Burger. He adored Carl, who had taken the time to talk to him at the wedding, and he had impressed his friends at Jarvis Collegiate with tales of their friendship.

"I wish I looked like Carl," he told me.

"You look fine," I assured him, "and I'm sure Carl would like to be you, going to McGill on a scholarship and heading for medicine. That's what I'd be doing if I wasn't such a moron at math."

"Carl wouldn't want to be anyone else," he said with assurance. "Skating with the Bruins and having everyone cheer for you when you get a goal, what could be cooler than that?"

I looked at his large green eyes behind his new horn-rimmed glasses, and his sincere little face, and thought of how I'd miss him.

"I'll miss you, Zoly, you know that. Good friends are hard to come by."

"Do you miss Carl?"

"Yes, I miss him a lot."

"You love him?"

"Yes, I love him a lot too."

Zoly sighed, but then we smiled at each other.

"We should," he said very seriously and softly, "try to be near people we love."

THE WORLD HAD changed overnight with 9/11. I watched pictures of the crumbling towers and was horrified at the thought of those jumping to their deaths to avoid burning. For a short time it made me stop worrying about Carl, whose absence made me ache.

Then at the end of September I received a call from Ma.

"I go to doctor. Frau Helbig come visit and she want me to go see doctor. She say I look sick, and when I tell her I am tired and coughing blood, she take me that day to her doctor. He take picture and say I have mess in my chest."

I felt my heart beating; it echoed in my ears and I could not breathe.

"Ma, you mean a mass in your lung, right?"

"Yes, doctor say it is in grade four."

Ma was in the house smoking when I arrived that weekend.

"I can't believe you're still smoking."

Ma sighed. "Sonja, if I knew things would turn so good, I tell you I would have stopped. Now it too late, so let me smoke."

"MA'S GOT STAGE four cancer in both lungs and it's metastasized to her liver, so it's three to six months tops. There's nothing they can do except make her comfortable near the end," I sobbed to Carl by phone that night.

"Jesus, that's awful, really awful. What is she, forty-eight? All those fuckin' cigarettes. What's wrong with some people? They never listen."

Carl Helbig, aged twenty-two, back playing with the Bruins.

I was, I was convinced, surrounded by lunatics.

Ma's illness filled me with aching grief. During the past year we had finally grown close and now Ma was dying, her lungs full of trees that had stretched their roots into her liver. I cried when I left to return to university that Sunday and then all the way back to Toronto.

"Don't cry, Sonja," said Ma, "this best year in my life because of you. I just wish I live long enough to see grandbabies."

I WAS TO go to see Carl play in Boston on October 15, my birthday. Both Mutti and Ma insisted. "You must go," they chorused together from Mutti's kitchen. An odd couple, I thought. Ma, appreciative of Mutti's, whom she now called Gertie's, medical concern, and Mutti sympathetic to this dying shrunken little Ukrainian, the unlikely mother of Carl's tall, clever wife.

I checked into my Boston hotel October 14 and immediately phoned Carl. "I'll be there by seven," he said, his voice eager and intense.

"Do you think . . . ?" I began.

"Didn't hurt Joe Namath," he replied. "Is this what they teach you at U of T?"

After my bath I didn't even bother to dress, and when I responded to the assertive three knocks and saw him standing there, his smile and eyes shining at me, I threw myself into him with such force that he staggered.

"Careful. Joe Namath's babes didn't do that." But his smile remained.

I helped him undress, my hands trembling. It had

been two months and I longed for him, for his body, his smell, his hardness, opening me up and plunging me into crying oblivion. When we had finished, I sat on the bed beside him, running my fingers through the now-clipped brush of hair and touching the still-obvious pink scar with tentative fingers.

"You'll be careful?"

"That's such a stupid thing for a girl like you to say. I can't be careful, then I'd be no good to them. They don't pay me the big bucks to be careful. You know I been playin' the game for fifteen years and I always played through the pain, and there were a lotta hits, dozens, and I never gave in, not till the one last February when I couldn't stand. I was 'a warrior,' remember, that's what my first coach called me."

He had only spoken to me of the game once before, that afternoon by the lake, when he'd spoken of playing through the pain, which I supposed were minor or sub-concussions, and I felt a shadow pass over my heart.

"Perhaps," I said, my voice high but soft, feigning a lightness I did not feel, "now that we're together you could be less of a warrior and just leave some of that to the bedroom, and promise me if you feel pain, you'll stop."

"Shouldn't have even mentioned it," he replied and rubbed my arm, then carefully lifted one of my breasts. "Did anyone ever tell you you've got great breasts?"

"Yes, you that first night, when you weighed them in both hands, comparing them to all the implants you'd run into."

"I know, I remember. I remember everything about that night. I even remember Paris and our fight in the chocolate bar."

He left after kissing me and giving me the special ticket for the section where the players' families sat. We would have a late dinner the next night to celebrate my birthday. I got dressed and left the hotel in search of a coffee shop. I didn't want to eat dinner alone in a strange city.

Outside it was dark and the grounds of the Boston Common were rich with clusters of thick trees, their leaves starting to rust at the edges. In the sky the moon, its grey scar tainting its silver brightness, seemed far away, as was the scattering of faint gem-like stars, but I directed my prayer toward them.

"God, I want you to take care of Carl. Please, God."

It was not the general diffuse instruction sent out casually in the now abandoned Greek Orthodox Church I had visited with Ma in Davenport, and that had been followed by my plagiarist detection, threatened expulsion, and loss of scholarship. This prayer was specific, precise, and focused. It gave God little choice. He was to render protection to Carl, the warrior who had played through pain too often.

It was after nine and there was only one couple in the coffee house.

"A toasted tomato and bacon on whole wheat, cut the mayo, and a glass of cranberry juice."

The waitress was a thin, nervous girl, with the name tag "Lucille" pinned to her uniform. So not a Lucille,

I thought. Her mother must have watched *I Love Lucy* reruns in the eighties. A Margaret or Victoria would be more appropriate. She was probably a student at Boston University who needed the money.

Lucille carefully placed the sandwich on the wooden table with its plastic tablemat and then the cranberry juice, but she moved too abruptly and the glass of juice tipped over, spilled over the table, and dripped cold over my lap and jeans.

"Sorry," said a flustered Lucille, mopping up the maroon liquid. "They just hired me. I'd appreciate it if you didn't mention it."

"It's all right," I said, thinking of my days at Matheson's, watching the red liquid drip from the table and the growing stain on my jeans.

On the way back to my room I picked up the *Boston Herald* and checked the sports section. In a small column on the second page was the headline "Helbig Returns to Bruins."

It merely mentioned the February concussion, the fact that Carl had been a top scorer, and that on that night he was the First Star Selection and was in line to be Rookie of the Year except for the forced absence due to the concussion.

I soaked my jeans in the basin of the hotel's bathroom, but the stain remained. I thought of the stained sheet at the Sinclair only four months ago and my heart ached from missing Carl.

Tomorrow night we would be together.

15
THE END OF PLAY

AT THE TD GARDEN, MOST of the players' family members sit together. They appear animated, supportive, and they all know one another. I introduce myself to the wives on each side of my seat and they welcome me with wide smiles. "You must join us more often," they chorus. Many of them never miss a game and they saw Carl's concussion in February. Some of the wives are Americans, while others are fellow Canadians who married high school sweethearts.

Carol, who sits to my right, is about thirty with short

hair and an overbite. She went to high school in Manitoba with Chris, one of the Bruins enforcers. They have three children.

"You can tell me what's going on," I say. "I'm not really up on it like a good hockey wife should be. I came into it late."

Carol smiles her agreement.

There is the lining-up of the teams and the playing of the national anthem.

A catchy song accompanies the players as they troop in.

"It's 'Parée,' a twenties' show tune. They play it when they enter and at the start of each period," explains Carol.

I watch them, listening to the loud cheers from the packed stadium as each player is introduced. Carl, number 10, receives a "welcome back" roar. He moves with the casual grace of the figure I remember from the Davenport arena, a grace that could be interspersed with dynamic bursts of frenzied speed. Carol's husband, a Bruins enforcer, who appears huge, is number 36.

"He has to drop his gloves tonight."

"What?" I ask, bewildered.

"They fight on the ice. The fans love it. Chris's nose has been broken three times and he's had two concussions. After ten years he's made only four goals, but he's spent hours in the penalty box and had dozens of suspensions."

Seeing my look of horror, she continues, "He's always such a quiet sweet guy, and gentle as a lamb with our kids."

I'm confused: skill and planned hostility with Broadway music and complex staging.

My eyes never leave number 10, then all of a sudden he scores, a treacherous and unexpected play on the net, with the goalie sprawled in vain to prevent it. The crowd erupts and his team surrounds him. The air is electric. He must be so happy, I think, so happy.

Then the music starts again, a strange chant. I give Carol a puzzled look.

"'Dirty Water,'" she explains. "They play it after every goal on home ice. It's the Zombie Nation."

Appropriate name, I think, but I say nothing. Carol is too good an interpreter to alienate.

At the beginning of the second period, Chris has his fight. His opponent is Veronikov, the Penguins' giant Russian. They swing at each other for several minutes and then Chris goes down. The crowd boos as he is helped back to the bench. I look at Carol and she is scowling.

"They're not booing Chris, they're booing Veronikov. It's a home crowd."

I watch them as they rush around with their sticks at 30 miles an hour, colliding, slashing, the ice gladiators, out for the kill. It's show business, I think.

The score is 4 to 6 in the Bruins' favour when, early in the third period, Carl scores his second goal of the night.

"He'll be the night's First Star Player," predicts Carol, "wait and see."

I watch Carl as he skates around to the resounding cheers, his stick held high with both hands over his head, while his team nudges their approval. And then I hear the chant of the Zombie Nation.

The tension is building. I cannot stand it. Why is he on the ice so long? He has done enough. He has done more than enough. Then, almost at the end of the third period, it happens. An elbow from the bastard Veronikov from behind. Carl is down, down on the ice. He lies still. His helmet is off. I see the maroon stain under his head. It spreads slowly. I hear someone say, "Career ender" from the row behind. It is announced that Veronikov has been exiled to the Siberia of the penalty box. I cannot breathe. My eyes are fixed on the motionless figure.

Carl is carried off on a stretcher. The crowd is hushed. Then they stand and applaud. The final act for number 10 is over. He can't hear you, I tell them silently.

I stand up to leave.

"Probably the Mass General's Trauma Center. Sorry, Sonja," says Carol.

My taxi follows the ambulance.

"Boyfriend?" asks the driver.

"Husband," I reply.

"Rough game. That's why they get the big bucks."

16
DÉJÀ VU

I HAVE BEEN HERE BEFORE. THE smell of antiseptic and menthol, the shining neon-lit corridors, manned from the little stations by the nurses with their modulated and controlled voices. Then the sparse room with its one chair, but this time the lights are on. Carl is not conscious; the lights cannot hurt him yet. He is unknowing, but he knits his brows. Is he racing toward an invisible net and does he hear the crowd?

They slide him into the bed so gently, so gently now, no more crushing, pushing, hitting; now is the time for gentleness. Be tender, the brain floats in its amber liquid, naked and battered.

There are two doctors, thin and bespectacled, in white coats. "You are the wife of the patient?" asks one.

I nod my head: I am cocooned in fear, my mouth is dry, and it is hard to speak.

Last night I was his wife in every way, his naked wife, opening up to him, savouring his intensity and smell, now gone, wasted on the shouting crowd.

I must stop these thoughts.

"Have there been previous concussions?"

"I think there have been several." I do not say he is a warrior and plays through pain. It sounds, and is, ridiculous—but true.

I force myself to continue. "Perhaps a series of sub-concussions, but the last concussion in February was severe, a complex grade three. They suspected a second brain bleed from two days prior to that, and then a post-concussion syndrome, followed with symptoms lasting for months. But he was cleared to play. He said he passed the ImPACT test. Dr. Folkes—I'm sure you've heard of him—they flew him to Toronto to examine Carl, and he viewed the MRS, which showed brain damage, as did the MRI."

"Of course we know Dr. Folkes. We didn't know your husband was his patient. You're a pre-med student or nurse?"

"No, I'm a university student."

I would like to add—but I'm reasonably intelligent— although I may lack judgment in many ways. A serious lack, I think. I should have been more emphatic, stronger, so stupid to back down because of his anger.

"Well then it's best you wait and talk to Dr. Folkes. Your husband has a nasty laceration here that needs some stitches, so we'll do that without further disturbing him. He may have had another brain bleed. We won't know until we re-do last February's tests."

"Dr. Folkes seriously recommended that he withdraw from hockey, but my husband couldn't be persuaded. I really tried."

I feel guilty. Although I know it's not my fault, I still feel guilty.

"It's difficult to persuade a young professional athlete to withdraw from all the adulation and excitement—and money—that goes with the game. And it's that abominable team spirit, we've seen it here before. Why not go and get yourself some coffee downstairs while we sew him up and check his vitals."

I am being dismissed, politely but firmly.

Downstairs at the cafeteria, I order a Coke and a bagel. My birthday dinner: twenty candles on a bagel. I take a nibble, but it sticks in my throat. I drink the Coke, which releases its pleasant bite. My head aches and I take an Extra Strength Tylenol, washing it down with the Coke. I must phone Mutti. She, Ma and Carl Sr. were all watching the game. I need to share my panic and pain and perhaps that will dilute it. She would not help me to dissuade him; now her precious son lies unconscious—stupid, stubborn, silly woman, never listening.

I hear her voice, high-pitched and tremulous. "How iss he?"

"He's still unconscious," I tell her. "There may be another brain bleed. It's as the doctor warned us."

He may have listened to her but perhaps not. But she could have tried. Instead, she blocked out everything but what she wanted to hear.

"I have to go. I'll phone when I know more." I want to cry, but I will not cry in a hospital cafeteria.

"WE ARE MONITORING him, Mrs. Helbig. We can phone you when he regains consciousness."

They do not say "if," they say "when." Surely that is a good sign. They expect him to wake up. They have attached tubes and apparatus to his arm, to prevent dehydration and blood clots, I suspect. The contusion is closed by black spider legs. Now he will have matching temple scars, but the left will be just a thin white line, while the right will remain a pink smudge that shines. I do not question these nurses. I know they want to be rid of me, but I am staying. The two doctors have gone. Carl Helbig is the designated patient of Dr. Dennis Folkes.

"When will Dr. Folkes be here?"

"We've put a call in, but he may wish to do an MRI and MRS before speaking to you. We'll contact you with any developments."

"I'm staying," I inform them. "I'll try not to be a bother, but I won't sleep if I go back to the hotel."

They shrug. I know they want me gone, but I won't go.

I sit in the one chair, watchful. When they leave, I go over and rub my finger on his forehead, gingerly ironing the frown between his brows.

"You mustn't frown," I whisper, "I'm here, and someday we'll be together." Then I trace his mouth with my finger and think of last night.

I see his eyes flicker, so slightly, almost not at all, and then I touch his hand, the hand not attached to the arm with the tubing. It feels warm and rough and I look at the square nails, cut short, and the index finger, the sizing finger, and think of where it's been.

"Sweetheart, it's me, Sonja."

His eyes flicker again. This time he half opens them but shuts them fast.

"The light . . . hurts."

I turn on the adjustable light near the bed and direct it away from him and then turn off the room light.

"Where am I?"

"In the Trauma Center of the Massachusetts General. You got hit, that bastard Veronikov. Remember?"

"Nope," he whispers.

"You got two goals, and when they carried you from the ice everyone applauded."

"Good of 'em."

He remembers nothing. Does he know me? I am afraid to ask.

"They're getting Dr. Folkes, he's based here."

"Who?"

"The last doctor you had. The specialist from Boston who

flew in to examine you at Toronto General. Remember?"

At that point one of the nurses enters, the one with "Donnelly" on her name tag, one of the nurses who'd been urging me to leave some thirty minutes earlier. A grey-haired woman with a pronounced, jutting jaw.

"He's conscious. Good. I thought you would have advised us, Mrs. Helbig. Carl, we've been trying to persuade your wife to leave, but she doesn't trust you with us. Now, tell me how you feel. How's your head? And I guess your eyes are bothering you, that's why your wife turned off the lights."

"My head's poundin,' poundin' like crazy."

"Then we'll give you some painkiller and a nice drink. Would you like to urinate, Carl? I'll just pull this curtain around you."

"No need for that," I say. "I'm familiar with his anatomy. Dr. Folkes—"

"He may or may not be in. Doctors have lives too, you know, although our staff is very dedicated, more so than most. It's after eleven, so he may wait until tomorrow. He'll order an immediate MRI, that much I know, and a MRS. Carl's probably best resting right now anyway. Dr. Stockey has ordered him Coumadin, it's—"

"I know what it is and does," I say. "It prevents blood clots."

"I guess you've picked up quite a lot of medical information married to a hockey player. It's the same with the football wives. They talk like osteopaths. You can stay here, but he'll be sleeping. He won't know you're here. Dr. Folkes comes in early. There's an Express Holiday Inn near here that may be more convenient. If you sleep, you may be more alert to what Dr. Folkes says. You'll be the smart one now."

I was always the smart one about hockey, but no one listened. Pointless to be smart in such a case. Walking around with unlistened-to smarts. It was a waste of time.

"I'll go," I say. "I know he's in good hands."

This is a lie to ingratiate myself, but it's no good to alienate all the nursing staff, especially Donnelly.

Donnelly walks over to where I'm standing. I wonder when her shift started: her breath smells tired and her eyes are a blurred and foamy pale green.

"How old are you?" she asks.

"Twenty," I reply. "I was twenty today. We were married in June."

"Not a good birthday for you. Nice you are married, though. Many young people today don't bother. My daughter won't get married and she's got two little kids. She says she'll marry him when he changes, but that won't happen.

"I'll be gone when you come back, but he'll be here for a while so we'll see each other again. Good luck on Dr. Folke's diagnosis. He's the best there is."

No good if you ignore what he says.

I give Carl a light kiss on the forehead. He does not speak again.

As I leave the room, Donnelly squeezes my arm and says, "Take care, my dear. Have some sleep for your birthday. I'll see you tomorrow night."

She likes me now and I like her. It can't be easy going through life with a jaw like that, yet she's had kids and is a nurse, an assertive one. It's like going through life and "not doing normal" and being smarter than everyone else, which I doubt more every day. My judgment is defective, obviously so. I engage in plagiarism, too arrogant to see the implications; then I marry Carl so he can support my education. But now I will be missing all my first term and will be going through life with a chest full of cut glass because of my concern for him. I did not expect I'd love him like this.

The room at the Holiday Inn is clean and quiet. It is after midnight.

Mutti is waiting by the phone. Ma is asleep on the sofa. The chemotherapy, which is supposed to give her additional time, drains her.

"He woke up, but he's in pain. The doctor's coming tomorrow and there will be tests, tests like before. I'll phone again. No, you must not come. Carl's in his own world, he doesn't need you here."

Mutti sounds relieved.

I am so tired I ache from it, yet my mind is full of questions. I should write out a list of them for Dr. Folkes. He will be disgusted that Carl went back and with me for not prevailing against his going. I did try, but perhaps not hard enough. It wouldn't have made any difference. In my heart I know this, so why am I torturing myself?

I turn the television on to Jon Stewart. He is making fun of some Republicans, but I cannot focus. I leave a message at the desk for a seven o'clock wake-up call. Then I lie here, alone in the Holiday Inn, wishing Carl were beside me. I don't cry. If I cry, I won't stop. I merely lie here, my eyes burning, feeling grasshoppers jumping in my head and with Jon Stewart turned down low for company. I must have finally slept. At seven, the wake-up call rings. I still lie here, wishing it were all a nightmare, now ended.

"WELL, SONJA," SAYS a smiling Dr. Folkes, "we meet again. As intelligent as you are, I did not wish for another meeting."

It is eight o'clock and I am sitting in Carl's room. Dr. Folkes has already been here and gone, but now is back again. The tests have been given and he has read them. I do not wish to hear the results. The room is dim and I go over to Carl.

"How are you, luv?" I ask.

"My head is killin' me."

"I'll ask the doctor for stronger pain pills."

Dr. Folkes beckons me outside and I follow him down the corridor and into a small office.

"Carl did not keep in touch with me so you must fill me in. What's happened since his discharge last February?"

"He seemed fine. We got married in June and spent a week in Paris. He may have suffered from headaches, but he didn't mention it, although he seemed to tire easily. One thing I noticed was he became quite anxious once when I left the hotel without him, really insecure, but he got over it. I attempted to persuade him not to go back to the Bruins, but he became very angry with me, almost hostile. It was impossible to get him to change his mind and he left for training camp in August. He seemed fine and told me he passed his ImPACT test with the team doctor.

"Last night he played in his first game here against the Penguins. After two goals he got an elbow to the head and went down. He was unconscious . . . it must have been at least an hour. He has no memory of what happened and has no memory of you. I think he knows me, but I'm not sure."

Dr. Folkes sighs. The serious stupidity of his patients, and of their so-called caregivers, appears to pain him.

"All concussions are different. As I recall last time, there were indications of damage, and I suspected Carl suffered a second concussion during his critical recovery period from the first. He had the usual physical symptoms and as I remember became angry when confronted with his condition. He was fortunate to have survived so well, and to have been fit enough to enjoy a honeymoon in Paris.

"You were both warned as to the hazards of his returning to play. Toronto General has, through the wonders of technology, sent me the results of his former MRS and MRI. I have compared them with today's tests. Now the damage is more widespread and there is frontal lobe involvement, which could result in memory loss and even dementia. No more warnings are necessary. Carl will not be able to play again even if given clearance by team doctors, which won't happen. I fear this time his previous and present symptoms may linger and prevent normal life functioning. You are . . . ?"

"Twenty," I answer.

"And a university student. If I were your father, I would advise you to set up a trust for Carl with any monies he's earned so far, and any future monies as a result of contractual obligations by his team, and hand him over to professional caregivers. And then get on with your life."

"You can't be certain. You said that every concussion is different."

I am choking and I feel a mixture of alarm and anger. Dr. Folkes's heft, which previously gave solace, now oppresses me. I feel foolish. He is a renowned specialist and he is being frank, thinking I am mature and intelligent enough to weigh my future options with detachment. I cannot do it because I am not the same person he spoke to last February.

"I can't write Carl off. We come from a small town in Ontario where his parents are well connected. He might get a job assembling machinery in the town's main plant, or even coach house league or high school hockey. We have a house and funds, and we'll be receiving money for a year according to his contract in spite of his disability. I cannot consign him to the garbage pile."

My voice is harsh and grating.

"You're shooting the messenger, Sonja."

"I deserve better than to receive glib clichés from you," I tell him.

Dr. Folkes is flushed. He is upset with me and with Carl. Carl has ignored his advice, both direct and filtered through me. Now I appear to be blaming him when Carl, with his own bravado, has caused what Dr. Folkes appears to believe is his own daunting future.

"We'll keep him as long as we can Sonja, then he's all yours."

THE NEXT DAY I telephone the university and cancel my courses for the first term. The registrar is sympathetic and agrees to defer my subjects until January, although some of my courses may not be available at that time. My scholarship was already gone, but that is not the problem. Money is not the problem. The problem is Carl.

His head pulsates—"pounds," he moans—and they have increased the OxyContin, but within an hour of taking it the pounding starts again. But now he knows me, at least that is something. I've cancelled The Four Seasons, and I'm now at the Holiday Inn Express, so I can come early in the morning and remain for the day. He likes me there. The nurses say he becomes restless without me. He still cannot walk to the toilet. He becomes dizzy when standing, but he hates the bedpan so now they are giving him laxatives. The OxyContin constipates him and I have suggested morphine, but they fear he will be addicted to the OxyContin and morphine may be worse. I no longer stay in the room. It is such an invasion of privacy to have anyone, even a wife, witness these forced bowel movements and enemas. And the old Carl would find it humiliating, although the new Carl appears indifferent.

"We've got to get him up," Donnelly says at the start of the second week.

Now we are friends. I bring her doughnuts and coffee from Starbucks and she calls me "Sony." Now that she has stamped me with her approval, the others have followed suit and they are sympathetic, patting me on the shoulder, and even bringing me an extra lunch and dinner tray.

It's Monday morning, and I have fed him his breakfast. We get him up, but he sways and getting him to the toilet is difficult. He finally shuffles in, supported on each side by Donnelly and me. And then he vomits in the sink. All the scrambled eggs and toast I so carefully fed him for breakfast down the drain.

"Feel nauseated, Carl?" asks Donnelly.

It's so self-evident that he merely says, "Fuck."

During the third week we walk the corridor together. His head still aches periodically and he becomes dizzy, but he is for the most part semi-functional—that is, he walks to the bathroom, feeds himself, and we talk . . . but not as we once did.

"I cancelled my courses until January."

"What for?"

"Because I want to be with you until you feel better."

"You shouldna done that. I never wanted you to do that."

"Don't you want me with you?"

He merely scowls. I know he does. It's a silly question.

"What did he say—about me playin' again?"

"Out of the question. There are other things, coaching, all sorts of things."

"You don't unnerstan'—not at all. I wanted to give you stuff. That was the idea. What else did I have to offer you? Now there's nothin.' You wanna be married to some guy who coaches kids an' can't read a book . . . who ain't smart . . . someone like you?" His voice is slurred, flat.

"This is silly talk, really silly, and you're getting yourself all upset. We're going home soon and everyone will want to see you: Jerry, Candace, Mutti, your dad, all your buddies, and I have to see my poor mother."

He just keeps shaking his head and telling me I don't understand.

But I do.

17

HOMECOMING

PLACES BECOME IMPORTANT BECAUSE OF the memories attached to them. For this reason I am glad to leave Boston. Although parts of it are beautiful, Boston will always be where Carl received his final concussion. And I shall always think of Paris as glorious, not only because it is but also because we walked its streets, boulevards, and riverbanks and fought and made love there.

Donnelly has given me a St. Christopher medal and we have exchanged email addresses. At times I envy the Catholics. They always believe God knows what he's doing and they have this little army of saints supporting them. I don't seem to have the inner track with God at all.

POST-9/11 AIR TRAVEL is so irritating, especially for those with disabilities. Carl is now considered disabled, a word I hate, but I still hope his problems are temporary. I try not to think of Dr. Folkes and his prognosis and advice.

"Do I look like a fuckin' terrorist?" Carl snarls at the security guard.

He has bent over to remove his shoes and I know he is dizzy. I smile brightly, too brightly, at everyone around. I am carrying Carl's medication from the hospital dispensary, his OxyContin, Vicodin, and sleeping pills. We are asked to step aside, our age and drug arsenal no doubt causing suspicion.

"Where'd you get these drugs?"

It's a ridiculous question when the name of the dispensary and Dr. Folkes are clearly written on the label. The temptation to answer "from a pusher on the Boston Common" is strong.

"My husband plays for the Boston Bruins and he had a concussion three weeks ago. These are for headaches and insomnia."

The security agent is a hockey fan and he saw the game. He hates the Penguins and most especially Veronikov. He is all over Carl.

"Veronikov blindsided you with his elbow. He should be suspended for twenty games, even the rest of the season. It's a real honour to have you here. If it didn't look strange,

I'd get your autograph for my son. He'll be real excited when I tell him I saw you today."

I feel like I could kiss the man. Carl brightens up and actually smiles for a few minutes before we board our flight for Toronto. We sit in executive class. I hold his large, warm hand and kiss its pale back with its little mauve knots— small butterfly kisses to coax a smile.

"See how lovely this is," I say, "I wouldn't be in first class or even flying but for you. We've even got three choices on the menu, and we're going back to our lovely new home." A home, I think to myself, that concussions built.

Carl must be convinced he has done things for me, it's essential to his self-esteem. He squeezes my hand hard and says, "You're the greatest, Sony." He's now taken to calling me "Sony" just like Donnelly did. But I'm much more than a computer to Carl.

No one meets us at the airport, as I told Mutti she should not even think of it. We wheel our bags over to the cold parking garage, one of them containing Carl's hockey gear—not that he'll ever play again, but he believes he'll go back. Even the plane makes his head throb and I give in and give him an OxyContin, which I know I shouldn't. It won't mix with the several glasses of red wine he insisted on having with dinner.

It's the third week of November and freezing. When we leave the airport and walk to the parking garage we can see our breath, and the air slaps our faces. It's after six and already dark. Small hard spikes of stars pierce the sooty sky, and even the shrunken moon, surrounded by a lavender haze, seems cold. I was only to have been away for three days and I'm now convinced the frozen engine of the car won't start.

"I'll drive."

"You've been drinking and taking OxyContin. If we're stopped, you'll be charged."

He can't drive for reasons much more serious than mixing alcohol and a painkiller, but why bring up things that will cause upset? Forced diplomacy was never my thing, but I am learning.

The car starts. We wind our way from the icy parking garage and turn east onto the 401 heading toward the 400. The heater kicks in and we drive through the night. I glance sideways and he is sleeping, mouth open, head hanging forward, a teardrop of saliva clinging to his lower lip. I want to adjust his seat as he looks so uncomfortable, and to turn on the news channel, even easy jazz, but it would disturb him. His face lacks any buoyancy. He looks almost . . . old.

Intrusive dark thoughts push into my mind: dyslexia was one thing, dementia another. Surely things will improve.

The Davenport turnoff appears before I expect it. I take it and drive past the trees knit with frost, others with black spruce boughs heavy with snow. Davenport's Main Street appears deserted, although it is only five weeks until Christmas; perhaps any shoppers are at the New Davenport Mall. We pass Mutti's bungalow and there are no lights on.

"We're almost home," I say, my voice full of false but firm cheer.

We turn onto our street and I see that every light in our house is on. As we get out of the car the door of the house opens, and people come tumbling out, accompanied by the background music of Pink's "Get the Party Started." I hear a muttered "Christ" from Carl before Jerry Henley embraces him. They are all there, all of The Choir members who are still in Davenport, many working at Dare's Machinery. And there is Candace Stewart, home from her social worker's course, strange in November, and a beaming Mutti and Carl Sr. Only Ma is absent, asleep at Mutti's perhaps.

Did Mutti not take in any of the information I had been giving her for weeks? Carl cannot tolerate noise and bright lights. Although The Choir means well, I am placed in the position of having to be the dampener of this spontaneous party, all to "Hanging by a Moment."

"Jerry, get the guys to bring in the bags."

Carl can't do it and I don't want to, but something practical has to be done before I force them out. Someone has made a pot of chili and there is a platter of Uncle Ben's Instant Rice heaped beside a salad bowl. Mutti obviously didn't cater this party; she only provided the access and information.

Carl is surrounded and he is scowling. I see the thin white line of his scar, then the bright pink patch on the other side. I think irrationally that his hair is growing out again. It is all irrelevant.

"Sony," he calls. He is drowning in a sea of human voices.

"You shouldn't have allowed this," I spit at Mutti. "Do you ever listen to anything I tell you?"

She looks shocked, but I feel no remorse.

"Sony," he calls again and pulls me into the downstairs bathroom. I know before he speaks his head is pounding, and that the music, the group's voices, and the room's lights are making it worse.

"Get rid of them."

"They love you . . . they mean so well."

"Get rid of them." His voice has a hoarse, jagged quality.

We come out and the room is hushed, the music silent. They may have heard us.

"We really appreciate you being here," I lie. "Carl's just out of hospital and really isn't up to any activity. He's exhausted from the trip home and he has to lie down. Please help yourselves to the food and I'll join you as soon as I settle him down."

We walk slowly upstairs and I help him undress after giving him another OxyContin. He settles himself in like a child, and I kiss his cheek and pat his shoulder.

Downstairs, the group is quiet.

"Sorry about all this," I explain when I join them. "The last concussion was very severe: he can't take noise and lights and the plane trip was difficult. You all mean so well and he loves you all. I'm sorry, perhaps in time things will improve."

They prepare to leave in silence.

Before leaving, some of them fill their plates and others pour themselves fingers of rye from the available bottles.

Mutti looks at me, her face frozen with concern. I have

hurt her feelings, but now, finally, she worries for Carl's future.

Jerry comes over. "Bad, huh?"

I nod. I am no longer detached. They are my friends now and I appreciate their concern.

I do normal.

18

THE WORST OF TIMES

I'M NOT FEELING WELL. PERHAPS it is stress, stress
related to Carl's problems and Ma's cancer. I'm tired and
in the mornings feel nauseated. Each morning I prepare
Carl's breakfast, his fresh-squeezed orange juice, whole
wheat toast, boiled eggs, and bacon, fried crisp. He eats
mindlessly, looking out the kitchen window at the heavy
snow-laden spruce branches and bare black maples, but
he does not see them. His eyes are fixed on space, as if the
air somehow has meaning.

Ma paddles in, a little wraith, so fragile a breath would

blow her away. It saddens me. The chemo and the cancer are devouring her.

"Eat," I command. "It will make you feel better. See, I've poured some maple syrup on your toast."

She nods, eager and emaciated and anxious to please. She still smokes out on the icy patio. I ignore it, too late for all that.

Every morning I walk with Carl to Mutti's and back again. It is only half a mile, but it exhausts him, and after he wants to lie down in our darkened bedroom. On the occasional sunny day, waves of snow lick the sides of our house, casting a blanket of glitter. On one occasion we drive to the lake. It is so silent there, everything hushed and frozen, with grey ice stretching out toward the far-off hills.

"Do you remember what happened here?" I whisper.

He shakes his head, his eyes fixed on the iced lake.

A WEEK BEFORE Christmas, Candace Stewart telephones and invites me to lunch. We end up at the Sinclair Hotel, the only choice for lunch in Davenport.

"How are you managing?" Her voice has a social worker ring, a mixture of sympathy and condescension, which I suppose will be further cultivated upon graduating with a BSW. I picture her with a series of abusive mothers and doddering seniors, asking the same question over and over, and barely listening to the reply. Still, it would be a relief to vent to someone, even if it were Candace.

"It's up and down. Carl was warned by a top neurologist not to return to hockey, and I begged him not to go back. Mutti was no help. We could have managed. Now, on most days, he's living on painkillers and in another world."

I hate my own voice, hate my disloyalty, hate my feelings of self pity. But it is cathartic.

"Ridiculous," spits Candace. "You didn't sign up for this. We all thought your marriage to Carl was the mismatch of the century, and that frankly there was a dollar motivation, but now we all feel sorry for you, we really do. You're showing him such devotion, and no one would blame you, or be surprised, if you just split and let Mutti take over. It would look good on her, it really would. I'm glad I escaped all this. When I look at the old crowd now and see their limitations, it makes me cringe. See my new guy? He's in third-year engineering. Engineers are in great demand; he's already getting job offers."

I look politely at the smiling face in the photo Candace shares.

"Nice," I say.

"You gaining weight?"

"Hope not."

"Stress eating," concludes Candace. "It'll do it every time. Just remember, if you want to vent by phone or email, I'm there for you. I do have social worker training."

I stand up. If I don't leave I'll strangle her for dessert.

"You're very kind."

I scoop up the bill.

CHRISTMAS COMES AND goes. Invitations to Christmas parties are politely refused and we don't decorate. I let Mutti do the Christmas dinner preparation. I buy us both laptops so we can always be in touch and assure Carl his spelling is not important. He grasps email, which is encouraging. Ma and Carl depress me, and I'm always at the point of tears, which I must hide from them. I had hoped Ma would help with Carl when I returned to university, but she is helpless and hopeless, and Carl hates her cooking, which has not improved. I'll take her with me when I leave.

IT'S THE SATURDAY after Christmas. It's only eleven, but Carl has gone back to bed. We fight about his drug intake, and I suspect he's found the phials I had hidden behind my books and added some of the capsules and pills to his hidden stash. He shows marked ingenuity when it comes to discovering and hiding drugs that I wish he would show in other parts of his life. Ma has gone with Mutti to her doctor, who has given her a special appointment at Mutti's insistence.

"A waste of time," she whispers to me, and turns down my offer to go with them.

I feel depressed, a heaviness and darkness that won't leave. I had made no friends at U of T, save for Janet Murdock, who, although very kind, was more a fellow diner and class colleague than friend and confidante. I had tried striking up conversations in the women's bathrooms and once, but only once, had approached a group of girls outside class. They greeted me with fixed smiles but did not involve me in the conversation so I casually walked away. I did not try again.

Gwen Andrews and Sophie Gallo were different. They had been at Mutti's Christmas party, which I always thought of as my boob unveiling, and at the welcoming party that had ended so badly upon Carl's return from Boston. They were Choir members, and they'd always been pleasant. They were fellow students I'd ignored at Davenport High but whom I'd nod to if I met them at the New Davenport Mall. Both of them had sent invitations to us to attend their respective Christmas parties, invitations that had been politely declined. I will, I decide, invite them both to lunch at the Sinclair. They can always say no. Anything would be an improvement after the recent Candace Stewart lunch disaster.

Mrs. Gallo answers the phone, yells "Sophia" in a thick Italian accent, and orders me to "waita a minute."

"Sophie speaking." She sounds almost prim after her mother.

"Hi, it's Sonja Helbig. I wonder if I could take you and Gwen to the Sinclair for lunch today? I apologize for the short notice."

A prolonged silence takes place, then a shocked but eager voice says, "That'd be really great, really awesome, really nice, Sonja. I'll phone Gwen to save you the trouble—if you like—and we'll meet you there."

I smile to myself. No hesitation here. So unlike me, reaching out.

They are both smiling and waiting for me at the table when I arrive. Sophie is short, dark, and animated, her black hair pulled back in a curly ponytail, with some brief tendrils hanging around her forehead and heart-shaped face. She sports a holiday-red pantsuit, lipstick to match, and staggeringly high-heeled black patent boots that give her a strange, mincing, tiptoe-like walk.

Gwen is my height but thinner and reminds me a little of Janet Murdock with her straight ash-blond hair, and taut, pale, almost makeup-free face. She is dressed more sedately, almost drably, in a tweed jacket, a round-necked beige sweater, and grey stretch pants. She'd been in the commercial stream at Davenport High but had attended my English classes, where she was noted for her silence. She's a clerk in the office of Dare's Machinery, while Sophie works the assembly line. I detect a slight air of superiority from Gwen toward Sophie, perhaps because of this, but they are friends nevertheless, or bantering companions, or really both.

"Things hard on you?" asks Sophie sympathetically after we all order a first round of vodka coolers. "We talk about you and Carl all the time, don't we, Gwen? We feel so bad, but we don't want to phone and bother you. You always kept to yourself, and we respect your privacy, you being so smart and all."

The words are ironic: the "smart" Sonja Danychuk, disgraced plagiarist, scholarship loser, worst waitress in Canada, and now with a drug-addicted husband whose brain she couldn't salvage, so clever she was not to be bothered by lesser lights, her potential friends, who she had viewed as a trudging army from her high, lofty—and lonely—perch.

"How are things going?" asks Gwen, shutting up Sophie with a look. "Is Carl any better?"

I will be honest. These are not future social workers but genuinely interested friends, and they deserve the truth.

"He's not good at all, takes too many pills for pain, both real or imagined. He remembers very little and can't bear to be alone or leave home. It's a never-ending nightmare. It would bother you both to see him like this. Jerry comes in and they watch mixed martial arts together—and drink. Jerry's such a good friend."

"Yes," says Sophie softly, "he was always into Carl, almost too much, almost lived through him, instead of living his own life. Pattie's dumped him: he was only an interlude for her. She's into sport professionals. She's got herself a Blue Jay now. I'll give her until the second inning, certainly not past the third, and no home run."

I pick up the ball, or bat. "Before the wedding, we went on a date with Pattie and Jerry and ended up at an out-of-town club. She forced Carl to dance with her and came on to him like you wouldn't believe, gyrating into him like crazy, with Jerry and me just sitting there, watching. Carl didn't mind—he was grinning away, insensitive clod—but I know Jerry didn't like it, and I was furious, especially when Carl was refusing to have sex with me until after the wedding."

"Carl Helbig refused to have sex with you!" they chorus.

All else is forgotten; both of them are obviously incensed and incredulous.

"Apparently he had me on some sort of pedestal, 'too much respect,' Jerry said, and feared things would 'go wrong,' if that makes any sense. I felt he was rejecting me, and perhaps I didn't stack up against the Tulas of this world."

"That makes me so mad, you'll never know," sputters Sophie. "I could tell you things—"

"But you won't," says Gwen, throwing her a hard look.

"If it makes you both feel better, we had the sexiest honeymoon on record, and the best sex in Canada until the latest hit. But I really appreciate your indignation—and support."

We all laugh and order a second round. I am, I realize, having my first cat-session.

"A woman needs her sex," says Sophie firmly. "Not that I'm any example. Vince Fanelli comes around every few weeks for a little poke, and that's what it is, a very quick little poke: a bump in the road. It happens on the back seat of his 1955 Jaguar, which he loves better than life, certainly better than me, and spends all his money on. He's too cheap to go to the Sinclair, or to a motel, but it's hardly worth it for two minutes of action anyway. Vince thinks foreplay is something that happens before the band starts playing. Don't ever listen to anything good about Italian lovers—they spread that rumour themselves—they've all been coddled to death by their mamas."

We all laugh again.

"My mother calls him 'Sophia's little male whore,' but she says it in Italian. She'd say more, but his mother's her best friend."

"Your mother knows?" I ask.

"My mother knows everything. She listens to every conversation and overhears every phone call. She absorbs my life through her pores. I have zilch privacy, zilch."

"On that note," says Gwen, "I think we should order."

"Let's get a bottle of vino; you choose, Sophie. You know people are meeting up online now," I say.

"With my luck, he'd be a serial rapist—or killer. What would I say, 'Italian-Canadian assembly line worker, located in small Northern Ontario town, short, dark, and fun-loving, seeks large, rich professional, with own home and big bank account, who can last for more than five minutes in any place that does not include the back seat of his new, fully paid for, Lamborghini.' Can't wait for the rush of replies I'd get on that."

We all laugh, but I think I detect a whiff of hopelessness, if not bitterness, in Sophie's voice.

"Gwen's eyeing Harold Dare," says Sophie in an obvious effort to change the subject. "He's her office manager. Now that would be the wedding of the year."

"Oh shut up, Soph," replies Gwen. "He doesn't know I'm alive. He took me for coffee once, and said he'd call me, but he never did. I must have bored him to death or his Mother Superior, Mommy Dearest, warned him not to socialize with staff."

I have an inspiration. "Hanging in my closet, and

depressing me all to hell, is a brand-new wardrobe from Paris, personally selected by Carl Helbig, who, though you'd never guess it, has the best taste in women's clothes. I'll never wear those clothes now, and you'll have to adjust them a little, especially around the chest, but they'll get Harold Dare's attention. They're way too much for Davenport, but Carl insisted."

Just thinking of it makes my throat fill and eyes burn: not even a year ago, but it seems like forever.

"I couldn't possibly do that," says Gwen, "but very kind of you to offer."

"Are you fuckin' nuts?" shrieks Sophie, her voice reflecting vodka and indignation. "Your mother's a seamstress. If I wasn't a dwarf, I'd beat you to it. That's your problem, Gwen, always being such a tight-ass."

"I don't have sex in the back seat of cars, if that's what you mean," retorts Gwen, "and I wouldn't have Mom touch a Parisian wardrobe. She'll recommend an excellent tailor; there's quite a few in Toronto."

Sophie looks at me and winks. Gwen is obviously giving the offer serious consideration.

"I don't want Gwen to know this," confides Sophie after Gwen goes for a bathroom break, "but while you're into doing good, I want you to give a thought as to how I'm gonna escape from Dare's assembly line into something more high-end. The pay's good, I make as much as Gwen, though she looks down on me, I know she does. I got money stashed, but it's a dead-end job, and I'm goin' deaf, in spite of the plugs. And my only prospect's Vince;

he's in the line too, and he drives me crazy. The only thing we got in common, we're both wops."

"I'll really think about it," I assure her. "I'll pick up some brochures from Humber, George Brown, and even Ryerson—or, better yet, I'll email you some links."

Sophie had never been a student, but she is lively and bright, even funny, and she deserves better than going deaf on the assembly line at Dare's.

When we finish our lunch and return to the parking lot, the girls become subdued, then Gwen speaks: "Let's keep in touch. Next time's on us, or separate bills, nothing wrong with that."

They both hug me before I get into the Challenger.

BEFORE I LEAVE for Toronto, I phone Sophie and tell her I hadn't forgotten about the brochures unless she'd prefer the links. I'll be getting brochures for both the summer and the next September's courses, and that she should think of sales, or even becoming a dental hygienist. There are so many possibilities. She can stay at my Manulife apartment for the summer months.

"Imagine you thinking of me when you got so much on your plate," she sings. "You're the greatest, Sonja. My cousin Dominic's got an apartment on the Danforth, so I'm okay, but I'd love to have you go over the pamphlets with me some Saturday when you're home. I'd rather not do the links on my own; it'll be easier with you." I think of Carl and the tutoring, and her familiar words ring painfully in my ear.

"You can help me decide. I'll drop in and see Carl, and bring him some of Mama's lasagna—not that he wants to see me—and I'll pray for your mama."

"He'd love to see you," I lie, "and I appreciate the prayers," which is true.

"Love yuh," she carols before she hangs up. People were into that now. I never had been, except with Carl, but it seemed like a good idea.

"Love you back," I say.

IT'S AFTER BOXING Day and the lunch with the girls at the Sinclair. I'm sitting with Mutti in her immaculate living room, where a little tree packed with ornaments is a reminder that at least some members of the Helbig family attempted to celebrate the season.

"I'll be going to U of T from Monday to Friday starting January 9," I tell her. "I'll have to take Ma with me; she can't help with Carl as I'd hoped. I suggest we get someone to come in the mornings to prepare his breakfast and then he can come here to your place each night for dinner."

"You are going away?" Her voice is heavy with surprise and disapproval.

"Only during the week," I explain. "Carl insists on it. He always wanted me to complete my degree. He was very upset last term when I withdrew."

This was the old Carl. The new Carl may not feel this way, but I don't tell Mutti this. Why make things even more complicated?

"It may be a gut thing, you baby him, Sonja. I make

plans for him to start on assembly line at Dare's. It will be gut for him to get out of the house and mix with others."

I am horrified and angry. She's so high-handed and without a word of consultation with me or Carl. A typical Mutti move, unthinking yet well meaning.

"I'll ask him."

"Don't ask him, Sonja, tell him."

It's January 5 and Mutti picks Carl up at seven-thirty. He is used to sleeping in and is groggy, but he eats his breakfast and looks like himself, with his leather jacket and blue jeans.

"Your phone is in your pocket. If anything goes wrong push 2." I write "2" on his hand with a ballpoint pen. I kiss him firmly on his cheek, avoiding looking at his temples. Sometimes I think of the times when we were close and I long for them. I miss our sex that didn't survive the last concussion. Looking back it was only for a short period, but what we had was wonderful.

"He's not fit to work," hisses Ma in Ukrainian. "Gertie Helbig is a mad Nazi. The boy is an invalid. He will kill himself on the machinery. This is Gestapo stuff. In Stalingrad they were forced to eat cement. It killed people."

The last three comments bear no relation to the first three. Ma may have chemo brain, or perhaps her cancer has metastasized to that area. This saddens me. I look at her, and her sunken green eyes glitter back.

"I thought you and Gertie were friends."

"What's that to do with anything?"

I shall be glad to leave, to hear lectures, and read the

materials on the list of required reading. It's time to find escape in literature again. I have managed to get into another modern poetry course, Poetry of the Nineteenth Century. And there is The Gothic Novel, with an emphasis on William Faulkner and Flannery O'Connor. This excites me. There is no reason Carl and I cannot keep in constant contact by phone and email, although Carl hates anything that reveals his woeful spelling.

It is only ten to nine when the telephone rings.

"Come. Now."

In the background I hear the roar of the machinery. What was Mutti thinking? She wasn't—deluding herself as usual.

He is outside waiting in the cold, looking into the distance as usual, scowling.

"My head is coming apart."

"We'll go home. You can have an Oxy and you can lie down in a nice quiet dark room."

Candace Stewart's pre-Christmas words, "You didn't sign up for this," come back with a sickening thud—except I did sign up for it.

CARL DOESN'T WANT anyone to come to our house and prepare breakfast; in fact, he wants no visitors at all.

"If you won't let anyone come, then I won't leave, or if I do leave, you can go and live with Mutti all week."

On occasion Jerry Henley or one of the old Choir members drops in, and they drink rye and watch mixed martial arts on the sports channel. It is Carl's only diversion. But he doesn't want to stay with Mutti, not under any circumstances.

"And you have to take a bath before I leave."

Carl now hates showers. They make his head hurt. But he will submerge himself in a prepared bath if I insist. I think wistfully back to the scoured quality that had endeared him to me early on. Now water has become his enemy. Then at two o'clock on Sunday afternoon, when I am packed and ready to leave, with Ma sitting in the car waiting, he does not want me to go.

"I'll be alone."

"The boys will drop in and you'll see Mutti and your dad every night. I'll email you every day, at least twice, and phone you every night, and I'll be back Friday."

He stands by the doorway watching, abandoned and disconsolate.

Ma sticks her head out of the opened window and yells, "She take me to hospital, Carl. Must die in comfort."

He remains in the doorway, making me feel guilty. As soon as we are out of sight I feel better. And then I feel guilty for feeling better.

"No wonder I feel sick lately, stress will do it." I think of Candace Stewart and shut up, but it is too late. The Davenport Philosopher makes her move.

"How you mean?"

"Nauseated, tired, even my boobs tingle."

"You pregnant?"

"Of course not. I haven't had sex since October 14, the day before my birthday, the day before Carl's concussion.

Sex is no longer in the realm of things Carl wants to do."

"In October. You on pill?"

"No, I went off at the end of August when Carl went to training camp. I thought it was making me fat, and it would take months for me to start to ovulate again."

"Periods?"

"No."

Could I have been this stupid? I glance at Ma, belted in like a wizened child: Ma and Carl, my two children, one dying and the other disabled. I don't need a third.

"When we came here," says Ma, speaking in Ukrainian as we whiz by the frozen snow-covered fields on our way to the 400, "we had nothing—except each other. I was the only one working, a night job doing dishes in the kitchen of the Royal York Hotel in Toronto, from eight to midnight every night. Then I get pregnant and your father, he go crazy. He make me drink a bottle of vodka and almost scald me to death in the landlady's bathtub when she go out. But nothing happen. Then he set up a doctor, for me to say I was bleeding, a threatened miscarriage he call it, and that I need a D and a C, whatever that mean. By then I was two or three months and I see the doctor, but I tell him the truth. Then I lie to your father, tell him it too late and doctor refuse, and that he should drink the vodka himself."

I sit transfixed behind the wheel. I'd never realized how close I'd come to not being here, to being part of a small pile of clotted blood and membrane, ultimately disposed of and forgotten, and it was Ma who saved me.

"He took you telling him to drink the vodka himself very seriously."

Ma hiccups a chuckle. "Yes, he never stop. But after you were born, he forget all about not wanting you and say you were the smartest little girl who ever lived, which you were, and he was your sole creator."

I stretch out my hand and hold Ma's tiny rough one, now a bundle of bones encased in loose skin, and squeeze it. "Thanks for saving my life Ma, but I'm sure I'm not pregnant."

Ma looks out at the fields, her shrunken face pensive, a small fold of yellow jowl sagging over the fox collar of her long-ago Christmas gift.

"Sometimes, Sonja, you can move too quickly to discard something precious, sometimes what you plan to discard can bring you joy." She said the word *joy* in English, as if to give it special impact.

I make the turnoff to the 400 and drive south, still holding Ma's hand.

AS SOON AS I get up, I email Carl on my new laptop. "Good morning, darling, are you OK?"

Within five minutes the reply comes. "Not OK. Brekfust suks. Miss U."

I scramble some eggs for Ma, but she says she's too nauseated to eat them and that the chemo, which is giving her herpes all over the inside of her mouth, is worse than the cancer. And that it is all a waste of time in any event.

I silently agree with her, but only suggest that she stop the chemo for a few days as food is more important than anything to keep her strength up. She gives me a sad cackle and asks, "What strength?"

The poetry class gets off to a fine start with Dylan Thomas, whom I really love, and I am glad to see Janet Murdock. We grab a coffee together and I explain about Carl and Ma. She offers to take notes on her computer and will print them off for me if I miss classes. She's such a kind girl. Jo has transferred to Waterloo University.

I pick up my novels for my Modern British Authors class, from Evelyn Waugh to Martin Amis. I am relieved that I feel excited, the first time for so long, and that I am still open to literature.

On my way home I stop at a Shoppers Drug Mart.

I email Carl at five o'clock: "Walk to Mutti's for dins." I've taken the car keys, which will annoy him as he still believes he can drive. I get a return email: "U tuk the dam kees." At this point I phone Mutti and tell her to pick him up.

I make a reservation to take Ma out for dinner to Pangyea, which is only across the street from Manulife and a far cry from the Sinclair Hotel. Normally this would thrill her, but now she says she's not well enough to even walk across the street, and that her mouth's too raw to allow her to eat.

"You have to force yourself," I say, "and give up the chemo." I offer to go downstairs to the drugstore and get her some benzocaine, which would numb her mouth, but she says, "No, Sonja, even if I swallow food, I throw it up later."

I don't want to lose Ma. I make her some canned tomato soup with a lot of milk, and some Ritz Crackers to soak in it. She smiles at me, showing her new veneers, which she got for the wedding only seven months ago, back when we all had hope.

"You're such a fine girl, Sonja, so good to your mother," she whispers.

I pretend I have to go to the bathroom and I sit on the toilet and cry. I know that she's going and there's nothing I can do about it. Carl has left me too. Much later I read,

Light breaks where no sun shines;
Where no sea runs, the waters of the heart
Push in their tides.

I ask myself how Dylan Thomas could have written this and still have drunk himself to death. Ma smoked herself to death in the absence of hope, but I don't understand Dylan.

I email Carl. "You OK?"

"Jerry here watting TV."

They are drinking rye. Carl mixes alcohol with his pain-killers and smiles at me when I tell him it's dangerous. He loves me to be concerned about him.

I tuck Ma in bed and give her two Tylenol with codeine ground up in jam as she says she's in pain. Her head rests on the pillow like a little girl, and when I kiss her cheek the skin slides over her sharp cheekbone and I smell soap and death, sweet, yet jagged and final.

"Love ya, Ma."

"Poor Sonja, too much on your plate," she sighs.

I go to the bathroom with my bag from the drugstore. The pregnancy test is positive. I cannot go ahead with this.

By Wednesday, Ma is in terrible pain and cannot get out of bed. She takes little sips of black tea but is becoming dehydrated, and the Tylenol is useless. I call an ambulance and go with her to Princess Margaret, where they attempt to hook her up to an intravenous, giving fluid and morphine.

"Little tiny veins," complains the nurse, trying to insert the needle. I see a purple bruise spread in the crack of Ma's shrunken arm. She smiles at me, and underneath my eyelids unshed tears burn.

"We're going to make her comfortable," explains the nurse, "a little morphine, she's so slight only a little will have an effect."

"She's only forty-eight," I say, a silly defensive comment, as if the years should insulate her from death.

"You're her only relative?"

I nod and sign a "Do not resuscitate" directive. What needless cruelty it would be to prolong Ma's suffering.

I go to the main-floor restaurant at Princess Margaret and collect a bagel, coffee, and yogurt with fruit at the bottom. I am bleeding memories. I go over the gifted coat, the Sinclair Hotel dinners, and Ma at the Helbigs, and how kind Carl was in the days when he still had kindness to spare. I hope I made it up to her for being the world's most obnoxious teenager.

I email Carl: "Ma dying."

He comes back with "Sory." There are no complaints about breakfast and missing me. He has risen to the occasion.

I sit by Ma and wait. I am missing my doctor's appointment. I email the clinic: "Family emergency. Will rebook."

Ma's breathing has become ragged. It is four o'clock, and outside the snow, like soft white feathers, floats down, surrounding the street lights, and landing gently on the shoulders of those trudging up University. Ma gurgles.

"It won't be long now," whispers a nurse.

By five, Ma is gone.

19

SEEING DR. ANDERSON

"AND WHY WOULD YOU BELIEVE you weren't pregnant?"

Dr. Harry Anderson, obstetrician and gynecologist, is round, smiling, pink, and bald, lacking the cadaverous quality of the surgeon and the heft of Dr. Folkes. He obviously likes his food, and it shows in his cheerful disposition and generous inclinations. He is kind enough to take me on Friday afternoon when his nurse tells him that my missed appointment was as a result of my mother's death. I have given my blood and urine samples and he has done an internal, which was like being probed by the snout of a pink, hairless, but very affectionate pig.

"It only happened once," I explain, "on October 14, the day before my birthday. I went off the pill in August to lose weight. The next day my husband had a severe concussion and I haven't had sex since."

"Doesn't seem fair, does it?" muses Dr. Anderson. "But it only takes a single act, as some poor little teenagers discover. Hopefully your husband will recover enough to function sexually and to help in parenting a baby."

"I can't have this baby," I blurt out. "I'm a student and my husband shows no signs of recovering. He is my baby. It's out of the question." I sound angry and argumentative, shooting the messenger as Dr. Folkes had complained.

Dr. Anderson has lost his smile. "These are personal choices, Mrs. Helbig, but if you choose the termination route, then you can't wait much longer. You're a healthy young woman and physically there seems to be no problem. I usually carry out an ultrasound in the fourth month to be sure. There's a clinic on Wellesley that deals with these other matters."

I obtain a card from Dr. Anderson's nurse and telephone The Family Planning Centre when I return to the apartment. I tell them I am three months pregnant and that my physician advises me it is a matter of some urgency. My appointment is the following week on

Thursday afternoon. This will give me the weekend after next to convalesce.

I gather up Ma's things and bury my face in her fox collar. I will take her clothes to the Salvation Army as it is too sad to keep them. She is to be cremated and all I will have left will be a little urn of ashes, like the ashes from the thousands of Camel cigarettes she smoked.

I pile my new textbooks in the car seat beside me and head for Davenport. I am weary at the prospect of the long drive, both there and back. Sometimes I feel Carl is getting worse, and I have a growing impatience with him that at times makes me feel ashamed. Ma brought about her own death, but I knew why. Carl could have saved his life but refused. And now I must bear the result of his stubbornness and stupidity. I must pay for a night of sex, amazing though it was, by having the result of it suctioned from my body—a little, pulsating, live pink butterfly vacuumed away like so much debris—because his maker, his father, has made his future life impossible.

My cellphone rings. Carl is hoarse with excitement.

"You gotta hurry or I'm gonna be late."

"What are you saying?" I phone back but he does not pick up.

I am stuck in traffic although it is only three-thirty. The predicted snow flurries have started and I turn on the windshield wipers. The blades click back and forth, relentless. I turn on the news. Northern Ontario will be experiencing some six to eight inches. Next weekend, I decide, I will stay in Toronto, and read poetry and Evelyn

Waugh's *The Loved One*: the funeral industry in California should be a diversion. I wonder what Dylan Thomas meant by saying that after the first death there is no other. Did he mean the enormity of loss cannot be duplicated? I think of Ma and then the loss of Carl's mind. Is he regressing or merely shutting down?

My cell rings again.

"Look out the window, it's probably a blizzard where you are. I'm doing my best," I tell him.

"I can't be late. Don't you understand?"

"Late for what? Just what is your problem?" My voice is strident.

"Fuck, you don't understand."

He hangs up.

The stream of traffic starts again. There was an accident ahead and everyone was slowing down to look. Plato was right. People need a philosopher king.

My cell rings.

"Stop bothering me," I yell and turn off my cell. I don't feel my usual guilt.

It is six-thirty when I pull into the driveway. The light is on over the door and Carl is standing on the first step, balanced on his skates, fully dressed in his Bruins uniform. His helmet is covered with snow and he holds a hockey stick in his gloved hand.

"We're late for the first period," he shouts. "Give me the keys to the car."

I approach him slowly and when I touch his face it is like ice, and his eyes are half hidden by snow. The fresh snow covering our cedar hedge sparkles in the porch light.

"They cancelled the game," I tell him softly. "The plane with the other Bruins couldn't land because of the snowstorm. You'll play next week."

We enter the house together and I go upstairs to start his bath. He sits obediently, waiting for me to remove his skates. I pull off his gloves and his fingers are rigid with cold. I take off his helmet and wipe the snow from his eyes. I rub each hand between mine, in turn, one after the other.

"Try to take off your skates," I beg, "You put them on, after all."

"You turned off your cell."

"It was the storm," I lie.

He removes his skates and we trudge upstairs. I slowly remove his shin pads, hockey pants, jersey, and shoulder and elbow pads, and he co-operates. He now stands before me naked, and I smell the sharp sweat from his armpits and the stench of stale urine from his tangled pubic hair. His penis hangs flaccid.

"You didn't take a bath," I scold, "not for a whole week. What will I do with you?" He smiles happily, savouring my concern.

As he sits in the tub I massage his scalp gently with my own lavender shampoo, wipe his eyes with a hot cloth, and soap his ears with my fingers. Soon they will be pink again. I lather his back, rub it with a cloth, and turn on more hot water as his arms are still cold.

"Wash your pits and down below," I order.

I think of Ma and her little joke about possible and I feel like crying. He is finally finished and he climbs from the tub, clean and triumphant.

"Why is it so difficult for you to do this on your own?"

He does not reply and declines my offer of food.

I lie down beside him. He always turns away from me. I place my arm around him.

"Can you sleep without your pills?"

He does not answer so I conclude he can.

"Do you remember in Boston, the night before the last game?"

He does not answer. It was the second bleed, he can't remember.

"What would you do if I were pregnant?"

There is a sharp intake of breath and I feel his back stiffen, then it crumbles, and I hear him sob, deep sobs, right from his gut.

"Carl, stop it. I'm not pregnant."

But he ignores me. "What good would I be to a kid? I couldn't even push him in a swing or play ball. I would be a shit of a father, lyin' in the dark, livin' on pills."

I rub his back gently, in circles.

"But I always wanted you to have my kid, I remember that part of it. He would be so smart. I don't forget everything."

My heart is bursting. Fuck hockey. Fuck everything.

"Go to sleep, darling. I'm not pregnant, so it's silly to talk about it."

"I missed you."

"I know. I missed you too."

THE WAITING ROOM of an abortion clinic is not like the waiting room of a doctor or dentist. It lacks the bustling efficiency. The magazines sit unread. Near the door sits a teenager; her eyes are swollen and she wears a nose ring. On her forearm is tattooed the name Chris, surrounded by the outline of a blue heart.

"Sometimes," said Ma, "you can move too quickly to throw away something that is precious, something that can cause future joy."

I stand up.

"You're next, Mrs. Helbig."

I am to go before the teenager, age discrimination in an abortion clinic.

"I've changed my mind," I say.

"You should have let us know," said the receptionist with a disapproving pout. "We changed our schedule to take you."

"Sorry," I say, "but I didn't know it would happen."

On the way out I hug the teenager. She stiffens in surprise, no doubt thinking I am mad.

"Good luck," I tell her.

Outside it is growing darker and the flakes are falling again. Light breaks where no sun shines, I think to myself.

THE NEXT MONTH I look at my ultrasound with Dr. Anderson. "You can see his penis," he says pointing, "and his arm is up."

"He's waving at me," I say, "thanking me for saving his life."

"As you wish," replies Dr. Anderson, smiling as usual.

20
OVERTIME

CARL'S DEPRESSION IS GETTING WORSE. I spoke to Jerry Henley about it after one of his visits. He suggested that Carl join The Choir for a brief game of non-contact pickup hockey at the Davenport Arena, as they reserve an after-hours session twice a month. It is a Saturday night and I help him get ready. He seems excited, actually smiling at me, and I suspect he thinks he is going to play for the Bruins.

"Nothing too rough," I instruct Jerry, "he gets dizzy

and nauseated, but it would be wonderful if he enjoyed this. It would really buck him up."

Ma's expression. Is it true, I ask myself, thinking of Oscar Wilde, that all women eventually end up like their mothers?

"Wanna come?" asks Jerry. He and I are now buddies, brought together by our mutual concern for Carl.

"No way," I say. "It would worry the shit out of me to watch."

I talk to Jerry now in what I think of as "Carl language," or what used to be "Carl language," and I swear as much as I can. It seems to relax everyone, including me.

Carl and Jerry have been gone an hour, and I have become relaxed enough to actually read *The Waste Land* when I hear them at the door.

Jerry looks at me and shakes his head. "Acting like a crazy man," he says softly, "all over the ice. Then he goes down and can't get up. Complains about his head all the way home—says it's comin' apart. But then he says, 'At least we beat the Canucks.' Right out of it. He thinks he's still with the Bruins."

Frontal lobe dementia, I think to myself, fear flickering in my throat, but I merely say, "Guess he's not ready, but nice try."

Jerry helps me take off Carl's skates, which he'd refused to take off in the change room at the arena, and he sits in his gear in a chair in the living room, looking into space. "Let's have a drink to celebrate," Carl says suddenly, "it's not often we beat the bastards like this."

Jerry looks at me and shrugs apologetically, as if in a strange and symbiotic way he's responsible for Carl's dementia.

I pour them both large shots of rye. "I'll go up and get your bath ready," I say to Carl. "It'll warm you up and help your head."

"I have," Carl informs Jerry, his voice bright, "the best wife in the world. Bet your wife doesn't give you a bath every weekend and wash every part of you."

Jerry is embarrassed. He lowers his head and gives me a furtive, almost shy glance. There is no wife.

"I'm sure she would if he asked her," I reply. "Lots of wives give their husbands baths, don't they, Jerry?"

I give Jerry a quick wink. I may as well make a joke of it.

"Christ," whispers Jerry, on his way out, "this is fuckin' awful."

"He has good and bad days," I explain. "He's not always delusional."

The bath is not a success. His head pounds and nothing alleviates the pain. I finally give him one OxyContin.

"What's wrong? You want me to suffer? I might as well be dead anyways."

"Take one more," I say, "but only one." I don't want to fight with him, not over one lousy pill.

March not April is the cruellest month, and not because anything is twitching and coming to life except Carl Helbig Jr., who grows restless. The wind blows bitter, and Sheila's Brush, the snowstorm that takes place after Saint Patrick's Day, March 17, to remind Canadians that winter is not yet past, takes place on March 20. On the last week of March I take Carl with me to Toronto to see Dr. Judith Weiner, a noted neuropsychologist affiliated with Mount Sinai Hospital. She has examined Dr. Folkes' MRI and MRS results, both from the February and October concussions. She orders another MRI and MRS and conducts a battery of tests and interviews throughout the week. She is crisp, immaculate, and clinically detached, and sits across her desk, speaking to me in her low but definite voice.

"There was a second bleed and some frontal lobe damage, followed by what appears to be pronounced dementia in certain areas. There may well be some chronic traumatic encephalopathy, which cannot be fully determined until a post-mortem. Should he die, I would urge you to donate your husband's brain to the researchers at Boston University."

I feel myself sag with depression and the heaviness of futility. Then I become angry. It is irrational, as I had already anticipated Dr. Weiner's dementia finding, but I cannot control the choking wave of powerlessness and fury that sweeps over me.

"Perhaps we could concentrate on his present quality of life," I suggest, "his bouts of depression and his great dependency on me."

As usual I am shooting the messenger, but I find the emphasis on Carl's brain post-mortem disturbing. I must stop looking for practical solutions from these medical people. They need to be pinned down like anyone else so they don't consider their patients an assortment of lab rats.

"His present medications?"

"Painkillers, OxyContin and Vicodin, Xanax, for occasional panic disorders, Ativan for anxiety, and Valium as a muscle relaxant. He's happiest when lying in a darkened bedroom, but will on occasion watch mixed martial arts on television provided he has a friend present, and will take a short walk with me. He lacks the initiative to wash and waits until I return home on weekends."

Dr. Weiner stares at me, her face expressionless.

"I don't prescribe drugs, but my colleague Dr. Leviticus would be glad to assist. My area of expertise is really diagnosis and lifestyle changes."

Dr. Weiner does not like me. She can't wait to shuffle me off to Dr. Leviticus, who will doubtless prescribe drugs with some firm instructions as to their use rather than advise me as to Carl's brain journey in its post-mortem state.

"All right," I tell her, "I realize you're a busy professional so I will keep this brief, but I must know how to manage my future—and Carl's. From a practical point of view, is there a chance of any cognitive improvement? Although there are obviously serious problems, can surgery, or any other drastic solutions, improve them? Please be frank with me."

Dr. Weiner frowns at Carl's file, as if my asking her to be frank imposes an onerous burden that she is reluctant to assume. "You are asking me for a definite prognosis. I can't give you one. A brain injury is not akin to a broken leg or arm. We cannot go in and clear away the damage. Sometimes, certain parts of the brain take over the functioning of the other parts, but naturally this is dependent on many other factors, including the extent of the damage. I am not unduly optimistic in this particular case. His test results show severe limitations and a marked inability to focus."

"He's severely dyslexic," I tell her, "and he's had attention-deficit as long as I've known him. These problems could affect the test results. He's been playing hockey since the age of seven. From what he's told me I suspect there's been a long series of sub-concussions, even concussions. He was the local hockey hero."

"You're his main caregiver?"

"I'm his real caregiver, but I attend classes here during the week. A local woman comes to fix breakfast, and he has dinner at his mother's each night. I'm not willing to stop my classes, a decision he used to support. And he only wants me around."

"Have you considered an institution?"

Is cruelty the criteria for Dr. Weiner's success? It's a rational question considering my situation, but I'm unfairly angry and affronted and have difficulty breathing.

"He's not reached that stage," I answer, "unless you feel he could receive some therapy."

"I was thinking of you, Mrs. Helbig. You've been married for less than a year and you're a student. I doubt if you thought you were marrying someone who would need you for his weekend bath, and whose idea of diversion is watching martial arts on television."

In other words, "You didn't sign up for this." Another

Candace Stewart, but with much more education and subtlety of speech.

"Carl was never an intellectual, Dr. Weiner, but he was kind, generous, and he loved me a lot. We were capable of enjoying life together. We had wonderful sex. Now all of that is gone. But he still loves me, as much as he is capable. I'm not willing to abandon my own life entirely, but I'm not willing to abandon him either."

Dr. Weiner stands up. "Anything else?"

"I'm five months pregnant. This may further complicate matters. I conceived before the last concussion."

Dr. Weiner shakes her head and tightens her mouth, her assessment of me as an intellectual student no longer existing. I am guided to Dr. Leviticus, who gives me a short lecture on the value of serotonin enhancers to combat depression, a prescription for Paxil, and another for the most viable current pill for insomnia. He will see Carl briefly to validate my information and the prescriptions.

There is something to be said for pill pushers: at least they don't waste time on autopsy reports and lifestyle changes that cannot work.

AFTER HIS WEEK with Dr. Weiner, Carl is visibly upset. He fears, correctly, that the results of Dr. Weiner's tests and interviews were not helpful. He has started on his antidepressants but sees no difference. It seems he expected some transformation that would lift him out of his depression and render him whole again.

"It takes weeks to kick in," I tell him, "and you can't

expect miracles. Besides, you can't expect to sit with Jerry and guzzle rye if you're on these."

He ignores me. I have become a nag and I hate the sound of my own voice.

"I'm glad we're leaving," he says.

Carl is only comfortable in Davenport. Our house is quiet, familiar, slightly isolated, and he feels safe there. He finds the bustle and noise of Toronto irritating and pain-provoking.

"You're getting seriously addicted," I warn him as I refuse to give him his second OxyContin on Thursday night, the night before we leave. "Are you sure you're in pain?"

"No. I'm great. I just want to get high. Okay?"

There are times like this when I get really angry, but they don't last and I have my little boy back, who smiles his delight at my concern and loves his bath.

On Thursday night, Carl gets his hair trimmed in Yorkville. Now he looks handsome, with his leather jacket and styled hair. I tell him so. Why does it hurt me when he looks handsome? Is it the present waste or memories of the past? It's both: the waste fills me with despair, even anger at times, and the memories choke me with gnawing sadness.

"Can we eat out?" It would be a break for me, and we are surrounded by restaurants.

"Nope."

So we order in pizza. It's just as well we're leaving tomorrow, I think. Toronto is wasted on Carl.

THE WEEKEND IS uneventful. Jerry comes over on Saturday night and he and Carl watch martial arts together and drink rye, which seems to have a much greater effect than usual on Carl.

"You're not supposed to mix rye with Paxil," I nag.

The next morning his head is throbbing so much he can't get up. I am instructed to produce OxyContin, but I refuse to give him the two tablets he wants.

"Then I'll take them myself," he says and produces two tablets he's hidden under the mattress, and chews them, all the time smiling at me. Then he complains that the OxyContin is no longer working and he wants one of his sleeping pills, as he is in agony and can only escape through sleep.

"You're not getting any more," I tell him. "It's too dangerous what you're doing."

I go downstairs to get him juice, but when I come back he is sleeping. Had he also hidden some sleeping pills?

As he sleeps, I take a shower. I lather my stomach and examine the swelling. I'm starting to show and I'm only keeping it hidden by wearing loose black skirts and long sweaters. Soon everyone will know and Carl will find out, and he will be upset as it will remind him of his short-comings. My skin looks so white, my hair so dark and my breasts so swollen, with their large brown noses bruised by my touch. Will little Carl suck the pain from my heart and give me joy?

I telephone Mutti and walk to her house. It is clean and fresh but very cold. There are ridges of low-lying mottled clouds and everything is hushed. A Sunday-morning quiet, I think.

Mutti answers the door in her dressing gown, although her face looks freshly powdered, and her hair is in short, tinted-blond feathers swept back from her face. In spite of her efforts, she looks old. There are fine lines around her eyes and her rosy skin sags around her jowls. Her eyes look filmed, and there is a prominent frown line between her brows. I think of her driving me back to the apartment, her head held high, her profile clean and definite. Now she looks old and it hurts me. I have underestimated her pain, which, regardless of fault, is as real and harsh as mine.

She embraces me, but it is perfunctory.

"Coffee and coffee cake, Sonja? I wait all day to hear what doctor say."

Always the little needle of guilt. I should have contacted her earlier, but it is news I'm not happy to share. I sit at the table, sip the strong coffee, and nibble at the coffee cake.

"Well, what they say?"

"He has considerable brain damage, mostly in his frontal lobe. It limits him. They don't seem to see a cure or an end to his headaches and dizziness."

Mutti sits back and nods her head. She looks defeated.

"They suggested an institution."

"And what did you tell them?"

"I said no."

Mutti nods her head with approval and reaches for my hand. "He much more happy when you are home. You know that?"

"Mutti, there are only another two months at my school; you can't expect me to give up everything." I try to keep the exasperated tone from my voice, but it is there.

"I know, I know. I wish he be more happy with me, but he want his Sony, like a little boy."

"Mutti, there is something you must know. And only you. I once mentioned it to Carl and he became so upset that I denied it right away."

Mutti leans forward, and for the first time her face shows some animation, a little life.

"I'm five months pregnant."

Mutti's face is flushed, the film over her eyes gone.

"I made arrangements but decided not to go ahead with it. I hoped that perhaps in the long term it would give us all joy."

Mutti covers her face with her hands and rocks back and forth. Through the small, jewelled fingers with Carl's square pink nails, tears flow.

"You are *wunderbar*, Sonja. No one like you—no one. Better to me than my own daughters."

"But you can't tell Carl," I insist again. "This is very important. He fears his inadequacies will interfere with his parenting and the thought of it will destroy him. Let me pick my time."

Mutti squeezes me as I leave and warns me not to slip although there is no ice. I have given her hope and that makes me feel better.

"I GET OFF early for the spring break," I tell Carl. "I'll be back Wednesday night and we'll eat at home. I'll bring us Chinese takeout from Toronto and heat it up here. The time will go fast."

I hide his pills in various coat pockets and boots and shoes in my downstairs closet, and then allocate the rest, with instructions, on the kitchen counter. He nods his head solemnly. He hates me to go and I feel guilty. I run my hand through his hair. "Great haircut," I say. "Come May, I'll be home all the time. You'll be sick of the sight of me. And I've got a whole ten days, starting Wednesday."

He sees me out to the car but for a change does not ask for the keys to the Challenger. I put my arms around him and we sway back and forth, then I kiss him on the neck. It is warm velvet. Perhaps, I think, they are wrong. Perhaps someday the neural pathways and synapses will re-attach, and they will find a way to do away with the porridge. Doctors are not always right.

THERE IS SO much to do in the three days before study week. I collect the notes from Janet Murdock for the lectures I've missed and see all my professors, explaining my absences.

They nod their understanding.

I leave on Wednesday afternoon at three-thirty after picking up cartons of Chinese food at Formosa. It is still cold, but there is a slight softness in the air, a faint promise of spring.

This morning I saw a robin on the campus searching for worms in the brown grass, and a toss of birds in the sky, which had pale patches of blue. I emailed Carl first thing this morning and reminded him of the Chinese food and that I have told Mutti not to pick him up. I don't check for a reply.

The traffic is better than usual as the weekend travellers have yet to open their cottages. I sniff the Chinese food on the seat beside me. Maybe it will still be warm when I arrive. I feel some twitching. "Are you waving at me again?" I ask. "I know you're there. I haven't forgotten you."

I'll tell Carl about the baby at the end of the term. Then I will have time to make him adjust, to see something good in it, to give it a positive spin, as they say.

At five-thirty I make the Davenport turnoff, and by six I am approaching the house. I feel the cardboard cartons. All warmth is gone.

There are no lights on in the house, and all is still when I unlock the door. Carl may be sleeping. "I'm home," I call. The silence sits, waiting for me. My throat is tightening and I hear my heart beat in my ears. I go upstairs to our bedroom. I walk slowly. I wish to postpone what I fear awaits me. There is no rush to discover what I fear.

The room is dark so I turn on the lamp. He lies there, looking into the distance. What does he see that he has been searching for so long? The empty phials are on the table, and a glass of rye with just a little left. There will be no bath tonight. I lie beside him and press my face against his. It is like ice. I remember cleaning off the snow, it was not that long ago. His chest is smooth and cold. I run my hands over it and kiss it. I wash it with my tears, warm tears on cold flesh. He lies, carved in stone, and his chill transmits itself to me: my arms become numb, my breasts cut from ice, my body transformed into a statue, the only warmth my burning eyes and my heart banging against my frozen ribs. I stay too long with this cold stranger, but I cannot leave, for then it will be real.

IT IS AFTER ten when I phone for an ambulance. The cold from Carl's chilled body stays with me, and my hand shakes so badly I can hardly punch in the numbers. I sit trembling, waiting.

"He's long gone," croaks the ambulance attendant, looking at me with hard, inquiring eyes. "You'll need a death certificate for Beringers, so I'll take him in and have a doctor sign. He's Carl Helbig of the Bruins, right?"

"Right," I reply. But I want to say that he was so much more, so very much more, at the beginning anyway.

His eyes are open when they lift him onto the gurney, so I go over and pass my hand over his frozen face.

"They'll glue them to," says the first attendant helpfully.

"Sorry for your loss," mutters the other.

After they take him away, the house screams at me in silence. I know I must see Mutti and Carl's father, because this is Davenport, and it will only be a matter of time before they're told. In the kitchen I check my computer. There was a message posted at ten that morning.

"Sory sony. Is to hard. Not yor falt. Love yu."

I press DELETE.

He waves to the world, my sweet baby curled inside me. He sees a happy place. He must not know his future presence made it "to hard" for his creator. I wonder when Mutti told him, perhaps Tuesday night. What were her words—stupid, stupid woman.

The night is a clot of darkness, so cold, with only crusts of snow marking the way to Mutti's. I am carrying Carl's cold, but I'm wrapped in the chill of this starless March night as well. I know that deep down in some hidden crevice of my soul there will always be this nugget of ice and it will never go away.

Mutti answers the door in her dressing gown, her face shining with night cream. She looks at me and knows and calls out, "Carl." Carl Sr. appears, also in his dressing gown. He looks at me, his face immobile, such a decent and gentle man.

"Our Carl is gone?" asks Mutti. "How it happen, Sonja?"

Carl Sr. turns to leave, his face now marble in the dull light, and I hear his sobs, terrible deep sobs, and I know this is a man who does not cry and these sobs are being wrenched from the depths of his grief.

"He took all his pills with rye."

Mutti does not cry. Her face is pale as suet, her lips thin with grief—and anger.

"It your place to stay with him. You selfish, put school before your husband when he need you so bat."

I can't listen, unwilling to bear an assault of guilt. I am already burdened. The guilt is hers, most of it, and I refuse to wear it like some wrap of thorns. Without saying or hearing more, I leave.

I cannot stay the night, the silence will oppress me, will wear me down. I take the keys of the Challenger and my wallet and get into the car sitting waiting in the garage. It springs to life under my fingers and I back it out into the empty street. I drive through the black waves of night, through the streets of Davenport, empty streets shining wet in the lights, past Davenport High and the Sinclair Hotel. Strange, now he is gone I see him as he was before that final game, the smile, the golden hair, the square jaw. I will miss him as he used to be.

I head for the water, the beach of rocks with the nearby forest of pine and spruce. It is almost midnight, but I do not want to stop driving. Once at the bay I see that the trees contain remnants of snow, ghostly trees, with their tattered shrouds. I get out of the car and the wind from the lake lashes against me, and I smell the spice of spruce and pine. I think of the ring and how it was a little tight as we sat together that day, before I told him I loved him, and on the day after, when we clung together on the rock with the wind blowing against us, and he spoke of our future children. I said I wanted to freeze the moment in time, to think of it when we were old together.

THERE IS NO one at the counter of the Sinclair Hotel so I ring the small bell and a rumpled young man appears. I obviously woke him up.

"I want a room," I say, "a room with a bathtub and a shower."

He looks at me with curiosity.

"Your bags?" he asks.

"No bags," I tell him.

The room is similar to our honeymoon room and I pour shampoo under the faucets of the bathtub, watching it fill with foam. I undress slowly, my body harsh with cold in spite of the car's heater. I glimpse myself in the mirror, my swollen belly and my breasts pendulous with their brown splashes of nipple.

"Great breasts," he would say. "Did anyone ever tell you've got great breasts?"

I wait for him to finish his shower as I watch from my hot bed of foam. He will emerge soon, his towel around his waist. It is only after I get in bed and know that he won't be joining me that I am able to cry, and then I cannot stop and I cry well into the night, for Carl, for his wasted life, and for myself.

I wake up, sodden from tears and lack of sleep, as reality seeps in. I feel the need for closeness, to talk, to share memories. I think of Jerry, his grief will mirror mine.

"Where are you?" he asks, his voice husky with concern. I know he knows, nothing remains secret in Davenport.

"At the Sinclair. Can we meet at the house later? Carl's mother has the key."

I break down sobbing, and Jerry answers, his voice as broken as mine.

"Sure. I'll meet you there around five. It's good you called."

Nausea mixes with my grief and I drive to the New Davenport Mall for toast and coffee, and then I drive out to the lake again, but this time I sit and watch as the temporary sun flickers away and the shadows start.

Before I head for home, I drive to Beringers. I'm told that Mutti has already been there and has selected the coffin. I start to become angry, and then realize the futility of anger under the circumstances and I'm glad she's done it.

"An autopsy is mandatory in these cases," Thomas Beringer tells me softly, "then the remains will be brought here."

Then I remember the brain, Carl's battered brain, to be sent to the forensic team at Boston University. I give instructions.

THERE ARE TEN of them from the original group at our house when I return. Mutti had given Jerry Henley the key, a reminder of that first night after the final concussion, when we returned to find them all there, but now without the music and raucous voices.

"We're staying," announces Jerry, "two of us all night. Can't have you sleeping at the Sinclair by yourself and driving round in the Challenger half the night."

In Davenport, news travels like lightning.

I start to protest, then think better of it. I smell tomato sauce strong and welcoming from the kitchen.

"Mama's makin' spaghetti and meatballs, I enlisted her, not that she minds," says Sophie Gallo. Mrs. Gallo, large and aproned, appears from the kitchen and embraces me. I feel her stout arms and smell a mix of basil and olive oil. She rocks me and I start to cry, leaning into her sponge-like warmth and finding comfort. Then they all surround me, cooing like homing pigeons and patting me, and I lean into them and we shake together with sorrow. Later they speak of Carl, as he was and not how he'd become.

"Remember that last game? The one against Etobicoke? That last goal?" They nod, brightening up, seeing the speeding figure once again. It was the last game for Davenport, the one I didn't attend.

"You mustn't blame yerself for any of this," whispers Jerry with rye-soaked hoarseness. "You were great to him, couldn't be better. If he'd been his self, he'd a done himself in months ago, rather than see himself turn into a dement. It's the old Carl we all miss, not like he was toward the end. What triggered it anyhow, him overdosing?"

"The baby, Mutti told him about the baby." My head is buzzing with rye.

"Crazy bitch, but imagine him not knowing, shows how far gone he was."

"I'm only telling you this. I'm going to say it was an accidental overdose, better for the baby."

"Appreciate your confidence," says Jerry, obviously pleased. He'd been such a good friend, the least I could do was trust him with the truth.

Vince Fanelli lights a cigarette and inhales deeply. It reminds me of Ma.

"People don't smoke in other people's homes anymore, it's very ignorant," lectures Sophie Gallo, "and a real insult to Sonja."

Vince gives me a sheepish and apologetic look and heads for the downstairs bathroom. I hear him flush the butt down the toilet.

"Don't worry, Vince," I slur upon his return. "I smoked two packs a week in second-hand smoke before I was five." Vince smiles his relief but doesn't light up again.

"Candace's mother says she's coming down for the funeral," says Gwen Andrews, "and we'll have to listen to how close her and Carl used to be. A few shags in the back seat of Helbig's Bug and she thought he was making some sort of commitment."

"He only ever loved Sonja," says Jerry. "He always told me that, he knew that much."

I start to cry again, but this time the tears flow easily, almost like balm.

"This kind of talk only makes Sonja feel bad," shrills Sophie, "and who the hell cares about Candace Stewart she's so high and mighty since she's in university it makes you wanna puke. Christ, imagine being a battered wife and having to turn to Candace Stewart for comfort an' advice—like bein' battered all over again."

For the first time there's a soft titter of agreement and even I smile, remembering Candace's disparaging remarks about her former friends.

"Sophie and Gwen will be sleeping here tonight," announces Jerry. Vince's mom will be here at ten to prepare breakfast, then we're having a potluck at Gwen's tomorrow night.

I lie in bed and listen to Gwen and Sophie snarl at each other before heading for their respective bedrooms. Sophie sticks her head in my bedroom door before finally retiring.

"You all right, sweetie?"

"As right as I can be, considering. I really appreciate your mom's coming, preparing dinner like that. I didn't thank her enough."

"No problem. You're family. She says to tell you not to drink hard stuff, though, vino is better for the baby."

Of course, what was I thinking? Lost in my own misery, not thinking at all.

Downstairs Jerry is urging everyone to leave, and per-suading Chris Devine, the only one sober enough to be the designated driver, to drive four of the drinkers home. I'm glad they're here. It is comforting. Perhaps I've joined the marching army. I lie in my bed listening to the voices of The Choir surrounding me. They were there for Carl, now for me.

THE NIGHT BEFORE the visitation I am alone with Carl surrounded by flowers. In his polished coffin, the scars, the forehead scars, are no longer visible, only his golden hair swept back from the last cutting less than two weeks ago. I touch his hair and it is thick, cool silk beneath my fingers. "Great hair," I whisper. I touch his face, so young and still, and run my finger down the marble cheek, along the icy jaw.

"You should not have done it," I whisper, my voice reproving. "We could have talked. Sorry I wasn't there for you, you must forgive me for that. I'll miss you." I touch his hands, to see his nails one last time, but they are clenched, frozen together.

"NO, HE WILL wear his dark suit, his wedding suit," I insist to John Beringer, who tells me Mutti had produced his Davenport hockey jersey. "No hockey jersey, he wore one much too long in life."

On the side of the coffin is a bronze plaque: CARL HELBIG JR. TWENTY-TWO YEARS. A Mutti touch.

It is a huge funeral, no quiet cremation here. Blankets of flowers and so many players; three of the Bruins are pallbearers. The Choir is there, all of the familiar faces, and Jerry Henley, beside himself with grief. We sob and cling to each other, Jerry and I, and I embrace The Choir members again. I am of their fabric, woven together, our humanity indistinguishable. My little guy will have them, aunts and uncles, who will be there for him. Candace is there, subdued and tearful, and I forgive her for being Candace.

They speak of Carl in the crowded church, of how he made Davenport proud, and of how he made two goals that last night, the night of the final concussion.

Cremations are so clean and neat, and I think of Ma and Pops being reduced to ashes, Pops residing in the cheapest urn provided by The Reasonable Alternative, and Ma residing in a more elegant one, both together on my mantelpiece in the Davenport house. I had no place to scatter Pops', not planning a trip to Ukraine in the future, and the Sinclair Hotel dining room where Ma had spent her happiest hours would be out of reach. Carl's internment is so different. Pristine and handsome, with his icy face and eyes glued shut, he is to be slipped into a yawn of raw earth, where, in his satin-lined mahogany casket, he will spin throughout eternity alone—and he hated to be alone.

Sitting through the service, the eulogy's emphasis on Carl's hockey career increasingly grates on my nerves, and my bitterness increases.

Outside the church, four reporters approach, one from the *Davenport Guardian*, the others from the *Star*, the *Globe*, and the *National Post*. One of the reporters is a woman, a writer of a daily column I had read while attending university. She has obviously been appointed spokeswoman.

"We apologize for bothering you at such a time, Mrs. Helbig, but we were wondering if you would care to make a comment on your husband's death at such an early age."

The remaining three, all men, shift and exchange uneasy glances, obviously expecting the comment that I am not prepared to speak at such a critical time. In fact, Jerry Henley, who is acting as my self-appointed body-guard, had already told them to "have the decency to get lost." But I will not do normal, as anger floods through me like a switched-on light bulb. In a clear, definite voice, a relic from my days as super-nerd of Davenport High, I speak to them.

"Carl's death at twenty-two was caused by his hockey career, which started when he was seven and went on until his final concussion at the Bruins opening game last October. Carl was a warrior who played through pain. I would like to send a message to all those parents who are investing so much in developing little hockey prodigies to consider the results of devoting their child's life—and brains—to this vicious so-called 'sport.'"

The reporters are scribbling and I notice one signalling to a photographer. In my mind I see a headline: "Grieving Widow Blames Hockey for Husband's Early Demise." I step into the car on the way to the cemetery, with a stone-faced Mutti and an ashen-faced Carl Helbig, no longer a senior, with Jerry Henley at the wheel.

"Sonja, Carl would not like what you say," mutters Mutti.

"Carl is gone. What difference does it make now?" I reply wearily.

"Sonja's been through a lot," says Jerry Henley defensively.

The word is out. After the gut-wrenching graveside ceremony, the dropping of the gravel on the polished lid, the reporters are back—with television cameras.

"Was your husband's death a suicide?" asks the *Star* reporter.

"Carl suffered from frontal lobe dementia. He could easily have become confused with his meds, especially when he was drinking. The report from the Boston University Forensic Unit has not been released, but from what several neurologists told me before he died, Carl had brain damage. This caused him pain and confusion while he was alive, and may have contributed to his death."

"You do realize," drawls the reporter from the *Globe*, "that attacking Canada's favourite sport won't make you popular. Do you intend to become an anti-hockey activist?"

"My comments were especially for parents of concussion-prone kids, and no, I'm not becoming an activist. No more questions, please."

"Whew, that won't score you any brownie points," says Jerry as we drive away in the car, aware of the disapproving silence from the back seat. "Guess all this puts an end to Uncle Jerry taking little Carlie to hockey practice."

"Perhaps baseball," I reply.

MUTTI IS ASHEN, her breath stale. "When did you tell him?" I ask as we leave the car.

She does not reply but eventually says, "He had to find out anyway."

Afterwards, we all sit together in the polished living room, drinking the rich coffee. His two sisters, Helga and Anna, have flown in from out of province, accompanied by their husbands. Helga's small, active, tow-haired children, who had played with Carl less than a year ago, but what now seems like only yesterday, run from room to room.

"He was such a bright little boy when he was six," muses Helga. "I remember his reading Dr. Seuss to us, *The*

Cat in the Hat it was, and we all thought he was a genius. Then there were problems. I wonder what happened."

"Hockey happened," I answer, not bothering to keep the bite from my voice.

The sisters look startled but keep drinking their coffee. The children scamper noisily over Mutti's polished floors, and I think of Carl, who could barely read Dr. Seuss in Grade 12.

Mutti sits, deaf to the children's happy cries, her head bowed. Sorrow has taken her and she is leaden with grief. Never an introspective woman, but I know she has regrets. But she will never disclose them. These, I think, are the worst kind, for they devour you, deep inside, late at night and early morning, just before the dawn.

"The baby will be seven weeks old when I return to university," I say. "Do you wish to care for little Carl during the week?"

"You would trust me with him?"

"Like no one else," I say.

"There, Mutti," the sisters chorus, "what a great idea."

Mutti smiles slightly, her first smile in days.

I DRIVE THE Challenger back to Toronto. Someone must drive it, and I cannot bear to sell it. On the side of the road, just before the 400 turnoff, a girl stands. She carries a sign that says TORONTO. I stop the car. She is perhaps eighteen, her hair bleached, with black roots showing, and she chews gum. She wears the usual uniform of faded jeans and a frayed duffle coat.

"Get in," I order.

She hops in beside me, obviously delighted and relieved that I'm not a man, intent unknown, offering the lift. I smell her perfume; choking and strongly floral, it permeates the car.

She chats with me. She has no job prospects as yet. Her boyfriend's gone to Alberta, but there have been no letters, not for months. Her mom's dead and her dad's address is unknown.

"Will there be a job in Toronto for someone with my energy and willingness to work?" she asks, her voice brash but somewhat unsure.

I let her off near Spadina and Queen. She has a relative who lives near there, a cousin.

Before she leaves I count out $500 in hundreds and fifties and hand it to her. Carl had always insisted I carry what he'd called "walking around money."

"I can't take this," she protests.

"Take it," I insist, "and promise you'll change your hair. Go to a good salon in Yorkville, it will help with employment prospects."

She laughs and asks, "When will I see you again, so I can pay you back?"

"No doubt we will run into each other," I lie. "And find some friends, good friends who'll have your back, who'll help you out and care about you."

She smiles as she waves me goodbye, and I smell the blatant floral perfume. It remains with me as I drive into the underground parking lot of the Manulife Centre.

IT IS NOW June and sometimes in the twilight I sit on the back steps of our house and wait. I do not know who or what I wait for. Perhaps Carl will come skating out of the copper sunset, hockey stick in hand, his golden head without his helmet. He will skate toward me, and I will see his smile glisten through the encroaching darkness and for a moment I will smell Irish Spring soap and Aqua Velva mixed with the fresh new grass of June, while inside me I feel our son turn and I await, await the future joy.

ACKNOWLEDGEMENTS

Many thanks to Taryn Boyd, publisher at Brindle and Glass, along with her in-house staff; thanks as well to editors Colin Thomas, Bethany Gibson, and Heather Sangster. I am grateful as well for the editorial help of Robert Karr, Ava Hillier, and Laurie Laughlin-Hillier. The enthusiasm of readers Betty Gorin, Jean Viereck, Jerry Peterson, Adair Lara, and Carol Dreleuch is appreciated. A special thanks to Joan Clark for her enlightened reading, and to John Metcalf for his early encouragement. I read and relied on a plethora of articles relating to concussions and hockey as set out in the *Toronto Star*, the *Globe and Mail*, the *National Post*, the *New York Daily News*, and the *New York Times*. Especially enlightening were interviews given by Dr. Charles Tator, neurosurgeon and concussion specialist, and of the surviving family members of deceased hockey players who suffered from CTE.

SUZANNE HILLIER is a former schoolteacher and retired lawyer who loves to cook for her family, cheer on the Toronto Blue Jays, and spoil her many grandchildren. Since retiring from her law firm, which she established in the 1970s, she has succumbed to her first love: writing. *Sonja & Carl* is her first novel.